Vic and Tory Merlin have at least some idea of what needs to be done, but accomplishing it is something else. Nonetheless they set out together, in a pickup truck and a white Caddy, to save reality as we know it . . . though not, perhaps, as it is.

*THE REALITY MATRIX is an incredible adventure novel—and it is also just plain incredible in its integration of the Tao of physics, computer modeling, cosmology, and games, among other things. Its people are memorably human,* ~~~mises~~ *. . . unusual.*

# JOHN DALMAS
# THE REALITY MATRIX

THE REALITY MATRIX

Copyright © 1986 by John Dalmas

A Baen Books Original

Baen Publishing Enterprises
260 Fifth Avenue
New York, N.Y. 10001

First printing, August 1986

ISBN: 0-671-65583-3

Cover art by David Mattingly

Printed in the United States of America

Distributed by
SIMON & SCHUSTER
TRADE PUBLISHING GROUP
1230 Avenue of the Americas
New York, N.Y. 10020

TO:

    J.W.C.,
    RON,
    JIM,
        and
    TOM,

each of whom made a lot of
difference. But especially to

    ROD,

who set the kettle boiling

# < ONE >

Striding strongly, Frank Diacono emerged from the timberline spruce forest into alpine tundra. Usually he felt exhilarated when he hiked the high country; now he felt vaguely uneasy—vaguely enough that he wasn't consciously aware of it.

He'd hiked a long way since noon, first up the dirt road that led over Schultz Pass, turning off it to climb the steep winding jeep trail to Doyle Saddle, thence along the foot trail that circled inside the rim of the broad crater where the snow had finally melted beneath the summer sun. To his right, the crater wall fell away steeply. The old crater bottom below was heaped with bouldery glacial moraine, partly clad with stands of hardy aspens—an epitomal frost pocket. Most weeks in summer found night frosts in its depths, though it was less than a hundred miles from that great blast furnace, the Sonoran Desert.

Diacono, who'd grown up in Philadelphia, was as addicted to the Arizona back country as the demands on an assistant college football coach allowed. He'd even audited courses in geology, forestry, and ecology to better know and understand what he saw.

Ahead of him stood his goal, Humphrey Peak,

highest of the peaks that ringed the crater. Its tundra was dusky rose in the sun's final rays, and Diacono quickened his pace. There was a notch between Humphrey and Agassiz Peaks, and for a little distance beyond it, the trail would be treacherous in twilight.

Another hiker was coming toward him on the other side of the notch, the only hiker he'd seen all day. The trail was narrow where they would meet, the slopes dangerously steep above and below, so when Diacono reached the notch, he waited there for the other man to get clear of the narrows. The other man was younger, and a bit in the old hippy mode, Diacono thought: slim but trail-rugged, his blond hair in a ponytail, a red bandana tied round his head.

The younger man stopped when they met, and sized up Frank Diacono's 240 pounds of bone and muscle. "Are you going on up Humphrey's tonight?" he asked.

"That's right."

"You going to sack down up there?"

Diacono nodded curtly, annoyed by what he considered intrusive questions.

The younger man got out of his way. "I guess you'll want to be moving along then," he said.

Diacono nodded and moved past. He'd gone only two or three steps when the other spoke after him. "Have you heard of the Indian spirit that lives up there?"

Stopping, Diacono looked back. Traditional Navajos and Hopis believed that a spirit, a god, dwelt there. The Forest Service protected the peak as an unofficial religious preserve for the tribes, restricting recreational development in the near vicinity. Not a superstitious man, Diacono nonetheless favored the action out of respect for tribal beliefs, and preferred the area without further disturbance anyway.

"I've heard of it," he admitted. "Why?"

The other man didn't answer at once, as if considering his words. Diacono waited, a trifle impatient.

"He . . . doesn't like people camping on top of him at night. Not white men like you and me, anyway."

Diacono nodded, his annoyance somehow gone now. "I like this old mountain," he said mildly. "I won't be leaving any trash up there or disturbing anything, any more than I would in church."

For several seconds they looked at each other, not more than six feet apart. The younger man was lean-faced, his tan reddish. Diacono was massive, blue-jawed, his black hair almost crew cut, his tan not red at all.

"Right," the younger man said, nodding. "Have a good one."

"Same to you."

Diacono turned and went on. The light was beginning to fade noticeably, and when the trail reached the crest of the rim, a brisk breeze hit him, thin and cold. By the time he topped out on the peak, night was settling in. The first and brightest dozen stars were visible.

On the top was a small walled space, intermediate between a rectangle and an ellipse, and about six by ten feet. The walls, of roughly fitted rocks, were some three feet high, with a narrow opening in the south end. A good place to sleep sheltered from the wind, Diacono thought. He assumed that hikers had built the wall and removed the surface stones for comfortable sleeping. It didn't occur to him that Indians might have made it for another reason.

Taking off his pack, he knelt within the walled space. The wind had increased, to twenty-five knots or better now. He ate a handful of gorp, chewed a piece of beef jerky until he'd mastered and swallowed it, then swigged water from his canteen. After unrolling his thin ground pad, he spread his down sleeping bag on it. Then he put his canteen and boots by the head of his sleeping bag, rolled up his jeans for a pillow, and put wallet, watch, and pickup keys in a boot. Finally, he zipped himself into the bag with only his face exposed.

The wind, he quickly decided, was going to be a nuisance. It continued to get stronger; even there behind the wall it actually rippled the nylon casing of his sleeping bag with little popping sounds.

But the sky was utterly clear, visible stars increasing by the minute. At more than 12,600 feet elevation, the star display would soon be out of this world; in Phillie, he'd never imagined such a sky.

While the casing of his sleeping bag popped in the wind, he fixed his eyes on one of the stars, the brightest in his field of vision, and began to feel ill at ease. The star moved, a common enough illusion when you lie on your back and fix your attention on one. He tried to hold it still with his eyes, but it moved erratically, jerking here and there over distances of ten degrees or more, pausing to glint, brightly stationary, for two or three seconds.

So large an apparent movement was new to him. Deliberately he withheld his attention from it, watching new stars gradually fill the empty darkness as the sky changed toward deep black. But any star he watched for more than a few seconds played the same trick.

As he watched, he became aware of anxiety, and gradually recognized dread. Blaming this on some mental effect of watching the stars, he closed his eyes. But that was no protection: Behind his lids were also erratic stars, and the dread intensified. Among these new stars were two lights, dull red, that gradually became more than stars.

They were eyes.

He opened his own to the night outside him. "Shit!" he muttered. Above him the stars jittered, and his sleeping bag rippled and snapped. Grimly he turned onto his side, bending legs and hips, and reclosed his eyes, determined to sleep.

And felt a growing *cold*, a cold deeper than discomfort, though he'd slept warm in this bag at much lower temperatures. Then the realization hit him, utterly illogical but with total certainty: If he spent the night there, he'd be dead before morning. It was that simple.

With an oath he sat up, fumbling for the zipper tab, and in seconds was stuffing his gear back into his packsack. Hurriedly he pulled on pants and put his canteen back on his belt. He didn't even take time to lace his boots, just wrapped and knotted the laces around his ankles, then fled, half running along the jumbly crest of a side ridge slanting down northward from the peak like a buttress to the crater.

The night seemed preternaturally dark, and he stumbled among low boulders until he realized he was at the head of the avalanche track above Abineau Canyon. Without hesitating he started down it, scarcely able to see the rocks at his feet.

Here the surface was slide rock, talus, most of the pieces flat plates and slabs that rocked and tilted at his weight or slid away beneath his feet as he scrambled downward among their dislodged clatter. But as he put distance between himself and the top, he calmed, slowing in response to the more immediate danger underfoot that could easily send him bouncing and sliding down the mountain.

It seemed lighter now, though the moon would not be up for hours, and he picked a zigzag course downward, finding and following the less steep ways. At last he reached the bottom of Abineau Canyon, and followed it until he came to a jeep trail. There, at the edge of spruce forest, he unrolled his sleeping bag again.

It occurred to him that the wind was not blowing

here. The sky was bannered and glittering with stars which were steady and impersonal. And for the first time since he'd left the notch and the other hiker, he recalled what the younger man had said about the god in the peak.

He closed his eyes and only darkness was there—darkness and whatever pictures he chose to put there. His last waking thoughts were a question and an answer: What had happened on the peak—would it have happened if the hiker hadn't said what he had? The answer, Diacono decided, was yes.

# ＜ TWO ＞

The West Hollywood night was softly lit by city glow off the overcast. The marine air was mild, vaguely moist, and heavy with night jasmine. Trees hemmed in and shadowed the narrow street—tall thin Washingtonia palms on one side, leafy trees shoulder to shoulder on the other. Along one curb, cars sheltered almost bumper to bumper beneath overhanging branches.

The buildings were two- and three-story apartment houses, their windows uniformly dark. A mockingbird called briefly, as if anticipating day.

At one end of the block a car stopped, and a young man, James "Lefty" Nagel, got out. The car was a Maverick, not new, its color uncertain in the night. A hammer in one hand, Lefty Nagel started walking in the street, a friend following slowly with the car.

They had worked this street two nights before. It would be funny to do it again so soon.

As he passed the left front windows of the first two cars, Lefty swung the hammer, smashing the glass, which rained down around his feet like crushed ice. The next car had only emptiness instead of glass in the driver's window. It was one he'd broken before,

7

and the turkey owner hadn't gotten it replaced yet, so Lefty struck the windshield as punishment.

In this wise he went halfway down the block, feeling invigorated, full-chested, godlike. A Toyota sat by a bank of shrubs. In his euphoria, he noticed nothing as he approached it except the clean new glass in its grimy side.

He raised and swung, and as the heavy steel head impacted, someone plunged out of the bushes and ran in front of the car. Lefty's eyes caught the movement and turned to it, even as his hammer drove through. It was the face and the terrible intention distorting it that held his startled eyes, as if the sword was peripheral in importance. He felt something strike his side, then his heavyset black attacker turned and ran, disappearing behind the bordering shrubs. With a squeal of tires, the Maverick accelerated past, gunning down the street and out of sight around the next corner.

For a long moment then, things were quiet; the next sound was someone vomiting a little way off.

*Jesus,* Lefty thought, *that was wild!* He looked down to see if he was bleeding. There was abundant blood; his body lay sprawled beneath him in a pool of it, nearly severed below the ribs.

Even then, looking down at his body from a viewpoint some six feet above it, Lefty Nagel took a long moment to realize what had happened. When he did, he howled—howled with horror.

But no one heard, or no one knew they heard. Only a cat on a nearby balcony rail looked in his direction. The mockingbird tried again to call the dawn.

The ghost of Lefty Nagel hung there numbly for quite a while, hardly seeing, hardly hearing. His buddy did not come back; actually, he had driven through a store window a few blocks away.

About ten minutes later a patrol car turned into

the street from Sunset Boulevard two blocks north, its flasher turning slowly, siren silent. It slowed abruptly when its lights picked up the body, then stopped a few yards away. For a moment the driver spoke into the radio, then both patrolmen got out. The entry door to the nearest apartment building opened, and the black man came over, his souvenir World War Two sword upstairs now in his bathtub. His body sagged; so did his face.

The ghost of Lefty Nagel stared at him, feeling no anger; feeling mainly grief.

"My name is Ernest Thoms," the black man said to the officers. "I'm the one that phoned you. I killed him."

"Mr. Thoms," said the corporal, "you have the right to remain silent. Anything you say may be held against you in a court of law."

Thoms was staring at the body in the street, showing no remorse, only a profound tiredness. "I'm the one that killed him," he repeated.

The remorse was Lefty's. If he could have cried, he would have. "I'm sorry," he said to Ernest Thoms, as an officer handcuffed the black man. "Jesus but I'm sorry. I don't know why I did it. I don't know why."

But Thoms ignored him, as if Lefty wasn't there. So did the police. Lefty didn't know what else to say; he realized now that they could neither see nor hear him. Only the cat on the balcony rail was looking at him, and Lefty hadn't noticed the cat.

They stayed until the ambulance arrived—all four of them: Ernest Thoms, the two patrolmen, and the ghost of Lefty Nagel. Then Lefty rode with his body to the morgue, not yet willing to leave it.

The paramedics didn't notice him either.

Leo Hochman left the Los Feliz Post Office—why the Los Feliz Branch, no one would ever know—and got into his delivery van. Leo had a house-cleaning business, and often the van held an industrial-grade vacuum cleaner, an assortment of pails, mops, and squeegees, buckets of solvents, and sometimes a steam cleaner for carpets. Today it held a pile of waxed cardboard boxes with a plastic tarp thrown over them.

He drove west on Franklin Avenue to the Hollywood Freeway on-ramp, careful not to encroach on the traffic signals, then went north on the freeway over Cahuenga Pass. After a few minutes he exited in the San Fernando Valley and drove to a large shopping center.

It was Saturday, early enough that there was still plenty of parking close to the L-shaped building, and he parked in the angle. A man and woman with three children were passing, and Leo Hochman waited a few moments, intending to let them get farther away. Instead, they went into the drugstore to his left; he could see them get in line at the ice cream counter.

He shrugged. Then he took the detonator out of the glove compartment and blew himself up with what later was estimated to be four hundred pounds of dynamite. The death toll was thirty-seven, including Hochman. Of the van, the biggest remaining piece was the engine block; only traces were found of its driver.

It was Monday before it was known who he'd been. Monday morning, the *L.A. Times* received a letter by registered mail, registered on Saturday at 9:48 A.M., nineteen minutes before the explosion. So did Channel Eight News, KFWB Radio, and the *Herald-Examiner*. In the letter, Hochman had said exactly what he was going to do, and where, and approximately when. It was, he said, in protest of the British presence in Northern Ireland—the "brutal Brittish oppreshion" [sic] as he'd put it.

"That's absolutely crazy!" said anchorman James

Fong Wu, after Channel Eight News was off the air. "Leo August Hochman? That's not Irish!"

Anchorwoman Sandy Steele looked pointedly at him. "Jim," she said, "that's absolutely crazy even if his name was Paddy O'Toole."

# < THREE >

Frank Diacono closed the file cabinet and picked up his office phone in mid-ring. "Diacono," he said.

"Frank, this is Bill. Just wanted to remind you about this evening."

"Don't worry, Bill, I won't forget—not with Sharon fixing lasagna."

"Uh, I'm not sure about the lasagna, Frank. She was thinking maybe she'd have gefilte fish instead."

"Gefilte fish? What's gefilte fish?"

"Damned if I know."

Diacono waited a beat. "Bill, you know it's not okay to put me on like that," he said, "a poor dumb dago jock like me." He went into his Mafia mobster impression. "I got friends that would be offended, you know? One short phone call to Vegas . . ."

"Gee, Frank, I forgot. I didn't mean to offend you. My profuse apologies."

"Profuse ain't enough, Bill. They got to be abject, too. Eh? And *never* forget the Mafia."

"You've got it, Mr. Diacono, sir. And lasagna it will be. I'll get on the hotline to Sharon right away."

"Seven o'clock?"

"Right. Oh, and Frank: Did you have a chance to read that story I wanted you to read?"

"Last night, before I went to bed."

"Good. Don't forget to bring the magazine with you. It's a collector's item."

"I put it on my dashboard this morning."

When they'd hung up, Diacono looked at his watch and decided to take a break. He went to the coffee room and poured his pint mug full, dropping a quarter into the money can, then took the coffee back to his office. He didn't, at the moment, feel like sitting around talking to whoever might turn up.

The magazine that Bill Van Wyk had loaned him was *Galaxy Science Fiction* for March 1952. Diacono had enjoyed SF novels since he'd been a kid, and frequently picked up one of the magazines as well. But Bill Van Wyk had shelves and shelves of science fiction paperbacks and magazines going back for decades. Fortunately, Bill could read a novel in under two hours; otherwise, he'd never get anything else done. Occasionally he'd push a book on Frank; he knew what Diacono would enjoy.

But the story he'd wanted Frank to read in the old *Galaxy* was not the kind Diacono liked, and Van Wyk must have known it. It was good—excellent, actually—but Diacono had more than once voiced a distaste for downers. And "The Year of the Jackpot" was definitely a downer—characters you cared about, a powerful concept, very well written, but a terrible ending.

The basic story premise was that lots of things in the world go in cycles, like weather and insects and diseases and violence, just for starters. The human craziness cycle had been important in the story. And when you got a lot of cycles peaking together, according to the story, they somehow reinforced each other so that they peaked higher than usual. In "The Year of the Jackpot," a whole lot of cycles all peaked at once, including the sunspot cycle, and then the sun went nova.

That was bad enough, but what was worst about the story—what bothered Diacono most—was the hero's premise that some cycles, at least, had no antecedent cause, but were a cause unto themselves. People *explained* such cycles, gave what they thought of as reasons, but the explanations seemed to be baloney, because if you attacked the supposed causes, the effects happened anyway.

Diacono was a jock, but he also had an IQ of 138, a lot of human sensitivity, and he was rational, so that last premise bothered him. It bothered him even after he reminded himself that it was just a story, the product of one man's imagination. And it still bothered him twelve hours after he'd finished reading it.

Because it bothered him so much, he might have resented Bill's getting him to read it, except that he knew Van Wyk: they were close friends. Bill wouldn't have asked him to read it just to annoy him. There was something behind the request that he'd probably find out about tonight.

The story's hero, Potiphar Breen, resembled Bill Van Wyk in one respect: Both were mathematicians specializing in statistical analysis. Bill Van Wyk had the kind of "home" computer that few college professors could afford. He'd come into an inheritance that allowed him to send his kids to Cal Tech and Oberlin. Playing with his computer had become an even bigger hobby for Van Wyk now than reading science fiction.

There was probably a connection, Frank decided, between Bill's interest in statistical analysis and his asking him to read the old Heinlein story.

Diacono shook the matter off and opened the folder on the Cedar City High School football team, in Utah. There were a couple of seniors there who looked like they could make it in the Big Sky Conference.

It was a beautiful January night in Flagstaff, Arizona. As Diacono got out of his pickup in front of Van Wyk's, he could see the towering triangle of Agassiz Peak glowing white in the moonlight, maybe five straight-line miles north and a mile higher than where he stood. A brisk winter wind made him shiver, and he thought of Humphrey Peak, screened from sight by the intervening Agassiz. If a person tried to spend tonight on top of Humphrey, he thought, he could die without the help of any unfriendly Indian god. It was cold enough here in town, a mile lower at 7,000 feet.

Bill Van Wyk answered the door chime. "Hey, Franco, come on in!" he said. He closed the door behind Diacono and helped him off with his jacket. "What'll you have to warm up on? The usual?" Bill asked as he hung the jacket in the entryway closet.

"Sounds good to me." Part of Diacono's attention was still on the mountain as they walked into the living room, where a couple was sitting.

"Do you guys know one another?" Van Wyk asked.

The man got off the sofa. "I don't believe so," he said. "I'm Dr. Justin R. Pingree, and this is my wife, Ursula."

Diacono wrapped his hand around Pingree's. Then Ursula extended hers, limp and moist. The thought occurred to him that an "Ursula" should be big, bold, and blonde, but this one was none of the three. Small and darkish, she came across as withdrawn. The wine glass beside her was empty. She wouldn't say much, he thought, but Pingree would probably talk freely and arrogantly. Flagstaff, Arizona was a relaxed, informal town, characterized as much by its huge sawmill and log yards as by its university. Faculty seldom introduced themselves as "doctor" there, certainly not in a casual domestic situation.

"I'm Frank Diacono," Frank answered. He plucked Simple Simon the Silly Savage from the room's largest chair and sat down, transferring the big Siamese cat to his lap. Simon wasn't having laps just then, and jumped down to disappear into the hallway.

"And what do you do, Mr.—what's your name again?" said Pingree.

"Diacono. Frank Diacono. I'm the defensive coordinator for the football team."

"I'd guessed something of the sort," Pingree said, "from your appearance. I'm associate professor of sociology. I'm afraid I'm not significantly informed on football." He sounded distinctly sniffy when he said it.

"Interesting," Frank said, and left it there.

Pingree looked guardedly at him through thick glasses. "Interesting? In what respect?"

"You're not interested in football, and I'm not interested in sociology."

Ordinarily, Frank Diacono was a mild man not given to antagonisms. He hadn't been even during his years as a linebacker in the National Football League. Violent, yes, but rarely antagonistic. He decided he might make an exception in Pingree's case.

"I didn't say I wasn't *interested* in football," Pingree enunciated. "I said I was not significantly *informed* on football."

"Sorry," Frank replied. "I didn't mean to put words in your mouth. I assumed that someone who was interested would be at least somewhat informed." He changed the subject. "Just what do you do in sociology?"

Van Wyk had come back into the room with a heavy glass containing Frank's drink. He'd overheard the conversation with Pingree and was eyeing Frank quizzically.

*Smirk, you bastard,* thought Diacono. *Inviting me over with a turkey like this.* From somewhere the thought occurred to him, however unreasonable, that Pingree's presence too might have something to do with "The Year of the Jackpot."

Van Wyk gave Frank his drink and sat down, ignoring Ursula Pingree's empty glass, and took over the conversation as if to avoid a Pingree lecture.

"I'm glad you wanted the usual, Frank," he said. "Justin thinks poorly of people who drink strange mixtures, but with you and I both drinking them, he'll have someone besides me to analyze. His Ph.D. is in sociology but his bachelor's and master's were in psych." He turned to Pingree and gestured at Frank's drink. "Aberdeen screwdriver," he said.

Pingree looked a bit uncertainly at Van Wyk. "And what is an Aberdeen screwdriver?"

"Scotch and orange juice." Van Wyk held up his own glass. "This is a Harlan County screwdriver. Kentucky whiskey and orange juice. I also serve Havana screwdrivers, if you'd like to try one—orange juice with rum."

Pingree was looking at his host with a carefully neutral expression, and Diacono realized the man had little if any sense of humor. Behind those thick lenses he was trying to figure out what significance might be hidden in Van Wyk's joking.

"Sharon says to tell you we'll eat in five minutes," Van Wyk went on.

Diacono glanced at Ursula Pingree. She sat somewhat birdlike, but blank, showing no hint of interest and little awareness of what was said. The times he'd come here with Candace, she'd gone into the kitchen to help Sharon, or at least to keep her company. Even declining with cancer, Candace had shown much more life than Ursula.

"Five minutes?" he said. "I guess I can hold out for five minutes." He changed the subject. "Your Heinlein story's out in my pickup. I forgot to bring it in."

Van Wyk nodded. "How about you, Justin? Did you read it?"

"Yes. Very interesting, although some of the xeroxing was faint."

"Interesting how?" Van Wyk asked. "What did you find interesting about it?"

"Well, clearly the author is not only an abysmal pessimist, but also regards mankind as a single psyche, in the Jungian sense. The single psyche—mankind in the story—has a death wish, and all the individual humans on earth must then perform in a manner contributive to that death wish, regardless of what their own individual purposes might be. The author carries it to ridiculous extremes, of course, as one might expect of a science fiction writer."

Frank could hardly believe the man had said it. *My god!* he thought, *the ass actually thinks that a novelist necessarily believes what he writes!*

"How about you, Frank?" Bill said. "What did you think of it?"

"I think Heinlein woke up one morning and decided to write a pessimistic story for a change, just to show people he could do it." Diacono glanced at Pingree, then turned back to Van Wyk. "Then he shifted the high-powered Heinlein creative mind into gear and wrote 'Jackpot.' What do you think?"

Sharon Van Wyk stood in the door. "*I* think," she said, "that you should all come into the dining room and sit down. Except Bill, who is herewith appointed to help serve the guests."

The food was excellent; Frank always found it so at the Van Wyks'. Ursula Pingree quickly finished her second (or third?) glass of wine, which seemed a little much for her. At any rate, Frank, sitting on her left, felt her hand on his leg, groping. Frank's fingers were very strong. Hiding his surprise, he reached across his lap with his left hand and snapped the back of her hand with a strong fillip by his index finger. She withdrew her hand promptly.

Shortly, Bill refilled the woman's glass. When they were done with dessert, they all went into the living room.

"Bill," Diacono said, "when are you going to tell us why you wanted Dr. Pingree and me to read 'Jackpot?'"

"Hmm. Right now is a good time, I guess." Van Wyk paused, looking inward as if for the proper place to start. "I read 'Year of the Jackpot' myself for the first time when I was twelve years old, and never forgot it. And not too long after that I read Asimov's *Foundation* trilogy. I was already interested in math; between them, they got me interested in statistical analysis, so I majored in math at Michigan State and took my Ph.D. in statistics at Duke.

"Like Potiphar Breen in the story, I compile data on various obscure and not so obscure fields, activities, and phenomena. It doesn't take that much time, with my computer and all the data sources I can access with it.

"Then, of course, I analyze it, and synthesize and test various indexes." Van Wyk wasn't smiling now. "And basically, what I've been running into the last couple of years is a lot like what the fictional Potiphar was running into in 'Jackpot.'"

Frank and Pingree were both staring at Van Wyk; Frank wasn't entirely sure his friend was serious. Frank looked at Sharon Van Wyk then, and she seemed as serious as her husband; he decided that Bill wasn't putting them on.

"Just a moment," said Pingree. "Are you predicting that the sun is going to blow up and kill us all?"

"I suppose that's an outside possibility," Van Wyk replied. "But what's a lot more likely is that the human race will blow itself up without celestial help."

For some reason, Diacono's eyes shifted to Ursula Pingree. For the first time, she showed an interest in something said—a furtive, frightened interest. Then she became aware of his eyes and quickly turned to her latest drink.

"Let me show you," Van Wyk went on, and getting up, led the other two men down the hall to his study. Ursula didn't follow. Sharon, presumably out of courtesy to Ursula, stayed behind, too. She was undoubtedly familiar with what they were going to see anyway.

Frank knew little about statistical analysis, and wondered if Pingree knew any more than he did. Bill sat down at the computer keyboard and began to touch keys. He didn't try to explain what came up on the CRT; the long chart that unfurled from the buzzing printer was what he showed them.

*Heinlein revisited!* Diacono thought, as Van Wyk explained the symbols and curves. TV and radio and politicians had displayed and stressed the bad, the ugly, and the calamitous for as long as Diacono could remember—the garish, the grotesque, the "newsworthy." The closest such people came to an objective overview were generalities phrased to support their own prejudices.

What Bill had here looked like the missing overview.

"Actually," he was saying, "there are some interesting differences between what I've got here and what Heinlein created for 'Jackpot.' For example, the cycles are pretty irregular, most of them. But it looks to me as if now, at least, they're responding to some exterior influence, some master factor I don't know about." He pointed. "The cycles are definitely beginning to coincide, getting in phase. And they're either reinforcing each other or they're responding independently to an increase in the master factor.

"For several years, things were definitely improving, you know. Not just economically; crime statistics were going down, for one thing, and while there still were plenty of loonies—well-publicized, of course— even the insanity statistics were falling.

"Then, about three years ago, there was a reversal in some of them, with others following not too far behind." His finger moved over the last year's curves. "And the rate of deterioration has been accelerating."

"Well," Diacono said, "and a merry Christmas to you, too."

"William," said Pingree, "I wouldn't be concerned about it."

"Why?" asked Van Wyk, turning to the sociologist. "Why wouldn't you be concerned about it?"

"Because," Pingree replied, "statistical analyses of unconstrained human activities are subject to too many factors and assumptions—for example, nonrepresentative samples and the dependence of what are assumed to be independent variables. In statistical analysis, if one cannot rationalize the results, they are probably an artifact."

Diacono grunted. "Following that reasoning, if gases are coming out of the sewer, and they really smell bad, and people are passing out around you and falling on the ground, it doesn't mean anything until you've got a chemical analysis of the fumes."

Pingree looked resentfully at Diacono, but if he intended to say anything, it was forestalled by the harsh sound of vomiting from down the hall. Pingree turned irritatedly in that direction. "I was afraid of that," he said drily. "My wife has overindulged."

They followed him to the living room, where Ursula was on her hands and knees. Sharon was emerging grimly from the kitchen with a roll of paper towels. Pingree pulled his wife to her feet without speaking to her and wiped her face roughly with one of the towels. He didn't even let her go to the bathroom to wash her face and mouth, simply excused himself and her, put her coat over her sagging shoulders, and rushed her out of the house.

"And a happy new year to you and yours," Diacono said after them when the door had closed. Bill and Sharon were still cleaning the carpet with towels. "Can I help you guys?" he asked. "Or would you prefer me to leave?"

"Stay," said Sharon. "I'd like to salvage the rest of the evening, and I've got some fresh coffee started." She got up and put out a hand to Bill. "Give me your towels; this is good enough for now. I'll spray with deodorizer if I need to, and shampoo it in the morning."

She went into the kitchen. The two men sat down.

"So why the seminar on the screwed-up state of the world?" Frank asked. "I presume it's the whole world, judging from the news lately." A major revolt in the Turkmen S.S.R., ruthlessly put down by the Red Army; intensified terrorism in Northern Ireland; a Shiite jihad in the Middle East; and the renewal of old secessionist movements, complete with bombs, in Scotland and Quebec—those were some of what Diacono had in mind. They fitted the trends of Van Wyk's mostly American data.

Van Wyk nodded glumly. "Basically it's hard to know something like that and not tell at least a few people. And when that Methodist preacher from San Diego deliberately crashed his plane into the stadium crowd at the Chargers–Bengals playoff game last month, to punish them for breaking the sabbath . . ." He shrugged and spread his hands. "Besides, I know it sounds dumb, but I guess I hoped one of you would say something helpful."

"Such as?"

Van Wyk shook his head. "I don't know. Pingree's

a sociologist. I suppose I hoped he'd say something like, 'Oh, yes, G.S. Heartburn analyzed this in a recent *Journal of Sociology*. It should reverse within one to three months, and things will improve rapidly thereafter.' "

"That's about as likely as a Baptist getting elected Pope," Diacono replied, "and if he had, I wouldn't believe him. Coaching is more of a science than sociology is. You're way ahead of people like Pingree, and you're an amateur." He fixed his friend with his eyes. "So now the other part of my question: Why did you include me in?"

Unexpectedly, ruefully, Van Wyk grinned. "Damned if I know. Maybe because you're my friend. Anyhow, it seemed like the right thing to do. Still does. I'm a mathematician, not a scientist; it's all right for me to act on intuition."

Diacono nodded thoughtfully as Sharon returned and sat down by her husband. "Insanity is insanity," Frank said. "Try to find the logic in insanity and it'll suck you right in. I don't know if that's apropos of anything, or where it came from," he added, "but it sounds profound as hell."

He looked at Sharon. "And speaking of crazy, I like you guys, even your old man. If you'll let me sleep in your spare room tonight, I'd like to sit here and talk for a while, and drink too much to drive home. I promise not to puke on your carpet, and I may even tell you what happened to me last summer on Humphrey Peak."

# < FOUR >

Sergeant Jerry Connor had gone to scores of accidents in four years on the California Highway Patrol, but it was the first serious accident he'd seen in the process of happening. The silver Fiat just seemed to take off—it left the ground on a divergent flight path and impacted the powder-dry hillside with a burst of dust. Connor hit the siren and flasher, and the traffic dropped back as the patrol car elbowed its way into the right-hand lane and onto the shoulder.

At the time it seemed like just another freeway accident—worse than most, but nothing strange. Connor jumped out with the first-aid chest while his partner reported the accident over the radio. Traffic was returning to its regular flow, more or less. Four or five civilian cars had pulled off onto the shoulder; now all but one slipped back into traffic.

Someone had gotten out of that one, ahead of Connor. She was running, pretty white dress, long blonde hair, a flower skittering through the coarse drought-bleached grass toward the wreckage. Connor broke into a gallop but she reached the wreckage well ahead of him.

Telescoped and flattened, the Fiat lay upside down

on almost the same spot as a wreck he'd been to a few months earlier, and maybe sixty yards from one the year before. And he knew that someone in it was just as dead as someone had been in each of the other two. The girl verified it for him before he got there, not by screaming, or even crying yet, but her face was white, wide-eyed, shocked, her knuckles shoved between her teeth. For a moment he felt her gathering grief.

The driver was very conspicuously dead, but Connor knelt for a moment as a matter of form, checking him out. That's when she began to cry, big wracking sobs. Connor got up and stood by uncomfortably, letting her get through the worst of it. His partner, who'd followed him, started filling out the accident report. After a minute or so she began to come out of it, her head bowed, her face wet and miserable.

Her name was Carol Ludi. She had just driven from Chicago by way of San Francisco, and her brother had met her at Castaic to guide her to his place in L.A. She didn't know how fast they'd been going, but she was sure they hadn't been speeding; he'd been taking it easy so he wouldn't lose her.

In most respects it was a routine sort of thing for Connor, but when he'd left, the accident hadn't dropped out of his attention the way they usually did. And it wasn't because the girl was pretty or because he'd actually seen the accident occur. It was because it had struck him that there was something strange about the accidents on the pass. He'd never looked at it before; probably, he decided, because people don't like to think about things that don't make any sense.

Fatalities are rare on the freeways, when you consider the immense volume of commuter traffic they carry. But on this freeway there were two short stretches that got more than their share. On just about any road there are places where accidents tend to happen, and these can usually be explained by something about the road or the terrain: places where fog tends to form or move in or there's a sun problem—something like that. But where Kevin Ludi had gone airborne, and on another stretch on the other side of the pass, there was no apparent reason for the unusual number of fatalities.

Connor brought it up with Benny Benitez, the oldest guy in the division. Benitez said it had been like that back before the freeway was built, when it was just an ordinary highway. Then it was mostly head-on collisions, and they blamed it on people passing slow-moving vehicles.

That wasn't the case anymore.

Next, on his own time, Connor graphed the accident frequency, starting with data about eight years old. The number of cars over the pass each day hadn't increased much, and for several years the average had been about one fatal accident every forty days.

But there was something odd about that average. With an average of one every forty days, you'd expect maybe two in two days sometimes, then none for maybe two or three months, and then another twenty days later—something irregular like that. But for five years of data *there had always been one on the sixty-third day*, give or take a day, with unbroken regularity. This regularity had been obscured by scattered random fatalities that might occur anywhere on the pass.

Then, about three years before the Ludi accident, the sixty-three day intervals had begun to narrow. After two years they had closed to one every forty-eighth day. In the last twelve months they had closed to one every thirty-sixth day.

Connor looked at the strip of taped-together graph paper and got a rush of goose bumps. He had no idea what all this meant, but somehow it scared him. He showed what he'd found to the lieutenant, who looked annoyed and said something about coincidence—"one of those little peculiarities."

Although it was an asinine response, Connor didn't argue; for one thing, he had no explanation of his own to push, and for another, he had no idea what to do next. Other matters crowded it from his attention, and for the next four months he thought of it less and less often. He might have effectively forgotten about it except for what happened next.

He was driving up the pass on a rainy winter day when he saw someone standing at the site where Kevin Ludi had been greased, and he had his partner pull off on the shoulder. There was nothing actually wrong with someone standing out there in the rain and mud, but it was odd. And he knew who it was, even at a hundred-plus feet, though her back was to him and she wore a hooded raincoat. He'd assumed Carol Ludi would have been back in Chicago months ago. He was tempted to go over and speak to her, but he was on duty and couldn't think of any logical reason to, besides which it was genuinely pouring just then. So they drove on.

But after his shift, he found the Ludis' address and phone number in the files, and when he got home, he called. While he was dialing, it occurred to him that he had no idea what he was going to say.

"Ludi residence. This is Carol."

"Hi, Miss Ludi. I'm Jerry Connor of the California Highway Patrol. You may remember me from, uh, your brother's accident. But this is *not* an official call. It's . . . personal."

There were several seconds of silence. "Yes?" she said warily.

"I saw you today," he said. "At the accident site. I'd like to meet you somewhere this evening and talk about it." There were several more seconds of silence, and he was starting to feel like a fool. What was there, in fact, to talk about? Maybe she'd say no, he thought, and save him further embarrassment.

She did say no. Actually, she said she already had an appointment for the evening, but the way she said it—very flatly—was like a no. And to Connor's surprise, he found himself digging in.

"How about before your appointment? Or afterward?"

Her next lag was even longer, but when she answered, it was thoughtfully. "Well . . . actually, there's no firm time set for it. This person is going to stop by when she can. Do you know where I live?"

"You're on your sister-in-law's phone, and I've got her address from the accident report."

"All right, you can come over. But you may be interrupted or have to wait."

"I'm on my way," he said, "and thanks!" He hung up, grabbed a banana, took a big swig from the milk jug—supper—and left.

The address was in the Hollywood Hills, and the storm had turned the narrow, winding street into a mountain stream. The house was one of the more modest in its neighborhood, worth perhaps half a million: Real estate costs are out of sight in the Hills. He turned his '82 Rabbit into the manicured jungle that was the yard and parked behind someone's BMW. Probably a visitor, he decided; on a day like this, the residents would have pulled into the garage. Jumping out, he sprinted through the downpour, pursued by a clap of thunder.

The entryway was roofed, and after he pushed the door chimes, he turned and watched the wind thrash the tall eucalyptus trees in the darkness while the rain splashed. Ludi's widow answered the door, and if Carol was pretty, this woman was stunning, the visual effect sharpened by a light German-Swiss accent. She had a dark tan that had not dried her skin, her hair was shiny black, and by the entry light, her slightly slanted eyes looked violet-blue. She looked like an athlete—a dancer or skater.

"You must be Sergeant Connor," she said.

"During duty hours I'm Sergeant Connor. Right now I'm Jerry Connor."

She smiled. "Come in, Jerry Connor. I'm Miki Ludi. Carol already has a visitor." She led him through a house decorated with plants. "I'm curious about your interest," she said. "Was there something peculiar about my husband's death? Or is it my sister-in-law you find interesting?"

He ignored the second question. "Nothing legally peculiar," he said, "but it has peculiar aspects." It didn't seem like the greatest thing in the world to say to a widow, but she'd asked.

She pushed open a door without knocking and ushered him through. The room was enclosed and snug, with built-in bookcases, a fire in the fireplace, thick throw rugs, and drapes that hid the dark stormy evening outside the sundeck door. Inside, two women sat opposite each other, both looking up at him as if in stop-action.

"Sergeant Connor is here," said Miki Ludi. Then she stepped back out, closing the door behind her, leaving him standing there awkwardly. Carol was staring, perplexed; it was her visitor who picked up the ball, standing and extending her hand. Carol stood up after her.

"I'm Laura Sigurdsson," said the guest.

Connor decided it was definitely pretty-lady night. Not only were Carol and the remarkable Miki lovely; Laura Sigurdsson was exceptionally good-looking, in her mid- to late thirties, with honey-blonde hair, greenish hazel eyes, and a delicate, symmetrical face. But he also got a sense of decisive and confident ability. She could easily be an executive somewhere; maybe, he thought, she was.

"Sergeant Connor," she said, "Carol and I were discussing something personal. Would you care to wait in another room?"

The way she said it wasn't cold or unfriendly, simply direct.

Carol spoke then. "Sergeant Connor came to talk about the accident. I . . . Maybe he has something we . . ." She didn't know where to take it from there.

Neither did Connor, but he started, trusting the ideas to come to him. "Call me Jerry," he said, "not sergeant. Like I said on the phone, this is strictly unofficial."

And the ideas came, surging out unforeseen. "When the accident occurred," said Jerry, "traffic was moving about forty-five to fifty miles an hour. I recall thinking at the time that it was slow for the conditions. And if Mr. Ludi had been going much faster, we'd have noticed. But he went airborne as if he was doing seventy, and the wreck looked like it."

Connor surprised himself with the statement. He hadn't even thought about that before, but it was right, without question. From there he went into the fatality frequency statistics, wondering where all this was leading. "And while I haven't checked the records, from the instances I know of personally, I think we'd find that the sixty-third-day wrecks—thirty-sixth-day wrecks now, or closer—we'd find that they're all cars that had just crossed the summit of the pass, within a mile."

Then the inspiration ran out as suddenly as it had turned on, and he stood there like a lump, waiting for someone to ask "so what?" and "why are you telling us these things?"

Instead, they looked at each other meaningfully before turning back to him. "Thank you, Jerry," said

Laura Sigurdsson, and stood again. "Miss Ludi, I'll recommend to my husband that he get together with you. What Mr. Connor told us makes it look very . . . interesting."

Carol excused herself to see Mrs. Sigurdsson to the door. Connor's attention stuck on the name Sigurdsson. It was familiar, but he couldn't place it. Sigurdsson was an unusual name in L.A.—not like Garcia or Wong or Miyake or Rosenbloom, or even Jones. He walked over to the bookcase and examined the exposed spines on the ranks of hardcover books. The books were mostly things like the classics and Brittanica, perhaps more for decoration than for reading.

A paperback lay on the coffee table, and when he glanced at it, he knew why the name had been familiar. The cover announced:

OLAF SIGURDSSON
MASTER PSYCHIC
by
Laura Wayne Walker

He picked it up. For Laura Wayne Walker, read Laura Sigurdsson, he thought; apparently the interviews had resulted in a marriage as well as a book. On the cover, Olaf Sigurdsson appeared to be in his mid-fifties and a bit unkempt, with a craggy grinning face and a thatch of gray hair. He wore a checkered lumberjack shirt and looked more like a good-natured North Dakota farmer than someone a beautiful, still-young authoress would marry, particularly since the book had been printed several years earlier. Sigurdsson would probably be sixty or more by now.

Carol Ludi came back in.

"I was looking at your book," said Connor, holding it up. "Why are you interested in a psychic?"

She sat down before she answered; Connor sat down opposite her in the chair that Laura Sigurdsson had occupied. "I want to get in touch with my brother,

Kevin," Carol said. "And a mutual friend recommended Mr. Sigurdsson to me."

"Is that why your sister-in-law interrupted you by ushering me in? She doesn't approve of psychics?"

"It's not that. She just tends to be direct. Actually, she and Kevin were both very interested in psychic phenomena and things like that. That's one of the things they had in common."

"How do you feel about psychics?"

"I suppose some of them are phonies; maybe most of them. But that doesn't mean Ole is."

Sigurdsson had been dubbed "the psychic of the stars" for his work, probably very lucrative, with entertainment personalities. Connor knew of him more for his work with police: describing criminals, reconstructing crimes, and locating missing persons.

"Why do you want to get in touch with your brother?"

She didn't answer at once, nor did she meet Connor's gaze. "That's what Laura asked me," Carol said. "She told me that dead people don't usually hang around as ghosts very long. They go and reincarnate somewhere."

"Umm."

"But I'm sure that Kevin hasn't. You see, sergeant—Mr. Connor—"

"Jerry," he said.

"Jerry, Kevin and I were very close. We were twins, and closer even than most identical twins. We didn't even have the usual childhood spats or jealousies. And since he . . . died out there, I've felt that he's been hanging around me, trying to tell me something. Something important."

She got up and started pacing. "I know that sounds crazy. But as I said, Kevin had been interested in psychic phenomena since we were kids. He believed in them. That was one thing we didn't share; I didn't have much of an opinion one way or another."

She stopped and faced Connor. "Well, I believe now. I'm positive he's been trying to speak to me, to tell me something. And I think it has to do with the accident."

"I see."

"You think all this is crazy, don't you?" she said quietly.

"Nope. I've heard about some interesting things Sigurdsson's done. But even if he's genuine, he still could rip people off. I mean, here's someone that feels a terrible loss, and convinces themself that their husband or mother or brother is still around. Someone with money . . ."

"But *I* approached *him!*"

"Of course you did."

"And I had to really *talk* to Laura over the phone just to get her to come out here!"

"Okay," said Connor gently. "But a little reluctance can help set the mark up. And she did come over."

She sat down again, shaking her head. "Oh, I understand why you look at it that way. But this friend of Kevin's that I was talking to, who told me about Ole Sigurdsson, has known him for years and years, and swears by him—both his honesty and ability. And she's a hardheaded business woman—a lawyer in the film industry."

"Right. Well, whatever." Connor got up. "Look, Carol—okay if I call you Carol? I'm interested in this too, so I hope we can keep in touch. Because whether there are ghosts or not, and whether your brother is hanging around or not, *something* is strange about the accidents on the pass.

"And I'd like to borrow your book, if you're done with it."

Driving down the canyon, his windshield wipers beating and splashing, it occurred to Connor that

Laura Sigurdsson apparently had become interested only after he'd told what he'd found, even though he was the law.

At seven-thirty the next morning, he called in sick for only the second time since he'd been on the Patrol. It was the first time he'd faked it. He'd gone to bed about four o'clock, having finished the book, and was in no shape to stand a shift if he didn't absolutely have to. Then he went back to sleep until almost noon, to wake up with Olaf Sigurdsson on his mind.

You couldn't be sure what was true in a book like that, he told himself, but it had certainly been interesting. He found himself inclined to believe a lot of it. Sigurdsson had been born in 1928 and grown up on the storm-swept coast of Iceland, in a stone house with a roof of living sod. The family had a farm of sorts, and a little fishing boat with sails as well as an engine, for harvesting fish from the rough and dangerous North Atlantic. Until age eight he'd been a normal farm boy, apparently; then he'd been kicked in the head by a horse. He'd almost died, and when he recovered, two things had changed. One, he'd become feeble-minded, and two, he'd become psychic. He'd still been functional enough to do the more routine farm work, with some supervision, but they didn't take him to sea with them when they went out for cod or herring.

Also, he claimed to remember being a notorious tenth-century Icelandic outlaw named Grettir the Strong. Grettir was famous partly for ridding a ranch of a dangerous and destructive ghost: the book told the story in brief, taken from an ancient Icelandic saga. And considering what happened to Grettir in his battle with the ghost, which was actually more of a zombie, it was surprising that Sigurdsson would have anything to do with ghosts, even if he only imagined having been Grettir.

When Sigurdsson was twenty-seven, his sister and her husband had migrated to the Scandinavian-American fishing settlement of Kitliat, Washington, and brought Olaf with them. And the farther they got from Iceland, so the book said, the brighter Olaf Sigurdsson became. By the time they arrived in New York, his intelligence seemed normal, but he was still psychic.

A good story, Connor told himself, whether it was true or not. He realized he wanted it to be, and looked forward to meeting the old man.

After brunch he went to the supermarket, and when he got home, there was a message on the phone machine. Carol Ludi had called: she had a 3 P.M. appointment with Ole Sigurdsson. She didn't mention where, nor had she invited Connor, but Connor wanted in.

His clock said two-forty. A phone call got only her answering service. It occurred to him to check the accident site and see if they were there, but that didn't make much sense: there was no reason to think they'd go there. So instead he made a cup of instant coffee and got out the *TV Guide*. After scanning the midday programming in disbelief, he left his coffee on the counter, went out to his car, and drove to the crash site anyway.

It was the sort of bright, fresh glinting day that can bless Los Angeles in winter. Carol and someone he assumed was Sigurdsson were standing in the breezy sunshine where the wreck had been, but Connor didn't get out and go over at once. He felt as if he'd be intruding just now, so he watched from the car. The old man looked bigger than he'd expected. The two were standing side by side, and it seemed to Connor that he could feel something heavy in the air, not good at all—something powerful and hostile.

When they turned and started back to the freeway, Connor got out and met them partway. Carol
was clearly surprised to see him. Ole Sigurdsson
looked calm and strong. There was a small stain on
his shirt, perhaps of coffee, but no sense of the slob
about him—just someone who didn't always notice
things like that. Carol introduced them, and Connor
shook the old man's big hand. It was like gripping
a two-by-four, its hard beefiness inconsistent with
Sigurdsson's rawboned frame.

"I'm glad to meet you, Mr. Sigurdsson," Connor
said, then added inanely, "I never met a psychic
before."

"O-oh?" The blue eyes penetrated. Suddenly the
old man laughed. "You never did, eh? And v'at the
hell you think *you* are?"

For a moment Connor didn't understand what
Sigurdsson meant, thought perhaps it was some obscure insult or challenge. Then it hit him, and he got
cold rushes from his scalp to his calves.

Sigurdsson's grin got bigger. "Ve vas yust going to
my place," he said. "You can follow us if you vant to.
I'll give you some real coffee, not that instant stuff."

Then, with abrupt vigor, the old man strode toward
his car, Carol hurrying behind. Connor slanted off
toward his own, preoccupied with what Sigurdsson
had said to him—"V'at the hell you think *you* are?"

That one simple sentence explained a multitude of
things for Jerry Connor, who thought he must have
been feeble-minded himself all those years, never to
have twigged on it.

It was because he didn't hear thoughts as such,
whispering inside his head like voices; never, or
seldom anyway, saw anything like a vision. He'd
never had a precognition with subtitles or fanfares,
had never seen in his mind a picture of something
happening, only to read about it later or see it on the

news. But there were all the times he'd gotten a notion to call Arnie or someone, to be told they were just getting ready to call him; the knack he had, sometimes commented on by others, of doing the right thing at the right time, like going to Ludi's just when Laura was there, or driving out here just now.

He cleared his mind of this as he buckled his seat belt, because Sigurdsson was already pulling his big white Caddy into traffic. Connor hurried to keep up; the old man drove like an Indy racer. Someone, Jerry thought, ought to give the Icelander a ticket.

Unlike his car, Sigurdsson's home was not large. It perched on the top of a very steep, very expensive ridge, with trees, shrubs, and shiny green ivy thick on three sides and a magnificent view across a canyon on the fourth. The psychic business must pay well, Connor decided, at least for Ole Sigurdsson.

Considering that Sigurdsson was a married man, the living room was a lot like bachelor's quarters—an old-timey, orderly, well-to-do bachelor. Glass doors stood open to twittering birds, the canyon view, and the smell of something or other in bloom; in southern California there was always something in bloom, even in winter. In one end of the room was a small brick box of a wood-burning stove, with a metal plate on top. Sigurdsson put two pieces of wood in it and an old-fashioned orange-red enameled coffee pot on top, and they sat down.

It was Carol that Sigurdsson spoke to. "Okay," he said, "let's see v'ere ve stand. V'at Kevin vanted to tell us is, there is something out there that kills people, makes them have wrecks, but he can't tell us no more because he don't know. So now it's up to us to find out.

"So he don't need to hang around no more, but he's still here. Right?"

She nodded soberly. It seemed to Connor that *he*

could feel Kevin Ludi, too; he just hadn't realized before what it was that he felt. The sadness, the touch of forlornness he'd felt before around Carol wasn't his own and maybe wasn't all Carol's, either.

"Vell, v'y don't ve let him go then?" Sigurdsson said. "Let him go hang around a delivery room somev'ere and pick up a new body?"

Her face got a stricken look, and Connor felt himself—or felt someone—wanting to comfort her. Sigurdsson's face was calm, his eyes steady. "He ain't stuck here from getting killed, you know," he said. "He's stuck to *you*."

She nodded.

"Is there something you can tell me about that?" he asked.

"I don't want to lose him." Her voice was small, face pinched, eyes haunted. She repeated a little more strongly: "I just don't want to lose him."

"Right. Did you ever feel like that before?"

She nodded.

"V'en is the earliest time you can remember not vanting to lose Kevin?"

She thought for a moment. "When we were ten. Dad and mom sent us each to camp—two different camps, one for boys and one for girls. We both cried." She looked at Sigurdsson and half smiled, ruefully. "It was really pretty silly, when I stop to think about it, but we were just devastated. And it didn't blow over in a day or two. We both got sick—bad colds—and both camps called our parents and they had to come and get us."

"Okay. Vas there an earlier time v'en you didn't vant to lose Kevin?"

"I don't remember. Probably not, or I would."

"Okay. Vell, yust close your eyes and see if you can spot vun."

She closed her eyes, her expression wary. "That's it," said Sigurdsson. "There . . . that vun." His voice was quiet, but held certainty and power. Conner wondered what the old Icelander saw that he didn't.

And then he felt it, and got a powerful cold rush again, his skin like a plucked chicken, his hair like electric wires. *What*, he wondered, *is happening? What does this old guy have going?*

Her mouth opened slightly.

"Tell me v'at you see."

"I see—two people. In a car, in the blowing snow. Everything is white and blurry, and I can't see very far. Their car is stuck. Or stalled. No, it's stuck."

She fell silent then, her face intent, seeing with her eyes closed, and after a few seconds Sigurdsson's voice nudged her gently.

"Um-hm?"

"I'm trying to figure out who they are. And where."

"Fine. Yust tell me v'at you see."

"Well, it must be really cold, because the snow is dry and blowing like dust. And I can only see a few yards. . . . Everything's white except the car. It's an old car, and they're sitting in it." She said the last with a note of finality, and sitting back, opened her eyes.

"All right. Is there anything else?" Sigurdsson asked.

"I don't think so."

"Okay. Vell, close your eyes and give a little look."

She frowned, peering with closed lids. "They're just sitting there," she said.

"Ya-ah?"

"With . . . The man has his arms around the woman. And there are . . ." Her voice faltered. "There are tears frozen on his cheeks and eyelashes. Little globules of ice . . . His lips are moving." Her face twisted, her own tears starting, and she began to cry silently. Connor got a sense of crushing grief that he knew wasn't his but that almost suffocated him. Sigurdsson just sat there, completely calm, eyes steady on her.

"She's dying," Carol said brokenly. "The woman
. . . freezing to death." She kept crying for what
seemed to Connor like a long time—perhaps half a
minute. Then Sigurdsson spoke again.

"Okay," he said quietly, "you're doing good. V'at
else do you see?"

"That's all," she said. She gave a quavery sigh and
opened her eyes. "That's all there is."

Sigurdsson's eyes were direct but mild. "Good.
Now go back to the beginning and run through it
again for me."

Her focus went off as if to an upper corner of the
room, and she closed her eyes again. After what
must have been another minute, she hugged her
arms around herself and began to shiver. Her skin
began to look waxy white to Connor's worried eyes.

Sigurdsson's words continued almost conversationally: "Tell me v'at you see."

"The same as before." Her voice was low, faint.
"He's holding her to him, and she's dying, and his
lips are moving. . . . And that's all I see."

"Fine." And then his matter-of-fact voice lit the
fuse. "How do you know she's dying?"

After a pause, she started to really shake. Not
shiver, but really shake—great big shakes, as if she
would come apart there in the chair. Her skin pulled
tight on her face and she started to moan loudly,
almost a wail. The shaking became a rocking: tilting
back, rocking forward. She did this for perhaps half a
minute while Sigurdsson said nothing, watching
calmly, alert, seeing God knows what, Connor
thought—maybe seeing what she was seeing.

"Because," she choked out, "because she's me.
I'm her. And he's, he's Stevie. Kevin, I mean."

That was the end of the moaning: the dam burst.
The grief and the crying were so powerful that Connor half rose in consternation. Her tears gushed and
splashed. Her nose ran. She blubbered. After about

a minute the whole thing changed: The tears continued for a bit but the terrible grief was gone. Her eyes turned first to Sigurdsson and then to Connor, and she half giggled through her tears. Fumbling out a tissue, she blew so strongly that it came apart in her hand; she held it up to show them.

"And do you know what he was saying?" She was smiling in genuine soggy-eyed amusement. "He was saying, 'I'll never leave you, no matter what. I'll never, never leave you.' " She hiccupped, then giggled again. "So what else would you expect? I died hearing those words, and he died a few minutes later, in a Saskatchewan blizzard. And we showed up twins in Madison, Wisconsin."

She looked down at the front of her dress, and her voice was firm and clear. "Ye gods! I look like I went three rounds with an open fire hydrant!"

Connor sat dumbfounded. How in the name of God had Sigurdsson pulled that off? He hadn't hypnotized her. What kind of power did he have?

"Maybe you better borrow vun of Laura's sveaters then," Sigurdsson was saying. "Ve don't vant you to catch cold." And before she could get up, he added, "You notice anything different around here?"

She paused, looked thoughtful, then brightened. "Kevin's gone!" she said.

"By golly, you're right!" Ole said. "You did good on that!"

She got up and kissed his cheek. "He's free and I'm free! And hungry! I'm going to raid your refrigerator before I go home."

She went into the kitchen and puttered around. They could hear humming, water running, drawers pulled; the refrigerator opened and closed. There was an occasional cheerful comment directed at them through the door. Sigurdsson was grinning broadly.

"How the heck did you do that?" Connor asked in an undertone.

"I didn't. She did. I yust prodded her along a little bit."

"Bullshit!" said Connor. "I feel like I've been a witness to sorcery."

"Not here you ain't. Maybe on the pass you saw some, v'en her brother wrecked."

When Carol came back in, her face was washed and she carried a baloney, pickle, and mayonnaise sandwich with tomato and lettuce. "Mr. Sigurdsson," she said, "you haven't offered us any of that coffee yet."

"Vell, I better do that then." He got up and took mugs from pegs on the wall, got cream and sugar from the kitchen, then poured three cups.

"What are we going to do about whatever is killing people out on the pass?" Carol asked.

"That's a good qvestion," Sigurdsson replied. "I vish I knew the answer to it."

Connor commented facetiously: "It sounds as if we're up against some kind of murderous computer that counts cars and trashes one out of every so many. That's it! It's a sort of computerized tollgate!"

He looked around and inwardly collapsed. Carol was looking at him as if she didn't think the subject was suitable for flippancy. Sigurdsson was eyeing him intently. "Not too funny, huh?" Connor said lamely.

"Maybe not too funny," said Sigurdsson, "but interesting. Keep going; you're doing fine."

Connor stared. "Are you kidding? You can't be taking me seriously!"

"Can you think of anything else that explains it so good?" Ole asked. "I think you put your finger on yust v'at it is."

Carol frowned. "But Ole, who could have put such a thing there? Even our most advanced science falls way short of anything like that, doesn't it? And what would the purpose be?"

"Carol," said Sigurdsson gently, "in my business you run into some things that don't fit very good vith history books or archaeology. I don't pretend to know much about it—yust glimpses, isolated incidents—but there vas some heavy games in the past—the *vay* past. And after v'ile the games ran down and people forgot about them, but maybe sometimes some of the machinery kept going."

Connor didn't know how to react to that; the whole concept was too strange and freaky. "Well," he said, "what do we do then?"

"Ve'll yust have to give that more thought." Sigurdsson got up. "Carol, I'm going to take you home. Or Yerry can if it ain't too much out of his vay."

"Not at all," said Connor. "I'd love to."

"Okay?" said Sigurdsson, looking at Carol. Then to Connor he said, "But give me your address and phone number so I can get hold of you v'en I need to."

It was beginning to get dark when Jerry Connor let Carol out. As he drove home, he realized he wasn't feeling well. He had an uneasy feeling that he identified as vague, unfocused fear. As if, he decided, there really was a game put into operation a very long time ago—a game that killed people, even now. It didn't feel like anything to mess around with, he thought. The smart thing to do was back off and leave it alone. One fatal accident in tens of millions of cars over the pass wasn't all that serious.

As he pulled up to his apartment house, he saw Ole Sigurdsson's big white Caddy at the curb across the street. When Connor had parked, they met in front of the building in the half darkness, and in mutual silence walked together through the planted courtyard. When Connor opened his door, the tiny red light of his telephone answering machine was flashing at them in the gloom. He went to it and started the playback.

"Jerry," it said, "this is Carol. I'm scared. Miki's out of town, her dog is growling, which he's never done before, the cat won't even come in the house, and no one answers the phone at Sigurdsson's. I know it sounds ridiculous, but I feel as if my life is in danger. Please call me as soon as you get home. Thanks."

"What'll I tell her?" asked Connor.

"Tell her I'm vith you and ve feel it, too. Tell her you and me are going out and handle it."

Connor knew what the answer would be, but he asked anyway: "Handle what?"

The tall old Icelander looked at him calmly in the dimness. "The tollgate," Ole said.

"Is that safe?"

"Hell, no! But it ain't safe not to, either. Your computerized tollgate got a security system vired in, and ve started it ticking today v'en ve put so much attention on it. That's v'at the hell ve're feeling. I think now ve better take the fuse out—either that or leave town av'ile."

Connor picked up the phone and got Carol. She wanted to go with them, but Sigurdsson told her he didn't want the delay, that he wanted to act immediately. Then Connor got his service revolver from the closet, feeling foolish as he strapped it on. *You don't even have any silver bullets for it,* he told himself.

They went in Sigurdsson's car, and things felt a little less oppressive as they drove. Traffic was moderate on the boulevard, and Sigurdsson had the signals perfectly: nothing but green all the way, and traffic just seemed to open for them. It was Ole, Connor decided; he felt the man's intention like sharp steel. Shortly he could see lights on the freeway overpass ahead; they'd be on it soon.

The car windows were open, and the January air was mild and sweet. Connor's earlier fears began to feel unreal, even silly. Then something small, triangular, and shiny came bouncing and clinking out into the street ahead, and with abrupt violence, Sigurdsson hit the brakes and jerked the wheel hard left. They careened sharply across the oncoming traffic and through it into a parking lot, accompanied by angry horns and squealing tires. There were loud crashes behind them, metal into metal, and then a different kind of crash.

They sat limply in the front seat, untouched, hearts racing. "A v'eel chock," said Sigurdsson. Connor stared at him uncomprehendingly till the Icelander elaborated. "That was a v'eel chock that come out in the street, from something parked on the hill."

They got out. It had been a wheel chock, all right, that had somehow slipped out and released an unattended moving van. The van had rolled down the slope then, out of the side street and into the boulevard, had hit a car broadside, been hit by two others, and crashed into a restaurant. Meanwhile, several other cars had run into one another.

Connor pursed his lips in a silent whistle as they looked at the devastation. If Sigurdsson hadn't been quick at the wheel, they'd have been demolished. "What do you suppose made that chock slip out?" he asked. Sigurdsson glanced at him without saying anything.

The boulevard was now blocked with wreckage, so they detoured. Once on the freeway, the Caddy moved out of the heavily built-up area into lightly developed hills. Whatever they were up against out here, thought Jerry Connor, it was more than a "simple" tollgate. It seemed to be a telepathic, telekinetic killer robot. He wondered just how far its abilities reached, and what its limitations might be.

"What do you think will happen next?" he asked.

"I ain't thinking," said Sigurdsson curtly. "I'm driving."

"What'll we do when we get to the pass?"

The words were hardly out when the car jerked sideways, seeming to rise above the pavement. Sigurdsson cursed in Icelandic and fought with wheel and will. The tires hit the pavement again and they bounced on the shocks. Sigurdsson's breath hissed out; Connor's guts were a hard knot.

Briefly, nothing more seemed to happen as they continued on. Then Connor became aware that the headlights of the northbound cars were paling; the traffic noise softened despite his open window, and the sense of menace was almost overpowering. He stared, his hair feeling as if it were standing on end.

"What's happening?" he murmured. Sigurdsson didn't answer, just shook his head. Two or three minutes later he pulled off on the shoulder at the head of the pass and they got out.

It felt somehow different outside, not like southern California at all. Ghost cars whispered by them on the freeway, and Connor thought that if the sound should fade out entirely, something terrible would happen. Overhead the sky glow of Los Angeles was gone, replaced by a blackness swashed with stars. It occurred to him that if he knew the constellations of 20th-century California, he wouldn't find them up there.

The lining of his mouth felt like flannel.

Beside him, Sigurdsson stood tall and doughty, scanning the hills around them. To Connor the hills seemed black and featureless, without lights, visible only in cutting off the sky, but Sigurdsson stopped panning, as if his eyes had found something. Jerry stared hard but saw nothing. They stood like that for a long minute, and it seemed to Connor that something was going on, but he had no idea what. The sense of menace eased notably, and the sound and headlights were returning toward normal.

"Let's go," Sigurdsson muttered.

They got back in the car and left. This time it behaved itself, and Connor decided that Sigurdsson's driving had definitely become more conservative.

"Ole," he said after a minute, "did people in the other cars out there feel what we did?"

Sigurdsson shook his head. "Not enough to notice," he said. "Maybe a few noticed it a little bit, but its attention vas on us."

"Whose attention?"

"V'atever it vas in the vatchtower back there."

*Watchtower*. Conner chewed on that briefly; he'd seen no watchtower. They sat for a while in mutual silence again. After Sigurdsson had turned onto Sunset Boulevard eastbound, Jerry broke the silence. "I felt the danger ease up just before we left. Do you know what caused that?"

"Sure. Somevun else come in out there—at least a couple of somevuns—vith power, and give us a hand. And no, I don't know who, or even v'at happened. V'atever ve did, ve did it cloaked off from ourselves, or cloaked off from me, anyvay. But the thing backed off; that's v'at's important."

*Cloaked from ourselves*. Connor decided this wasn't the time to ask what that meant. He did almost ask if everything was all right now, but realized it wasn't. Instead he said, "What do we do next?"

"You got any vacation time you can use?"

"More than three weeks. But it'll take at least a week before I can get off. Maybe two."

"Put in for it. Ve need to take a trip."

"A trip? Where to?"

"I don't know yet. Ve're going to find whoever it vas that helped save our ass out there."

"What are we going to do that for?"

Ole turned and looked at him. "I ain't got no idea. That's part of being an operating psychic: You got to go vith your knowingness, your hunches, even if you don't know v'at the hell it is you know.

"But I can tell you this: Somehow or other ve're up against more than yust the thing at the pass. That's yust a little shirttail of it—sort of a symptom."

# < FIVE >

Its mountains look too perfect to be real; even their asymmetry seems idealized by any Earth standards, as if designed. Forests of towering leafy trees cover the steep slopes to the edge of the large, fjord-like, deep-blue lake, mostly beachless. This landscape and the innumerable, equally idealized others in its universe could be collectively thought of as Olympus, but their inhabitants are more players than gods.

At one point the mountains do not plunge into the water. There a valley comes down with its stream to the lake, a valley U-shaped without benefit of any glacier ever. Near its mouth spreads a rich lawn-like meadow, almost a putting green, never having known a caretaker, yet innocent of weeds, though not of tiny flowers that sprinkle it with color, blue as flax, yellow as buttercups. Structures of marble are scattered artfully, their style reminiscent of Hellenic Greece, but gracefully gracious instead of imposing, with roundness the principal motif.

All in all it looks like a Maxfield Parrish painting, rather than like any place on Earth. (Parrish was an insightful man, more than he knew.) Everything here is beautiful.

But for the beings who base in the Maxfield Parrish universe, interest and adventure are elsewhere. In a metaphorical sense, the Maxfield Parrish universe might be thought of as a balcony or mezzanine, although the analogy is weak; video arcade might fit better. At any rate, for a very long time, its "occupants" have had most of their attention in another universe, just as on Earth, some people spend much of their time at the theater, or playing video games.

Over the ages, the avoidance of boredom has been highly developed by the immortals dwelling here. Intricate and ingenious machinery and rules have evolved, and play engrosses the inhabitants almost totally. But of course, the Maxfield Parrish universe requires no maintenance, no production, no service; it exists and functions without attention.

Actually, from the standpoint of play, its inhabitants could almost as well be based in empty blackness, but the Maxfield Parrish universe is better than limbo because it is aesthetic. It has been there since long before the universe of interest, and in it, bodies require no care or feeding.

In the Maxfield Parrish universe, interpersonal communication has nothing to do with the compressibility of air, although its rules of communication have some things in common with speech. For example, it is subject to the volition of the "speaker." However, it is also subject to the volition of potential "listeners:" unwanted communication is not received. Nor is spatial proximity necessary, although it is often enjoyed.

In the instance of interest to us, several who were part of the conference lounged together on the turf. Together with conferees elsewhere they numbered nearly a dozen, and by agreement they all had fully removed their attentions from the other universe, which might loosely be termed "the stage," "the video game," or "the playing field." "Later," when they returned their attentions to the game, they would return them to the exact time from which they'd withdrawn them, unless they decided otherwise. As nearly as their conversations can be put into words, their assorted inputs went something like this:

". . . I'd say we're doing nicely. We have four gathered in one group and four in the second, and I'm quite optimistic about developing the third."

(Sense of laughter.) "If we pull this off, it will be the biggest coup in the history of Tikh Cheki. The reality generator is well on its way to a phase three."

(Another.) "The key is to outmaneuver The Four. And I must say, things don't look very promising."

(A fourth.) "I disagree. Would you like to wager? I'll bet a class-two penalty against a dropout that we pull it off."

(Thoughtfully.) "Unrealistic."

"I don't think so, for two reasons: the energy has been bled off the Balthor Incident, and The Seven Lords of Chaos were extradited."

"It's still over-optimistic. The chances are, they didn't happen soon enough for this cycle."

"Well, then, a wager. If you're right, you have little to worry about."

"No, thank you." (Sense of grinning.) "I never bet against myself."

(Another.) "Does anyone here have any changes or additions to suggest with regard to either our strategy or our tactics?"

There was a general negative response—a sense of "we're doing excitingly well, given the obstacles," and "we actually have a chance to win now!"

(Another.) "I'm going for a swim before I put this body back in the closet. Anyone care to join me?"

Of the several on the site together, all but two got up and ran to the lake. They wouldn't swim for long, though. Their real interest was on the playing field.

# < SIX >

It was a bright warm day for January—seventy degrees at 10:53 A.M. Ole Sigurdsson was driving east on the Sunset Strip, hardly noticing the glass-faced towers, the shops and cafes, a huge entertainment sign promoting "Bilbo and the Seven Orcs." He was watching for a street sign.

The boulevard changed, its buildings and mood becoming less flamboyant. Trees lined one side. Seeing the street he'd been watching for, he turned south on it. If some powerful, hateful entity had any attention on Ole just then, it was too slight to be apparent to him.

A block farther he surprised himself by turning a block east, out of his way, then half a block south again. Pulling to an available length of curb, he stopped. Just ahead was a site of strong psychic trauma, flagged by the standing waves of emotion left by murder. Briefly, Ole sorted out the elements; they matched a news report he recalled from television a few months earlier.

Then he drove on and parked a block north of Santa Monica Boulevard. Behind him, on the front porch of an elderly house, hung a varnished wooden sign, the words routed into it and painted white:

MADAME TANYA—PSYCHIC

Auras Read, Fortunes Told

Questions Answered

Trees shaded the emerald yard; rose bushes, blooming yellow, white, and red, guarded the walk; bougainvillea rioted wildly scarlet over the porch roof and down a trellised end to the ground. Madame had a green thumb.

Ole Sigurdsson knew a number of professional psychics, from as far away as Indonesia and Lapland, and as near as Beverly Hills and Hollywood, but almost all only casually. Anna Jennings, AKA Madame Tanya, he'd never met, had only heard about, but she was reputed by her peers to have more psychic ability than most.

Ole's telepathic ability was neither controllable nor precise, so he'd phoned her. Now, walking up her front steps, he glanced at his watch: eleven sharp. Nearly exact promptness without effort *was* one of his rather consistent talents.

He pushed the button on the doorpost and heard the buzzer inside. Shortly, Madame opened the door. "I'm Ole Sigurdsson," said Ole. "I called you a v'ile ago."

Madame Tanya was not a typical homemaker, nor did she use makeup the way she did through any illusion that it beautified her. Simply, many clients expected it. Lipstick too vivid, eye shadow too thick, eyebrows plucked and penciled to a thin black line, and clothes that might have come from a gypsy wagon, all were useful parts of her image. When a client left, the image stayed with him or her; it helped them remember to talk about Madame Tanya and her considerable abilities.

Most of her business came to her from word of mouth, although occasional appearances on local radio and TV talk shows had certainly helped. She was good, both as a sensitive and as a showperson, in her living room and in the studio.

She looked Ole over, her eyes seeing physical things that most people wouldn't have noticed, her "inner eye" noticing other things that very few indeed would have picked up.

"Olaf Sigurdsson," she said, pronouncing the first name almost like "Olive." "What brings a celebrity psychic from Bel Air to a palm reader in West Hollywood?"

"You tell fortunes," he said. "V'at do you see for me?"

She grinned up at him. "You haven't showed me your palm yet."

He smiled slightly. "If you needed to see my palm, that vould really be a surprise."

She laughed, then gathered her attention and frowned thoughtfully. "I don't want to sound corny, but you're going to take a trip. You'll leave tomorrow, with a young man and a good-looking young woman with long blonde hair. The young man wears a . . . bandage of some kind. A cast, on his arm. And I see desert, and there's a 'dobe ranch house, with trees around it, and a windmill. Two windmills; now that's interesting. And a water tank on stilts. Any of that mean anything to you?"

"The trip does, and the company, but ve don't expect to go for a veek or so yet. The rest of it don't ring any bell at all, but it feels right v'en you say it.

"V'ere is this place in the desert?"

"Damned if I know." She concentrated again. "Arizona someplace, that's all I get on it. Yeah, Arizona."

"Vell, if finding it is in my future, I von't vorry about how."

"I don't guarantee it's in your future. It's just what I got in answer to your question. Fortunes aren't what they used to be." She peered at him interestedly. "Don't you see futures?"

"Now and then, for this vun and that vun. Never my own. Mainly I help people straighten out their lives. I used to be a Noetie, you know—a counselor vith the Institute of Noetic Technology. I see more the pasts of people and places, and things in the present that other people don't, or things somev'ere else."

He paused. "V'at do you mean, 'fortunes ain't v'at they used to be'?"

She cocked her head. "How do you feel about how things are going lately?" she countered. "With the world, I mean."

"To hell on a bobsled," he said. "So vy ain't fortunes v'at they used to be?"

"Well, the last couple of years I've been running into people with short futures. I mean, it's everybody that comes to me to get their fortune read. Mostly I get that their future just . . . stops a little way up the line; whatever it is that happens then, I can't see. I don't get a date on it, but it feels like, oh, about half a year from now.

"But the funny thing is, it feels as if there's a weak alternate line for them, too, not strong enough—maybe too improbable—for me to read.

"This hasn't screwed up business yet, because mostly I just tell the near future anyway: next week, maybe month after next. I bat a lot better that way; the odds start to slip when you forecast farther ahead than a few weeks. It's that way with me anyway. If I get something really interesting a few months up the track, and it's not too heavy, I give 'em that, too. But these days, if they insist on anything long-term, I have to fake it.

"So the way it looks to me, six months from now there's not likely to be any more future."

Ole nodded; all this was new to him, but it felt

right. "You get anything on me besides a trip vith two people and a ranch house?"

She looked at him as if evaluating. "Actually, there's more, but I can only kind of feel it. It's . . . heavy, but not . . . it doesn't feel all that terrible. Necessarily. Whatever it is, the outcome is undecided." She shrugged. "I'd never lay that on an ordinary client, but you asked, and you're different."

"But there's still vun track vith a future on it, eh? Vell hell, that's hopeful; it could be vorse than that. I'll vork on that vun. You get anything else at all?"

She shook her head. "Not a damn thing . . . Except be sure to check your answering machine when you get home. It's important."

He nodded. "V'at do I owe you?"

"Nothing. It's a professional courtesy."

"Okay. So v'at's your favorite charity?"

"Huh? Oh." She grinned again. "Next to me, the Salvation Army, I guess. I'm reaching the age where I appreciate an outfit that helps old derelicts . . . There is a favor maybe you can do for me, though. My house is haunted lately."

"Ya, I noticed. It's the guy v'at got chopped by a sword last summer, yust a few blocks from here. How come he's hanging around you?"

"Because I noticed him. He's on a big guilt trip, and nobody but me paid any attention to him. He makes it kind of sticky around here—all that guilt. Do you suppose you can get rid of him for me?"

Ole looked past her, his line of vision above her shoulder. The ghost of Lefty Nagel appeared then, like ragged, semidissolved cheesecloth to Ole's perception. That was a good sign; instead of still carrying around his old physical appearance, Lefty had adopted a "ghostly look." Ole said nothing out loud to him; sound wasn't necessary, and their exchanges were much faster than speech. Within three or four minutes the guilt blew the way Carol's grief had, leaving Madame Tanya's lavender hair electrified. She looked at Olaf Sigurdsson with appreciation and increased respect.

"What the hell did you do?"

"Oh, ve yust looked at a few things, me and him. A modified Noetie action ve done together."

"Well, I'd say we're even now. More than even. You've got something on account with me."

Ole looked at her thoughtfully. "You know," he said, "I vouldn't be surprised if I drew on that, vun of these days."

When he got home, he checked the messages on his machine; there were three. The first was from a Mrs. William Benning, telling him there'd been a cancellation; if Mr. Sigurdsson wanted to talk with Mr. McBee this evening, it was now possible. He should confirm right away. The second was from his wife, Laura: The Burriston script for *The Lantern of God* was a disaster, and she'd be at the studio until very late. The third message was from Jerry Connor: His patrol car had been broadsided by a drunk driver, and his right arm was broken. He was now on sick leave and would be available for the trip as soon as Sigurdsson wanted.

Ole took a deep breath, remembering Madame Tanya's predictions of an arm in a cast and a next-day departure. The two expected delays—the approval time for Connor's vacation and the wait to talk with McBee—had both unexpectedly evaporated. He dialed Benning's number and confirmed a McBee conference at eight. Then he called Carol Ludi at her sister-in-law's health salon, where Carol was the administrator. Finally he phoned Laura and told her what was happening.

After that he sat on the sundeck overlooking the canyon and relaxed with a scotch on the rocks. It occurred to him that Lefty Nagel was hanging around him now, not particularly noticeable because the grief and guilt were gone. Ole could have run the ghost off but decided to let him stay for the time being. He didn't know why; it just felt right.

Then he fell asleep on his recliner, knowing the sun would waken him in half an hour or so when it moved around to shine in his face.

Jerry Connor couldn't drive with his arm broken, so Carol picked him up at his Van Nuys apartment and crossed the hills via Coldwater Canyon Drive. She wasn't about to take the freeway over the pass. They arrived in front of Benning's Culver City home with fifteen minutes to spare, and waited in the car until Ole arrived at seven fifty-six.

Benning's wife let them in. She seemed like a regular housewife-mother type with her head on straight, not like the wife of a spirit medium. Jerry wondered what kind of people she usually met at the door, and whether any before him had carried a police shield in their wallet.

She left them in the living room, where a ten-year-old boy and an eight-year-old girl were watching television, oblivious to the newcomers.

Three minutes later, Benning walked in, wearing bedroom slippers. He was about thirty-five, a machinist at McDonnell Douglas, and he'd been taking a nap. Sometimes, he said, these sessions ran late, and he had to get up at six in the morning. He led them into what might once have been a bedroom, and asked if they had a tape recorder. They didn't, so he seated a cassette in his own, gave Ole brief instructions on its operation, and sat down opposite them.

To Jerry, the machinist sounded like Oklahoma a generation removed—very middle America.

"All right," said Benning to Ole, "we can get started in just a jiffy. I'll need $200 in advance, cash or

money order, like my wife told you over the phone.
If you don't feel all right about what you hear in the
first five minutes after McBee takes over, you can
wake me up and give me $30. I'll give you back your
advance payment then and we'll quit. When the
session is over, you can have the cassettes of it for $3
each, and any copyrights are yours. Mr. McBee can't
use them, and I'm just the medium.

"Now, have you got any questions before we start?"

Ole shook his head. "I don't think so. I'm ready."

"All right. It may be a couple minutes before Mr.
McBee takes over, so I need you to be quiet until he
talks to you. He'll tell you when to start asking
questions."

Benning leaned back in his old naugahyde recliner, then tilted it and closed his eyes. In the
silence that followed, Jerry Connor became aware of
the throbbing ache in his lower right arm, broken
only eleven hours earlier. Briefly, he wondered if he
was rushing things, coming here tonight and leaving
town tomorrow. Quietly, he took a pain pill from a
pocket and swallowed it dry.

His eyes watched the sweep second hand on the
wall clock. It had made less than one complete circle
when Benning spoke again. But the voice—its pitch,
its timbre, its accents—was utterly different from
before, reminiscent more of Calcutta than Oklahoma.
The words chased each other more quickly than Connor was used to, though they were easy enough to
understand.

"Thank you, beloved," the voice said. "I am with
you now. If you will ask whatever questions you
have, I will answer those which I may. There may be
questions, however, which it is not proper for me to
answer. What is it you wish to ask first?"

*He's hedging already*, thought Jerry.

Ole summarized very briefly the deaths on the
pass and their statistical pattern, but did not mention

Jerry's speculation on the cause. He also summarized what Madame Tanya had told him about futures. "So v'at I vant to know first is, v'at's going on?" he finished.

"Ah. There is . . . machinery at the point of which you speak, beloved. On the pass. Very old machinery, in the order of millions of years, left over from a very ancient game, from a cycle long before that in which you now find yourself. It has been operating at a uniform rate until very recently, when it began to accelerate. Next question, please."

*Does he know that,* Jerry wondered, *or did he put it together from what Ole told him?* He watched Benning's relaxed face for any sign of the effort of thought as Ole put the next question.

"Okay. V'at speeded it up?"

"Its rate of operation is influenced by the output of another, much older machine, which we may call the 'surprise generator.' This surprise generator makes it possible for the people of this planet to lead more interesting lives. And under certain conditions it accelerates. Those conditions now exist, beloved, and therefore its output of, um, aberrative impulses is speeding up. This has resulted in acceleration of the tollgate. Next question, please."

*God,* Jerry thought, *if he ever decides to go out of the spirit business, he could write science fiction.*

"Okay," Ole said, "v'at vere ve running into last night that tried to kill us? V'at kind of being vas that?"

"It is an artificial construct, one which might be called a robot sentry. It was designed to protect the tollgate, and was activated by your awareness and attention. Next question, please."

Jerry sat thunderstruck: *The tollgate! He'd called it the tollgate!*

Ole said nothing for a minute, his brows gnarled in thought. Finally, he focused again on Benning/McBee, who still lay slack-faced. "This surprise yenerator—does it have anything to do vith v'at else is happening? You said it's accelerating; so is craziness. And Madame Tanya said ve maybe only got about half a year before there ain't no future. Is that because the surprise yenerator is speeding up?"

This time it was Benning/McBee who had a long lag before answering—at least it seemed long to Jerry Connor. Finally, the medium's mouth moved. "Beloved, there are things I may not tell you. There are rules governing these things and much else. You have discerned something independently which allows me to answer this question, but I will not talk about it any further than that. Yes, the surprise generator *is* responsible, as you surmised, for the phenomena which you call 'increased craziness.' Next question."

"Wait a minute!" Jerry interrupted. "Ole has this idea that the world may end or something in six months, and somebody or something is killing people on the pass and tried to kill us last night. Do you mean to say you can't tell us what you know because of some stupid rules?"

"Thank you, Jerry Connor. I appreciate and admire your exasperation. But Mr. Sigurdsson, and you two as his teammates, are embarking on a game which we might call 'save Earth.' You may not heretofore have realized that fully, but it is so. The name is not fully appropriate, but from your point of view it might be called that. And indeed, almost everyone on Earth has an interest in that game, actively or passively, though few of them know consciously that there is such a game, as a game.

"Such games have rules. Human beings are so deeply conditioned to those rules that they do not even know the rules exist. To them there are only *inabilities*, which are the rules agreed to long ago and continuingly, and which are closely enforced.

"Meanwhile, Mr. Sigurdsson, and you, his teammates, may conceivably win the game, but this will *not* happen should I break the rules for you. God bless you, beloved. Next question, please."

Jerry sat back, confused. Sigurdsson changed the line of inquiry. "Ve're going to the desert tomorrow, but ve don't know v'ere. All ve know is, ve're looking for a 'dobe ranch house in Arizona somev'ere; ve don't know v'ere it is or who lives there. Can you tell me either vun? Or better yet, both?"

"It is not allowed that I tell you either. My position is one of neutrality always. If I should become polarized in favor of one side or another in my actions, or give what might be called 'operational guidance,' then I would become part of the game, and I do not wish to be so. Also, it would jeopardize your own efforts. But I can tell you this: there are others in the game who wish in turn that you will arrive at that place. If you do not try hard, but *allow* yourself to go there, not demanding it seriously of yourself or of God, you will probably arrive."

He paused, and it seemed to Connor that McBee was consulting silently with others. It was nothing that Jerry could see or hear, but it seemed that way to him. Then Benning/McBee spoke again. "There is one thing further I can say. It is in the nature of a riddle, and it is as far as I can go in this matter." He paused. "When you see the sign of the triumphant sorcerer, you will need to seek no further.

"I will tell you now that this interview must end soon. The entire subject is one of which I may not speak at length. There are too many opportunities for damage. I will answer two more questions."

Jerry Connor looked at Sigurdsson, then at his watch. He wasn't sure they'd gotten their $200 worth, but more than five minutes had passed; they couldn't get it back. Ole spoke again.

"There's somevun v'at came vith us tonight. He's

kind of hard to notice. I think he's adopted me. Vy did he do that? Does he have a part to play in any of this?"

The next sound from Benning/McBee startled all of them: a peal of laughter, the laughter of delight. "You are testing me! Yes, beloved, he did indeed adopt you, because you relieved him of his burden, one which he was unable by himself to put down. As you already know, you can send him away if you wish, and he will go. But he would like to help you in his turn. I may say no more about that.

"And now you have one more question. Perhaps Miss Ludi would like to ask it; she has not spoken yet."

Jerry's scalp crawled. It occurred to him that neither his name nor Carol's had been mentioned to Benning unless Ole had named them over the phone. Yet Benning/McBee had referred to each of them by name.

"Mr. McBee," said Carol, "we need to appraise what you've told us, but we don't know anything about you. Who or what are you?"

"Hoo-oo! Hoo-oo! An excellent question, beloved! Very well; that I may certainly answer without care.

"There are many spectators without bodies who are also outside your universe or indeed any universe—spectators of the games played by men and other embodied spirits, here and on other worlds. I am one of those spectators. We are in some ways like the people who watch your sporting contests. For example, we are far greater in number than the players, and we may not interfere in the games ourselves. However, noninterference is not a difficult or onerous constraint, because we do not have favorites. To have favorites would draw us into your games. But also we do not have the *inclination* to favoritism, because we have chosen to remain outside.

"Our position outside the games allows us to perceive far more than the players, at one level, are allowed to know. And really, beloved, that is the basic difference between those like myself, and those like you who have chosen to operate bodies and play within your universe.

"But now I must end this interview. You have the potential to succeed in your objectives, and either you will or you will not. Your best chance lies in not striving excessively, but simply in doing what seems appropriate at any given time. God bless you, beloved."

A few minutes later, Ole, Jerry, and Carol stood by the curb, deciding the time and place of their next day's departure. When they had done that, Carol looked thoughtfully at Sigurdsson. "Ole," she asked, "did you mention our names to Mr. Benning at any time?"

"You noticed that too, eh? No, I never did. Only mine. I told him I vas coming vith two friends, but I never said either of your names."

"Are you sure?" Jerry asked.

Ole cocked an eyebrow at him. "Positive," he said.

"Did you tell the fortuneteller our names?"

"No. And I never told her I vas coming here, either."

"You said something about someone else who came with you tonight," Carol said. "I didn't understand what that was about. And Mr. McBee said you'd helped this person. That wasn't me, was it?"

Ole grinned and shook his head, then looked at Jerry. "Did you feel anyvun hanging around?" he asked.

"What do you mean? Like Kevin hung around?" Then waves of chills hit Jerry Connor again; for the first time, he felt the presence of Lefty Nagel. Ole laughed out loud looking at him.

"Okay, you got him. Carol, I got adopted by a

ghost today. I helped him kind of the vay I helped you and Kevin, but this ghost decided to stay vith me, and I agreed he can if he don't make no trouble. His name is Lefty."

"Can't ghosts be dangerous sometimes?"

"Not for me they ain't; not anymore. But now and then vun of them can be unpleasant. Those are the vuns—they ain't very common—that can cause physical effects. The vuns that can knock dishes off the shelves and throw the furniture around—things like that. Those are the vuns people ask for help vith the most."

He looked at each of the two younger people in turn. "I think ve learned something useful from McBee tonight," he added. "V'at ve're getting into here can sound pretty vild and danyerous. But if ve can go at it vithout getting up-tight, ve got a better chance to pull it off."

Two hours later, Jerry Connor was in bed. Ole had taken him home and given him a "treatment" for his arm. When he'd left, Jerry had awkwardly packed, then mixed himself a vodka collins and thought for a while. If Carol had brought him home, he might have asked her to stay—or he might not. He was really interested in creating a future with her, not simply an affair—if there was going to be a future.

The future. *Tomorrow*, he thought, *we'll be headed for we don't know where, looking for we don't know who, and we'll probably have a left-handed ghost with us.*

He wondered if he was crazy; it didn't feel right for a dream. Mr. McBee was a spirit, Benning a medium, Madame Tanya a fortuneteller, and he didn't know what to call Ole—a master psychic, he guessed. And a week earlier he didn't really believe that any of those things existed as genuine. He still wasn't a hundred percent sure.

But there was the pass and its fatality statistics. You couldn't argue with those. And what had happened last night on Ventura Boulevard and on the freeway were real without a doubt. While the world . . . the way things had been going lately in the news, it was easy to believe that the world might end in half a year.

Jerry Connor hadn't prayed since he'd graduated from Saint Ignatius High School. He decided to give it another try after all those years.

# < SEVEN >

Ole wasn't actually grumpy, but he wasn't smiling or saying much. It wasn't that the gray sky and steady drizzle had gotten to him. Rather, he'd wanted to make an early getaway—be on the 210 freeway by nine, headed east out of metro L.A. But Carol had needed to repack; she'd had more luggage than Ole was willing to take. The luggage of all three of them had to fit into the Caddy's big trunk, he'd said; the back seat was for relaxing and sleeping, not for suitcases.

Part of it too was the six-month deadline that Madame Tanya had implied. And he didn't have an inkling of where they would go, once they crossed the state line into Arizona. Last night's easy confidence had weakened, and the psychic vision that he'd used so effectively to guide others seemed now to have gone on vacation.

Informed of the space limitation, Carol quickly and efficiently trimmed her gear to camping clothes, hiking boots, and a few other relative indispensables. While she was sorting and repacking, Ole phoned Jerry and told him to do any repacking he needed to do before they arrived to pick him up.

Ole's treatment for his broken arm the night before had begun with about twenty minutes of what Jerry mentally termed "laying on of the hands." It hadn't seemed like any big deal at the time, but it had relieved the ache and throbbing considerably. Then Ole had run through the traffic accident with him, using a procedure a bit like he'd used on Carol, although the results were less dramatic. That, Jerry had decided, was because the incident dealt with pain, not grief.

This morning Jerry and his arm both felt a lot better. He hadn't even taken an aspirin.

With Carol's baggage in the trunk, Ole started for Jerry's, and like Carol the evening before, he avoided the pass, taking Laurel Canyon Boulevard across the hills to the Valley. On the way, they passed a shopping center that had been extensively damaged the previous September by a terrorist bomb. The construction crew either wasn't working today or was working under cover to keep out of the rain; corners and edges of heavy plastic coverings flapped in the wet and windy grayness.

"Hnh!" said Ole.

"What?"

"V'at do you mean, 'v'at?' "

"You said 'hnh,' and I wondered what that was about."

"Oh." He said nothing more for several seconds as he drove, while Carol waited. "Vell," he said at last, "ve got another visitor."

"Visitor?"

"Ya. Another ghost. Lefty yust picked him up v'en ve drove past the shopping center back there."

"Ghost? At a shopping center?"

"Ya, v'ere the construction vork vas back there. A guy bombed it last summer or fall and killed a bunch of people. I guess vun of them vas still hanging around; anyvay, Lefty picked us up a ghost there."

He said nothing further for a minute or so, driving more slowly than was usual for him, while Carol sat wondering if this was real or not.

"God damn!" Ole blurted suddenly. "It's the guy v'at blew the place up! No vonder he's got so much shit stuck to him!" He glanced at Carol. "Excuse me for svearing like that."

"That's all right, Ole," she said. "It really is. I understand." *You should have heard some of the girls I went to school with,* she added to herself. *Especially junior high.* "But thanks anyway." She touched his arm and smiled. "It was thoughtful of you to consider me like that. Especially since I threw your schedule off this morning."

He glanced at her, and a grin crept through his dourness. "I voke up grouchy today. But I'll get over it; I am already. Maybe next time I'll remember to tell people ahead of time v'at's vanted."

He pulled over to the curb. "Excuse me," he said. "I got to stop and help this guy. Don't talk till I tell you, okay?"

She nodded soberly and sat back. To her surprise, the next thing she knew, she was waking up; Ole was looking at her curiously.

"Okay," he said, "ve're done vith that." He pulled out and drove down the street.

"Is he all right?" asked Carol.

"Ya, he's in good shape now. But he's staying vith us, like Lefty." He looked at her. "Did you dream anything v'en you were asleep back there?"

"I don't think so." She looked at her watch; it had been about ten minutes. "Mr. Sigurdsson?"

"Ya-ah?"

"Why did you invite me on this trip? What help can I be?"

"I'm yust riding hunches, Carol. Psychics do that, you know. I like as much information as I can get, but even then I ride my hunches. The biggest trou-

ble vith this trip is that I ain't got no more hunches
than I got information—damn little of either vun."

His eyes moved to her face for a moment. "The
vay it seems to be," he said, "is that people know a
lot more than they know they know. It's like there's
a shield or a curtain, vith part of you on vun side and
part on the other. The part this side don't know very
much, even though the part on the other side seems
to know yust about everything. So the part of a
person that's on this side got to figure-figure to make
up for not knowing.

"But a psychic, he gets more looks or sniffs or
ideas from the other side than most people do. Some
people are natural athletes or natural musicians or
v'atever, and some of us are psychic."

He turned into Connor's street, then added thoughtfully: "Maybe somevun like McBee, maybe he's all
on the other side of the curtain. Maybe v'at's special
about him is, he's got an outlet to the everyday side,
our side, through Benning."

They saw Jerry waiting in the entryway of his
building, out of the wet, with an old duffel bag at his
feet. "And Carol," said Ole, as he pulled up to the
curb, "don't say nothing about our new ghost. I vant
Yerry to have a chance to notice him by himself."

# < EIGHT >

It was eleven-thirty, and at Northern Arizona University the training room was empty. The walking wounded from the basketball team, the ski team, the gymnastics and wrestling and ice hockey teams, had been there and gone. Frank Diacono walked between its familiar tables and past the battery of whirlpools to the small office of the assistant trainer. The door was open.

"Morning, Lew," he said. "Got a minute?"

Lewis Quahu looked up from his morning report. "I've always got a minute for you, Frank. Are you going running this noon?"

"Yeah." Diacono stepped in and closed the door behind him. That told Quahu this wasn't an ordinary visit, but he did not change expression. He was of medium size, brown, and twenty-five, from Fourth Mesa on the Hopi Reservation, 120 miles northeast of town. He and Diacono were not really close, but they were friends who often kept one another company on their noontime runs—cross-country if snow didn't interfere.

"But just now," Diacono went on, "I'm looking for information."

"What do you need to know?"

"I understand you're pretty traditional—as a Hopi, I mean."

Quahu didn't actually move his shoulders, but his voice carried a shrug. "I guess so. For someone with a master's in physical therapy, who lives two hours' drive from the reservation, I'm pretty traditional."

"What do you know about Indian spirits?" Diacono asked. "I'm interested mainly in the one in the San Francisco Peaks."

The Hopi looked at him. "The traditional Hopi belief is that there's one there."

He looked the big man over. Lewis Quahu was very selective of whom he talked to about such things. In fact, he'd never talked about Hopi beliefs to an Anglo. But when one of the football team that fall had decided derisively to name him "Big Chief Quahu," Diacono had nipped it in the bud. He'd collared the player and asked him if he'd like a "friendly little rassle." It had been obvious that beneath his calm exterior Diacono had been angry, and when the young man declined, Diacono had asked if he'd like some close personal supervision during conditioning workouts. The harassment had ceased.

So looking now at the slightly uncomfortable defensive coordinator, Lewis Quahu made a decision. "Sit down," he said. Frank lowered himself into a chair. "Specifically what's your interest?" Quahu asked. "Maybe I can help you."

Diacono told him what had happened on the mountain the previous summer. As he talked, he watched Quahu for any sign of how the Hopi was receiving this; when he was done, he still had no inkling. "So what I want to know," Frank added, "is, was I hallucinating—or is there really an Indian spirit up there? Do you personally feel that there is?"

"There's a spirit up there, all right, but I wouldn't necessarily call him an Indian spirit. He's just a spirit; a powerful one. People refer to him as an Indian spirit because Indians know he's there and pay him respect. And he's friendly to Indians."

"How could *I* get to know him on friendlier terms?"

"Why don't we go up there together next summer?" Quahu suggested. "I've got a steam bath in my house. We can fast and steam for a couple of days to purify ourselves, and then hike up there."

"Does it take all that?"

Quahu didn't answer at once. "I'll tell you what," he said after a few seconds. "There's a guy, a Caucasian down around Phoenix, who was really into 'Indian spirits' a couple of years ago. He got to know my Uncle Ernie, who's the medicine chief of the Eagle Clan at Fourth Mesa, and some medicine chiefs of other tribes. Ernie said this guy could really talk to kachinas, as good as anyone he'd ever seen. He said the guy is a really powerful medicine man, and the only Anglo he was ever willing to talk to about Hopi beliefs.

"That's probably the guy you should get with. I'm not all that expert, and a medicine chief probably wouldn't talk to you about it. If you think you're interested enough to go down to Phoenix and talk to him, I can probably get you his phone number from my uncle."

"I'd appreciate that," said Frank. "I really would." He looked at what he was saying while he said it. It didn't make any sense to him, but there it was.

"Okay," Quahu said, "I'll call my uncle tonight. He may have the guy's number, but if he doesn't, he'll remember his name and the town he lives in, and you can probably get the number from Phoenix directory assistance.

"I'll call you when I find out. If you don't hear from me by nine tonight, give me a ring. I might need to be reminded."

Diacono nodded and got up. "Thanks, Lew," he

said. "Let me know what the call costs you, and I'll pay you back."

Quahu shook his head slightly. "I'm doing it for a friend," he said. "I wouldn't take money for that."

Diacono returned to his office wondering why he'd done what he'd just done. It was as if he was operating on a hidden purpose, hidden from himself. All he knew for sure was that it had felt like the thing to do, and that somehow it had grown more out of last Friday night at Van Wyk's than out of that summer night on the mountain.

Which made no sense to him at all.

But Frank had always tended to follow his hunches; he'd never been too much of a head case. He seldom worried about what to do, or regretted what he'd done. Just do it right, that was the thing.

This was foreign territory for him, though, and he told himself it was okay to feel uncomfortable about it.

# < NINE >

Hustling through the rain, Jerry Connor put his
duffel bag in the Caddy's big trunk and got in the
back seat. When they hit the Ventura Freeway and
he still hadn't noticed the new ghost, Ole mentioned
it to him, then said nothing more.

The Icelander seemed distracted now, as if driving
on automatic. He'd intended to continue on the Ventura to the 210 freeway, but inadvertently got into a
wrong lane and ended up on the Hollywood Freeway
instead. He didn't even notice what he'd done for
half a mile. But the Hollywood would do; he'd just
have to put up with the heavy traffic inbound to
downtown L.A.

They hadn't gone many miles when the first incident occurred. Chased by a police car, a Mercedes
sped the wrong way onto the Vermont Avenue off-
ramp. Two off-bound cars took the guard rail with
squalling horns as the Mercedes gunned down the
ramp toward them, headed insanely north toward
the southbound traffic. Someone in the Mercedes
was shooting at the police cruiser. On the freeway,
Ole swerved into a momentary opening to his left.

The truck that had been behind him wasn't as

lucky; the Mercedes crashed into it and exploded in flames. The patrol car swerved off the ramp and up the muddy, ivy-grown bank, stalled, and rolled sideways down into the flaming shambles. Cars were skidding on the rain-wet pavement, into or around the fire or into each other, and Jerry's ears were filled with the impacts and tearing of metal as he stared in horror out the back window. Then they were through the underpass, and the disaster was out of sight behind them.

Ole wasn't visibly affected. Carol still covered her face with her hands, while Jerry discovered he'd been holding his breath, but the Icelander drove calmly, intently on.

On I-10 the traffic was lighter and faster, and things were uneventful all the way to Pomona. There a pickup just ahead of them was tooling along with a load of office furniture at about sixty miles an hour when its tailgate fell open. A file cabinet tipped out, hitting the pavement about fifty feet in front of the Caddy. Ole yanked to the right, barely avoiding it, but the pickup swerved right, too, heading for the shoulder as another cabinet, strapped to a dolly, fell off. A large desk, standing on end, toppled and followed the cabinet. Ole swerved left, and the car behind him, its driver less quick, smashed into the second file cabinet while the desk bounced and tried to go through the windshield.

After that—incredibly, considering the destruction and carnage—Ole seemed positively cheerful, apparently because they seemed to be leading charmed lives. He even began whistling something neither Jerry nor Carol had heard before, something with a rollicking old-country ethnic sound to it.

Sixty miles later, just short of Banning, the rain stopped. Between Thousand Palms and Indio, clouds gave way to sunshine.

At Indio they stopped to eat.

"Ole," said Carol when they'd sat down in a booth, "do you think we're going to make it?"

Ole grinned at her. "V'y not? Ve come a hundred and sixty miles all right, in spite of crazy people and strange tailgate latches. Ve going to get there yust fine."

"Leaving a trail of wreckage and bodies all the way," she said with a shudder.

"Maybe it hasn't given us its best shot," Jerry suggested. "It hasn't thrown the Caddy around yet like it did the other night."

Ole's blue eyes glittered. "It ain't the same thing that's after us," he said.

"It's not?"

"It sure don't feel like it. Not to me, anyvay. Give a look; does it feel the same to you?"

It didn't, Jerry decided. He'd just taken for granted that it was the same. But everything that had happened today seemed entirely of this world and time, not some other; it had felt physical, not sorcerous—not directly sorcerous, anyway.

A waitress interrupted them with menus, and they ordered on the spot. When she'd gone, Ole looked at the young sergeant and the pretty administrator and grinned again.

"Ve ain't doing too bad. Ve handled v'at ve needed to today, and the other night v'en ve needed help, ve got it. I got the feeling that v'en ve get to that ranch house, there's going to be a regular team of us. Ve going to be hard to beat then."

Jerry grunted. He knew he was going to sound like a nerd, but there was something he needed to say. "I hope the rest of the team is worth more than I am. As a psychic, I don't amount to much; I don't shoot worth a damn left-handed; I can't drive with this broken arm . . . I can't even sign a check with a signature my bank would recognize!"

"Um," said Ole soberly, "maybe ve should have a

pity party. Ve could sing three verses of 'poor, poor thing' for you. But I ain't going to; you'd probably break my head vith your cast." He turned to Carol. "How you doing, kiddo?"

"Not so badly now. We did come through the morning all right, didn't we? Even if some other people didn't."

"Do you think the worst is past, then?" Jerry asked.

Ole shook his head. "Could be. I got no idea. But ve done yust fine so far. And ve can handle vorse than v'at ve seen, if we have to."

The waitress arrived with coffee. When she'd gone, Ole looked at the younger two. "Look," he said, "I know this is heavy stuff for you. It is for me, too, and I been into strange stuff since before you were born. But look at it like this: If things are as bad as Madame Tanya says, ve might as vell take a run at it. And if it ain't like that, then ve got a really vild vacation going here. *I* think you're both the right partners for me, even if you don't, but I can't prove it to you. That's yust how it feels."

He looked pointedly at Carol. "And remember, *you're* the vun v'at brought *me* in on this. And you," he said, turning his eyes to Jerry, "are the vun that got us involved vith the tollgate and the surprise yenerator. You guys *picked* me to vork vith you, probably for good reasons you don't even know yet. V'ich is fine; life's been more interesting these last couple of days than it's been for a long time. And yust now I'm feeling optimistic.

"Don't take me serious if it don't sound reasonable to you," he added. "This is yust a psychic talking. But for v'at it's vorth, I got a hell of a good batting average."

Jerry decided to leave it at that. "Do you have any idea yet how we're going to find that adobe ranch house we're looking for?"

"I know how ve're going to start. I'm going to drive like a sightseer vith all the time in the vorld. Anytime I get a notion to, I'll take a turn—left, right, or double back. And if either of you gets a hunch, tell me." Ole paused. "I'll make you a bet: I bet ve eat supper in that ranch house tomorrow night."

Jerry smiled ruefully at him, then grinned. "What the hell," he said, "this *is* a lot better than watching television. And I get to spend a lot of time with Carol." He paused and looked around. "And you too, Leo. Or . . ." He stopped, confused. "His name is Lefty; how come I called him . . . Hey! Is that right? Is the new ghost named Leo?" he asked excitedly, and the chills hit him again.

He'd spoken loudly enough that a truck driver and an elderly couple looked over at him.

"You got it," Ole answered, grinning widely. "Leo's his name—Leo Hochman. By golly, you surprised me." He turned to Carol. "Call the caterer and tell her ve're changing the pity party to a celebration. Our novice psychic yust graduated from first grade vith honors!"

They spent the night in the nearly nonexistent village of Greasewood, Arizona, after hours on mostly secondary and lesser roads, some of them gravel. No one had felt the faintest inspiration, not even, apparently, the ghosts.

Before they'd retired to their separate motel cabins, Jerry and Carol had strolled along the desert road beneath the kind of night sky that L.A. hadn't seen for a century. Carol repeated for him Ole's thoughts about a curtain or shield, and a person being partly on one side and partly on the other. Jerry found it interesting but not particularly convincing. There seemed no point to such an arrangement.

Afterward, in Jerry's cabin, Ole treated the broken

arm again with the laying on of hands. This time the waves of sensation were slight, but when Sigurdsson was done, the ache was entirely gone for the time being.

It was breaking day when they left Greasewood, with a few stars still gleaming in the clear desert dawn, and an unaccustomed chill in the air. For forty miles they saw no further building and no paved crossroad. Then they crossed another blacktop, on which an empty cattle truck approached. The truck turned left onto their road and followed them.

Jerry felt ill at ease about the truck. Riding in the back seat, he turned and watched it; it was closing on them. He wondered whether to mention it to Ole, then saw the Icelander watching it in the rearview mirror. It wasn't as if it threatened them, Jerry thought. But it did, he felt, have something to do with them.

The blacktop was narrow and irregular, with rough, unpaved shoulders. The desert surface here was rolling—the vaguely eroded pediment of low ragged mountains close by to the north. The truck driver clearly wanted to pass, and remarkably, Ole slowed to accommodate him, crowding the unpaved shoulder with his outside wheels. The truck accelerated and passed them, jouncing on the bad pavement. When it was safely past, they saw the driver's plaid-sleeved arm waving his thanks.

"How fast is he going?" Jerry asked.

"Probably sixty-five," said Ole. "Fast for a road like this vun. I guess these cowboys drive trucks like they vas race horses."

Shortly, it disappeared over a small rise ahead of them, and a minute later Ole slowed abruptly, hitting his brakes. Jerry had felt something, too. When they topped a second rise, they saw the truck on its side in the ditch a hundred yards ahead. Nearer, in and by the road, lay a cow and two calves, wiped out; blood and entrails smeared the pavement.

Ole steered through the carnage and pulled off on the shoulder across from the truck. Its driver, a young man, was dead. Apparently the first cow he'd hit had been thrown high enough into the air that it had come down on top of the cab, caving it in and killing him. This cow lay in the ditch not far behind the truck.

Ole stood quietly regarding the dead man for more than a minute—communicating with him, Jerry realized, doing for the man's spirit what he had done for Carol and himself, and Lefty and Leo.

After that they drove on to the nearest village and reported the accident. When they'd eaten, they went on, sober and untalkative. The low mountains that had flanked them for miles fell astern. Their next change of road was unexpectedly abrupt. They saw the crossroad coming, marked by an unobtrusive sign. The sign meant nothing to any of them as they passed it, but suddenly Ole braked, stopped, backed up to it some sixty or seventy yards, and turned right.

"What is it?" Jerry asked. "Did you get something?"

"Nothing clear or strong," Ole answered, then said no more. Some ten miles farther a dirt road led off to their left, marked by a mailbox, and a sign which read "Pumphandle Ranch 14 mi." Ole hesitated, slowing, then passed it and went on. Roundbacked mountains grew ahead of them, also on their left, and some miles farther they passed another dirt road. Its sign held only a cattle brand and the notation, "9 miles."

Jerry wondered what cattle found to eat here. The dominant vegetation was teddy-bear cholla—viciously spined cactuses resembling five-foot-tall trees—and the multi-stemmed, thorny, wide-splayed ocotillo. Scattered saguaros stood tall above them, the trademark of the Sonoran Desert. Here even the plants were clawed or fanged, and that which crawled was likely to be venomous.

Soon they were paralleling the roundbacked mountains, now about three miles away on the left. They all saw the next dirt road at the same time, innocent of any marker save a mailbox, but they knew, each of them, that it was theirs—knew before they saw the name. Ole slowed, stopped. The hand-lettering on the large mailbox announced: VIC & TORY MERLIN. Jerry stared, then groaned.

"The triumphant sorcerer," he said. "Victory Merlin."

"Good grief! No!" said Carol. "I don't know much about Mr. McBee, but the last thing I expected from him was a pun! Especially one of the worst I ever heard!"

# < TEN >

They sat for a few moments with their eyes absorbing the weather-beaten mailbox, then Ole turned the Caddy onto the dirt road and headed toward the mountains nearby. Soon they entered a small canyon with a trickling creek that disappeared into the gravel at its mouth. Along the canyon bottom were scattered clumps of cottonwood, and somehow it seemed to Jerry that they had been planted there by some pioneer.

About a mile up the canyon they came to a set of buildings that were once the headquarters of a ranch. There was the adobe house they'd sought, almost encircled by box elders which in summer would shade it. A small microwave dish sat on its roof. Next to the house, and taller than the box elders, stood a conventional farm windmill; the water tank beside it stood on a platform for gravity feed to the house. Nearby was another windmill, with long latticed vanes, apparently to generate electricity. But now the air was still, the vanes motionless. From somewhere came the sound of a gasoline engine, perhaps a backup generator.

Two vehicles stood in the yard—two pickups. One

was a tall, new-looking, four-wheel-drive model with a camper shell. The other was older, a work vehicle, also with four-wheel drive but without the camper shell or oversized snow tires. Ole pulled the Caddy in beside them.

*Well, we're here,* Jerry said to himself as he got out. *Now what?* So far, everything had matched the predictions, right down to McBee's atrocious pun, but this was where the prediction ended. What if the people here told them to get off the place? But no, McBee had said that someone here wanted to see them.

The ranch house door opened, and a wiry man with a short grizzled beard stood waiting in the doorway. He looked fiftyish and wore scarred lace-up boots, faded jeans, and a gray twill shirt: a desert rat. While walking toward the house, Jerry noticed that the taller pickup had a current Northern Arizona University parking decal on the windshield and a power winch on the front bumper. *A mountain man,* he thought, *to go with the desert rat.*

Ole stopped at the edge of the low porch.

"Can I help you folks?" asked the desert rat.

*Oh man,* Jerry thought at him, *you aren't going to believe this.*

"Ya," said Ole, "I'm pretty sure you can. Ve come to talk about—the surprise yenerator."

"Well, that sounds interesting." The man's glance encompassed all of them. "Come on in. We've been waiting for y'all and never even knew it."

To Jerry Connor, the reply fitted all the other strange occurrences of the past three days. The man held the door open and they trooped in, Connor feeling as if this had to be a dream. They were in a large living room with throw rugs on a floor of worn, closely fitted planks. The ceiling was high, supported by rough-sawn beams—vigas. A big adobe fireplace in one wall held a slow fire. Besides themselves and the man who'd let them in, there were four people in the room—eight in all now.

One of the two women seated there got up. "It looks like we're going to need more coffee," she said. "Y'all just take whatever seats you'd like." She walked briskly from the room. Jerry tentatively identified their accents as Texan.

The man introduced himself as Vic Merlin. The woman who'd gone to the kitchen was his wife, Tory. The others were from Flagstaff—a mathematics professor, his wife, and a football coach. Jerry recognized Frank Diacono as an ex-NFL star, an all-pro linebacker. In turn, the Merlins and Van Wyks had read the book on Ole.

By the time the handshakes were over, Tory Merlin was back. "I've put the big pot on," she announced, "but it'll be a while."

Tory Merlin was about five feet two and a hundred and ten pounds, her carroty-red hair dulled by gray. There was power in her that he wouldn't want to cross, Jerry decided. She had an eye that would see through any pretense or cover and knock off your hat on the other side.

"You don't need to rerun the introductions," she added to her husband. "I heard them in there." She sat down and turned to Ole. "So you're Ole Sigurdsson! We always thought it would be neat to meet you someday. Matter of fact, it seems like I know you from somewhere—you and him," she added, indicating Jerry.

"Maybe so," Ole said, "but I don't remember it."

Tory shrugged. "Vic and I sometimes do things we don't see that clearly, or don't remember afterwards, although we're getting better. I don't know how it is for you, but for us sometimes, operating psychically is like working in the dark."

Ole laughed. "By golly, I sure as hell know v'at you're talking about there."

Tory looked around. "Did I hear something about a surprise generator? What's that all about?"

Ole looked at Jerry and grinned. "V'y don't you tell them? You talk better than me."

For just a moment Jerry froze as every eye in the room turned to him. *Why me?* he thought. *Ole talks all right.* But he began, and the tension disappeared. He talked for fifteen minutes, not omitting Ole's remarkable handling of Carol and her brother's ghost. Telling about the encounter on the pass, he noticed Vic's and Tory's eyes move to each other. Again a cold chill flowed over him, leaving his skin pebbled. He decided they'd found the ones who'd helped them out with the tollgate sentry.

"Well," said Tory when he'd finished, "y'all had a pretty eventful few days. The coffee'll be ready by now," she added, "but you'll have to serve yourselves." She got up and led an exodus to the kitchen. A few minutes later they were back with assorted cups, and coffee that even Ole would approve.

"It sounds like you folks were supposed to come here, all right," Vic said when they were seated again. "Frank here just finished telling us another interesting story." He turned to Diacono. "Maybe you'd run through it again for these folks."

Diacono nodded. "Okay, although it doesn't seem to fit in with Jerry's story in any way I can see—not the way Bill's story will." He paused thoughtfully, then described his evening on the mountain, and of getting in touch with the Merlins through Lewis Quahu's uncle.

He glanced at the Van Wyks, then turned to Vic. "The funny thing is that as soon as I heard about you, it felt to me as if I had to bring Bill and Sharon along, even though it didn't make sense at the time, because as far as I know, they're not particularly interested in Indian lore. But they didn't even argue. Now it looks as if this meeting is turning out to be more important to them than to me." He looked at Bill Van Wyk. "Do you want to tell them about your work, Bill?"

Van Wyk was eyeing Ole Sigurdsson. "You bet I do," he said. "It's amazing how we came together like this—like witchcraft." Then he gave them a five-minute rundown on his research on cycles. "It fits perfectly with what the fortune-teller and the medium told you," he finished.

Even Tory seemed impressed. She looked at her husband. "Well, you'd better tell them what *we've* been doing the past four years out here—besides reroofing the buildings, growing vegetables, shooing rattlesnakes and scorpions away, chopping up firewood, designing and building the wind generator, and a few other odds and ends."

Vic nodded. "Right. But first I'd like to thank you all for being here. It feels like the time's arrived to do whatever it is we've been getting ready to do. About us: We bought this place four years ago—these buildings and 160 acres to go with them, part of the Stokes Ranch—and moved out here from Phoenix to do research where we wouldn't be disturbed. Before that I was personnel relations chief at Bourdon Electronics. Before that, Tory and I were 'Noeties' —noetic counselors and counseling supervisors with the Institute of Noetic Technology. Before *that* I was supervising editor of *Energy Weekly Review*, which I got into from having been a technical editor at Viggers Electronics.

"I've been interested all my life in what makes people what they are, and why they do what they do. In fact, I started college as a psychology major, but some of the psych professors were pretty crazy compared to my professors in science and math and

English. And it seemed to me like, if psychology really understood very much about the basics of the mind and human behavior, the people teaching it would be saner than most. So I transferred to chemistry; I was pretty sure the people there knew what they were talking about.

"And meanwhile I got into reading on eastern religions, Edgar Cayce, the occult, and things like that.

"Later on, while I was working for Viggers, Tory and I heard about Leif Haller and the Noeties, and got interested enough to visit their Washington D.C. branch. We ended up getting a lot of noetic counseling from them; we only lived about twenty miles from there in Maryland. Three years later I quit Viggers and we joined the staff at the Noetie central organization in California. Leif Haller had come up with some neat knowledge and techniques—powerful, the most comprehensive and workable mental and psychic techniques I'd run into up till then. They did some neat things—helped a lot of people.

"But there was something wrong there, and after a couple of years we couldn't keep looking the other way. It seemed to us like they'd taken a wrong turn somewhere down the line and couldn't turn around. They weren't making any more real advances, and the organization was going sour. And it seemed like you couldn't get the kind of changes made that were needed."

He paused to drink some coffee, then lit a cigarette. No one broke the silence. Jerry noticed that Ole looked particularly intent.

"So we moved to Phoenix, and I went to work for Bourdon Electronics as technical editor. But mainly because of my training and experience in Noetie counseling, I got to be everybody's unofficial counselor and squabble fixer there, until I got enough of a reputation for handling those kinds of things that Old

Man Bourdon established the position of Personnel Relations Director and put me in it. I was a one-man department.

"The work was pretty interesting and it paid well, but somehow it wasn't very satisfying. Sometimes Tory and I, occasionally with our sons, would talk about where Haller and the Institute might have gone wrong. There were plenty of things we could point to and say this shouldn't have been that way, or that didn't make sense, but none of them was basic. None of them was the cause.

"So I started doing some research. I looked at times when there'd been a major change in Noetie technology—changes in direction or emphasis. There were several of these, but one of them looked to us like the most critical. Then I looked for what had happened just before that, something that might have led to it.

"One thing that had turned on for me while I was a Noetie counselor—not something I was taught, but something that just turned on by itself—was to see things from the past. Quite a few Noetie counselors get so they do that. Like Ole apparently does, a lot of times I can see things from the past of a person or place, sometimes as still pictures and sometimes like holographic movies. But I'd only done this while counseling a person, or incidentally while doing something like driving past a Civil War battlefield.

"Then, when I started exploring what you might call the unrecorded past of the Institute of Noetic Technology, I started running into things I never expected or even imagined, and they led a lot farther back than the Institute. So instead of a little investigation to satisfy our curiosity, I'd gotten us into a major project.

"That's when we bought this place and I quit Bourdon's, so I could work on it pretty much full time, in a place that's about as undisturbed as you can find. Since then I keep pulling the strings I uncover, seeing what they lead to. They hardly ever have anything to do with the Institute anymore; it turned out to be just a starting point. I just sense back to what feel like key points, and sort out what I find there; so far, I've got about four thousand pages of research notes on a word processor.

"Sometimes I've had to take a couple of weeks or a month off to recover, or get over a case of psychic block, like writer's block. I work in the garden, cut wood, and things like that. Overhaul the transmission. Some of the stuff I've run into is pretty heavy; sometimes it's kicked back on me and I've had to stay in bed for a week or so.

"Tory works with me, but I'm the point man. Mostly I probe alone, and she bails me out when I need it. And she and the boys help me sort things out afterward. We've come up with some pretty advanced psychic procedures and drills."

He looked at Ole, their eyes meeting. "One of the things I ran into was the history and nature of reality," he went on. "And while I never ran into a surprise generator, there's sure enough a *reality* generator.

"The reality generator we're interested in is the one for this sector of the universe. It's got a whole network of output terminals, and what it generates is a matrix—the Tikh Cheki Matrix—which is reality as we know it. But someone could have patched a surprise generator into the reality generator."

Vic grinned. "As soon as you said 'surprise generator,' I thought, Wow! That would sure explain a lot of things!"

He looked around at the others. "Being in the Tikh Cheki Matrix is like being part of a giant video game, but it's a lot more complicated than Pac Man. The reality generator's got all the laws of nature programmed into it. In fact, that's what natural laws are, and that's all they are: parts of the program of the reality generator. And all that reality is, actually, is the Tikh Cheki Matrix.

"Something that injects irrational or other destructive impulses—confusion, chaos—into the matrix, would account for some of the things that still haven't made sense to us." He looked at Van Wyk. "If the surprise generator is speeding up, that would account for the statistics you've found." He turned his glance to Jerry. "And for the accident statistics you turned up, and for the fortune-teller's dead-ended futures.

"The present reality isn't the first reality we've had. There's been a long sequence of realities; the Tikh Cheki series is just the most recent set. Now, whenever the ratio of disorder to order gets too high in a matrix, the existing reality erases and the generator generates a new matrix—a new reality. That's probably where the Hindu belief in cycles of the universe comes from: The world ends and a new one starts. And generally the new one doesn't include any physical evidence of past civilizations: even the old iron ore and fossil hydrocarbon deposits get replaced.

"And in between cycles, modifications get put into the program to try to take care of some of the things that were wrong with the reality just past, while still keeping things interesting and challenging."

He scanned his small audience. "The reality generator is actual physical machinery, but it exists on what we think of as 'the other side of reality.' It's like it's on the other side of a wall. We don't have the language to talk about it exactly, but that's a pretty good simile.

"There are installations scattered around all over the world, but the central one is right here in the Southwest. It's almost as if they were in the same space as here, but they can't be seen by most people. They're in what's been kept of the reality that existed when they were installed, quite a few realities ago. You can think of it as being like the part of a building where the wiring and pipes and central air system are that keep the building functioning, but in this case it keeps the building itself in existence, too."

Vic's eyes went to Diacono. "And now we're coming to your Indian spirit. There are gates—access points from this side to the generator installations—and the gates have guardians who are pretty powerful beings. They're what people refer to as Indian spirits, or 'the old man of the mountain'—things like that.

"If there is a surprise generator tied into the reality generator, and I expect there is, and if we wanted to disconnect it to get less insanity, we'd have to go to the other side of reality to do it. We'd have to go through the gate where it's at, and then we'd have to disconnect it, and that means we'd have to get approval from its guardian."

"Wait a minute," said Jerry. "Assuming . . . assuming what you've said is real—and the past few days have sure as heck expanded my view of reality—then even if there weren't any guardians, how would we get through?"

"Oh, we could get through all right," Vic said. "I've been through two gates; Tory and I both have. We decided not to try the one under Humphrey Peak, where Frank was, because that's the central installation for this planet, and we were a little afraid of it. But we've been through the one in the Davis Mountains in West Texas and the one up at Sipapu."

"Sipapu?" Frank said. "I've been to Sipapu, and I didn't see anything I'd think of as a gate."

"Right. People have various things that keep them from seeing things like that or, in the case of Sipapu, of recognizing what they are. You just about have to have some preparation."

Frank remembered what Lewis Quahu had said about fasting and steaming. "What kind of preparation?" he asked.

"We'll show you, if you'd like." Vic turned to Ole. "From what Jerry said about how you handled Carol and her brother, you're a Noetie, too."

Ole nodded. "I used to be, for about five years in the late sixties and early seventies. Vorked up to a Class Five counselor. I still do it sometimes, like vith Carol, but I left the Noeties in seventy-three." He grinned. "Actually, they kicked me out. I had this bad habit that I made my own decisions and did and said v'at *I* thought vas right. They couldn't have that."

Vic grinned back at him, then looked around at the others. "I need to sit down with Ole alone for a while and go over some things with him," he said, then turned to Ole. "Is that all right with you? With your talents and your Noetie training and experience, I don't think it'll take much to teach you some techniques that Tory and I've developed. And we could sure use your help."

Ole's big grin was in place. "Sure," he said. "It sounds interesting."

"And if it's all right with Tory," Vic went on, looking around at the others, "she could tell you about what you might call the operating diagram of a human being. It's part of the preparation you'll need to help disconnect the surprise generator. If anyone isn't interested, or if you'd rather not get involved in something crazy like this, you can go outside and take a drive or explore the canyon or do whatever else you'd like."

No one got up.

"Looks like we've got a full house," he said to

Tory. "Now, if any of you-all decide to leave for any reason before we're done, we can work out the transportation."

*And that,* thought Jerry Connor, *is about the least coercive recruiting proposition I've ever heard.*

He didn't even think of leaving.

## < ELEVEN >

Jerry had gone to bed early—they all had—then
found he wasn't sleepy. Part of it was that, with his
broken arm, he couldn't lie on his stomach, which
was his best position for going to sleep. But mostly
his mind was too restless. So he got up from his
pallet on the living room floor and tiptoed out, careful not to waken Ole or Frank or Bill Van Wyk.

Carol and Sharon had been put up in the guest
bedroom. And the two Merlin sons, Kelly and Nor-
man, had returned home to their rooms from some
undefined weekend project at Bourdon Electronics,
where they still worked, commuting forty miles daily
each way. So the male visitors had been bedded
down on foam pads.

Jerry's watch said it was only eleven, but standing
there by the pickups, looking around, it already felt
colder than winter nights in L.A., as if it might even
frost by morning. The sky was black and rich with
stars, the Milky Way a white swath across its depths.

He started to walk; he would hike down the road,
out of the canyon onto the broad desert basin. The
exercise, he told himself, would do him good, and
bed was no place to sort out his thoughts.

It had been the damnedest day of his life, even more so than the previous three. He'd been exposed to a whole new . . . He groped for the word. Cosmology? Cosmogony? A whole new theory of what the universe was and how it came to be. It was so fantastic that he'd have rejected it out of hand a few days earlier. Now, with it, things made sense that otherwise made no sense at all.

The video game universe.

And like Ole had said, if it was bullshit, at least he was having something different for a vacation than fishing at Puerto Peñasco.

Tomorrow, one of them—Vic or Tory or maybe Ole—would be giving him a "session," some kind of mental preparation that Vic had developed that would, among other effects, enable a person to go through a gate. There would be several such sessions. So far, Jerry didn't know gate from goat—not that kind of gate. And crossing to "the other side of reality" was too unreal to him even to feel nervous about. Intellectually he accepted it: his recent experiences had loosened his old preconceptions, and besides, it was real to Ole. But at the gut level, it was too remote to impinge on him.

Ole had been shut up with Vic for almost four hours. Meanwhile, Tory had drawn some diagrams on a chalkboard for the rest of them, and talked to them about what was done in sessions, and what it was all about. Then she'd answered questions. After that they'd amused themselves by browsing through the Merlin bookshelves.

According to Tory, operating a body was a sort of team thing. It wasn't as simple as "you've got a body" or "you are a body." A long time ago—a whole lot of lifetimes ago—they'd lived in a different universe, and each of them had had a body they could use to go around in and have experiences and sensations through. They hadn't *needed* bodies—they could create sensations subjectively and feel them without a body. But it got to be the thing to do: wear a body.

And over time they got into games and surprises using bodies. *And into making things more and more difficult to do,* so they'd be more interesting and challenging. Finally, they weren't really operating bodies directly anymore. They'd ride around in them, with a sort of crew operating them, each crew made up of semi-independent entities. And each crew member had the potential to get into disagreement and even feuds with the other crew members, depending on the handicaps they and you had drawn and the penalties laid on you.

And the body and its crew members were here in this reality. But you, the captain, just had a sort of extension of yourself in this reality. Most of you was out of sight and forgotten in a totally different universe from your body. Not just on the other side of reality, but in a totally different universe.

It was harder than playing Pac Man, too, because you didn't have control levers or buttons. All you had in this universe was your attention, and your intention, and your awareness. The crew ran the body, based on a kind of rough script or life plan, sort of an outline that the scriptmaster entity filled in as he went. The only way most people had of influencing what the crew did was by intending, and by putting their attention on things. And one of the problems was that most people's crews had two script entities, two navigators, so to speak, each of whom was likely to have different ideas about the script.

You couldn't force your crew; very few people could even talk to it. You simply experienced the emotions and sensations of life under your script, and did what you could toward controlling things by putting your attention on what you wanted to do or be or have. What you wanted to *have* was the master factor; be and do tended to fall into line with have.

And using attention was tricky, too, because if you put heavy attention on something—tried to force something—it skidded away from you. It worked best when done lightly, the lighter the better.

All this had sounded to Jerry like a hell of a way to run a ship or live a life. He'd asked Tory who'd written his script, and she'd said you ordinarily picked one out of a kind of script library between lives, and maybe modified it. Then your script entities had the job of trying to adjust it later as you and your crew went along through life, to fit what you ran into and what you put your attention on. Scripts generally tended to become pretty confused even early in life.

What Vic or Tory or the newly trained Ole would do with him tomorrow was help him cull and revise parts of his script, get rid of certain control machinery he was operating under, and clean up his crew members of their rivalries and gripes. The idea was to reach the point where he could *tell* his crew what he wanted and have them pay attention to him.

It occurred to Jerry, walking down the dirt road beneath the stars, that the sane thing to do would be to get in Ole's Caddy and get the hell away from there. But the notion had neither fire nor force. Because, as wild and crazy as all this was, at least the part about the reality generator fitted the events of the past three days better than any conventional wisdom. And Van Wyk and Madame Tanya were right: you couldn't run away from it. The future on Earth was damned short unless, as McBee had put it, they won the game. So the least he could do was hang around and see what tomorrow brought.

When Ole had come out of his session with Vic, the old Icelander looked five or ten years younger. He'd had a good grin before, but right then he'd looked as if he'd just eaten the universe. Then Ole had taken Carol in one room, and Vic had gone into another with Diacono. Tory had taken Sharon into the old bunkhouse, each carrying a chair. He and Bill would have to wait till tomorrow. And he had felt what? Jealousy, because he had to wait!

Diacono had come out looking like a different man—cocky instead of restrained; cheerful instead of sober. Sharon had been next, and came out looking totally in charge of herself, but he didn't know her well enough to say how much of a difference that was. Finally, Carol had come out. Previously there'd been a certain sense of childlike vulnerability about her, a certain shyness, although it had decreased after Ole had handled the thing between Kevin and her. Now the little-girl shyness seemed to be gone. She'd looked around the room with bright calm eyes, as if she were seeing things newly and differently.

Tomorrow would be his turn.

He was introspecting too strongly to notice much around him at the time, and didn't see Carol below the road, sitting on the trunk of a fallen cottonwood uprooted by some past flooding of the creek.

"Hi, Lefty!" she called. "Couldn't get to sleep?"

He jerked out of his reverie and walked down to her. "Hi. How come you called me Lefty? Do I look like a ghost?"

She laughed, her eyes night-shadowed but somehow bright. "No," she said, "but with your right arm in a sling, it seemed to fit."

"What happened in there today?" he asked. "What was it like?"

"It doesn't describe well. Good though. Rough in spots, but good. You'll find out tomorrow."

"What does it feel like, now that you've done it?"

"Good enough that I don't want to go to sleep yet. Good enough that I look forward to more of it tomorrow." She patted the tree trunk beside her, and he sat.

"What did you think of Tory's lecture?" he asked. "And the stuff Vic told us before that?"

Her face was near his in the night, half turned to

him. "It felt weird at the time," she answered. "Too far out. But it seemed as if I should go along with it for a while and give it a chance. Now it feels lots more real to me. *Lots* more."

"Why? What makes it feel more real now?"

She was grinning. "You're never going to figure it out tonight, so there's no point in trying to explain it." Her eyes were on his, suddenly playful. "Besides, there must be something better to do on a beautiful night like this."

He stared, surprised, but only for a moment uncertain. Reaching across her with his left arm, he drew her close and kissed her, his lips exploring softly at first, then more firmly as she responded. After a minute or so she disengaged his arm and they stood up, to walk slowly back toward the buildings, holding hands, not talking much. Instead of going into the ranch house, she led him into the empty bunkhouse.

From their assumed location in and above and around the Caddy, Lefty and Leo watched the couple go in. It stirred vague sexual feelings, despite their having no bodies, but the feelings were without intensity. They were content for the present with their condition, and they realized now that they could recycle if they wished—withdraw to the mezzanine and arrange to become the "souls" for newborn baby bodies and begin a new life.

But they had decided to stay, to help Ole and the others in whatever ways they could. They'd eavesdropped on lectures and sessions during the day just past, and the result was to make them relatively powerful, as ghosts go. Further, they realized that this little group of humans was undertaking to undo exactly what had destroyed their recent lives. The knowledge gave them both interest and a sense of purpose.

Now, with unexpressed agreement, they lifted upward past the box elders and windmills and beyond, to float gently above the canyon and enjoy the view. The night was softening with the newly risen, somewhat gibbous moon. Without bodies, their perceptions could have been somewhat different as they looked with a 360-degree viewpoint over the desert and hills, but mostly they translated and experienced their surroundings rather as if they still saw through eyes.

Still, they perceived things that eyes might not have. Thus they saw a glowing golden spheroid appear a little distance away, above the crest of a ridge. After watching it for a moment, they approached it curiously, cautiously. Cautiously because, though its beauty drew them and they felt nothing they identified as a threat, it did not feel quite right.

A light flow of friendliness came from it, and it projected toward them what looked like the inner cylinder of a vacuum bottle that appeared transparent in the moonlight. Inside the bottle it was blacker than the night sky, but it was a blackness scintillant with stars, as if it held a universe within.

They were intrigued. The golden spheroid flowed a gentle sense of approval, as if their curiosity was acceptable, and the two ghosts jointly surrounded the bottle to examine it more closely. With a suddenness that exceeded their speed of awareness, Lefty and Leo both were sucked into it. Inside were no stars; those had been artifice. There were only themselves, tiny now like two fireflies flitting sluggishly against the field that was the bottle.

The beautiful golden spheroid turned into what looked like a small oily cloud and drew the bottle into itself. Then the cloud flicked away and was gone.

# < TWELVE >

For Connor, Carol, Diacono, and the Van Wyks, the next day was spent closeted individually with Vic, Tory, or Ole. Ole in turn was closeted intermittently with Vic. These second-day sessions were mostly short: One might go in for five or fifteen minutes, then come out for half an hour or longer before going back in. In between, a lot of coffee was drunk and there was a lot of talk and laughter.

There were also numerous catnaps on sofa, floor, porch—anywhere convenient. Sometimes one would waken with a sense that much had gone on during sleep; sometimes a meaningful dream would be remembered. A fifteen-minute nap might feel like two hours, or as if one had closed his eyes for only a minute or two without sleeping.

At seven-thirty that night, after an impromptu cold buffet, they got ready to leave. They would attempt a gate—see what they could learn and what help they might get. If they were lucky enough, it might even be the installation with the surprise generator.

Planning was minimal. Bill and Sharon Van Wyk would go home: Bill had two classes scheduled the next day. Vic told them they might be called on to help from a distance—that they should not be alarmed if they felt an urgent drowsiness, or periods of vagueness and absent-mindedness. Tory would remain at the ranch as an anchor or beacon, an able and stable connection to everyday reality. The rest would go on to Sipapu—the gate through which, according to Hopi legend, the ancestors of the Hopi nation had come into the world.

Vic considered three the most favorable number of people to try the gate. Because Frank was strong and country-wise, he'd be one. Ole's psychic advancement was definitely desirable, and as a semiregular jogger, he ought to be fit enough for the physically strenuous trek.

Jerry's broken arm would be a serious handicap on the rugged canyon climb, so he would guard the pickup with Carol, and they would lend off-site psychic support, along with Tory and Sharon and Bill.

Except for Tory, the support team members weren't at all sure what "off-site psychic support" involved, but Vic assured them that they would if the time came.

The expedition would go in Frank's pickup. It was not until they were ready to leave that they missed the two ghosts. Under other circumstances, Vic or Ole might have taken time to investigate. But Lefty and Leo were not part of their plans, and ghosts, once relieved of any compulsive attachment to a place or body or living person, were prone to recycle, so their absence was passed off as irrelevant.

Frank would drive; he knew the way. Sipapu was remote, and the route unmarked, but it was known and appreciated among connoisseurs of the Arizona back country.

Two hours after leaving the ranch house, they topped the Mogollon Rim on Interstate 17. On the high plateau, brawny pines stood deep in snow. The air was mildly wintry. Frequent cars passed them headed homeward toward Phoenix, skis and sleds secured on tops or backs. In a sense, thought Frank Diacono, he and the others were already in a different universe from the people in the cars they passed. Perhaps some passing child, asleep or sleepy after a day of sledding, was picking up their mission at some subliminal level as they passed; what dreams or strange feelings might such a child be having then?

Diacono stopped in Flagstaff long enough to drop off the Van Wyks, pick up some hiking gear, and fill his gas tank, then headed north on Highway 89. For some miles as he drove, he could see the frozen snowy bulk of the great mountain nearby on his left, and wondered if its formidable spirit was aware of them. If so, what was it thinking?

Psychically he reached, and it seemed to him that it did notice, knew their mission—that it was friendly but not partisan, interested but passive. Had he stayed on the peak that summer night, unprepared as he'd been, perhaps he *would* have died. But not, he thought, from enmity; rather in the manner of someone stumbling amidst high voltage equipment. He had been susceptible, he decided, and the old man in the mountain had chased him away before it could happen.

With the thought came a rush of goose bumps. He turned and saw Vic smiling at him from his thicket of beard, friendly eyes laughing under bristly brows. Frank grinned back, but neither man spoke just then. Meanwhile, Ole slumped gangling by the door, asleep, his head bobbing now and then with the movement of the truck.

At length Vic broke the silence. "Ole's had the hardest weekend of any of us," he said quietly. "Tory and I needed to get one of you as close to our operating level as possible, as a psychic and a counselor, and Ole had the background. In two days he learned most of what it took us several years to find out. Psychically we brought him as far as we know how."

"How far did you bring the rest of us?" Frank asked.

"A long way; more than you realize yet. You'll have it when you need it; it's all there. On this side you're still pretty much cloaked from yourself, but that'll reduce. You can already operate a lot more freely than you could before, even if it feels like you're doing it blind."

Frank nodded; it felt right to him. The things he'd looked at and done under Vic's guidance, in session, had changed him a lot. In two days all of them, even Ole, had changed conspicuously before each other's eyes.

He wondered what was going on in the camper shell between Jerry and Carol. His body stirred at the thought, but he didn't feel actually horny. Two days ago he probably would have. Now—she wasn't his girl.

They came out of the forest onto a vast rolling grassland marked by scattered, rounded cinder cones of the Flagstaff volcanic field. The snow was less deep here, the south slopes burned bare by the sun. He had to look back over his shoulder to see the high peaks now. Nothing strange or dangerous had happened on the road—nothing like the incidents that Jerry had described. It occurred to him that whoever their adversary was might deliberately let them continue unhindered: *"Come into my parlor," said the spider to the fly*, he thought. He glanced at Vic Merlin again; the man's eyes were straight ahead now, but it seemed to Frank that only Vic's body was there, on hold and idling, and Vic himself was elsewhere.

An hour later they checked into a motel at the high-desert village of Tuba City, and Vic set his alarm clock for five-thirty. Frank phoned Coach

Barkum's office, knowing he'd get an answering machine he could lie to unquestioned, and left a message that his truck had broken down in Albuquerque—that he might not be back before Wednesday.

Then he paused by the phone booth for a last look at the night. Around him, the patchy snow had been worn thin by desert winds. The moon had risen, and some sixty miles southwest he could see Humphrey Peak lighted by it, impersonal now, as if its guardian slept. Tomorrow . . . He had no idea what tomorrow might bring.

Dawn was grading into day when they left Highway 89 just north of the tiny Navajo village called "The Gap." The road they took was not on their map, probably not on any map, not even with the symbol for unimproved dirt roads. It had not been put there by the white man's engineers but by the wheels of Navajo sheepherders' wagons and later by Navajo pickup trucks.

No one had wanted to ride in back this morning because visibility was poor from the camper shell. So all five were crowded in front, like a Navajo family on an outing, Vic and Carol sitting on laps because they were the lightest.

Frequently the road forked or branched; always it wandered. There were no road signs, and although the country was desert grassland, it rolled enough that they could not usually see the road for any distance ahead. Occasionally they came to a Navajo cabin with horse shed, corral, and sheep pens; otherwise, the country seemed empty. Jerry and Carol were impressed that Frank could find his way.

After an hour they topped a low, broad-backed ridge and stopped. Frank pointed. "Up ahead is the canyon of the Little Colorado River. Sipapu is in the bottom of it, a few miles above where the Little Colorado runs into the Grand Canyon. We get there

by climbing down a side canyon called Salt Canyon;
that draw off to our right is the head of it."

He shifted back into gear and continued for a little
way along the ridge top, then pulled off to the side
and set the parking brake.

"And this," he said, "is where we get out and
walk."

Vic put on a pack that held a lunch each, plus a
few dried trail rations and three towels. Each man
carried a belt canteen. Jerry and Carol walked with
them down into the draw, to the point where it
reached the headwall of Salt Canyon. There and over
several other stretches, Frank assured them, the way
was not a hiking trail but a thinly marked scramble
and climb.

The three began working their way down. After a
few minutes, Jerry and Carol lost sight of them and
hiked back up the slope to the truck. Neither felt
good about staying behind.

At the pickup, Carol stood slowly scanning the
desert plateau, empty as far as she could see. Jerry
practiced drawing his revolver left-handed, dry-firing
it, until he felt comfortable that way. At length they
both got into the cab, saying little. He turned the
radio on. The only station he could pick up decently
featured country and Indian music and an announcer
who spoke what they decided must be Navajo—tonal,
with sequences of vowels, its consonants mostly soft.
After a little he turned it off.

They wondered where the three hikers were now,
how far down the three-thousand-foot descent, and
how difficult it was. Neither had even a concept of
what the gate would be like.

Eventually the three looked down from a bulging
prominence at their first good view of the Little
Colorado River. Ole and Vic were glad to sit on a
rock and rest. The river, only a few hundred feet

below them now, was a milky turquoise blue. Ole guessed that it averaged about forty feet wide there—a lot of water in that country.

"How deep is it?" he asked.

"You can wade it in most places," Frank said, "but generally, we'll float or swim. In lots of places the saltcedar jungle is so thick with fallen trees and regrowth that you actually can't walk along the shore, and in places the cliffs come right down to the water."

"V'at makes it that milky blue color? It don't even look like real vater. It looks like some painting v'ere the artist didn't get the color right."

"It's full of dissolved carbonates. Tastes like mineral water, but it's okay to drink."

They started down the last stretch, the route marked only by an occasional small rock "cairn," usually just two or three stones stacked up. Often, keeping the trail was more a matter of picking the only way that presented itself as it wound downward through narrow clefts or among great stones. At last they came to near-white sand and a thicket of green saltcedar, where the turquoise river rushed smoothly by between tall boulders, rock shelves, and sandy beach.

They stood by its edge for a moment, then took off their boots and clothing and stashed them behind some saltcedars. The elevation was less than three thousand feet there, and the late morning temperature about sixty degrees—cool but not wintry. And the exertions of the trail, even downhill, had generated body heat to spare. Vic's thin, wiry legs contrasted markedly with Frank's massive, hairy ones; Ole's looked stronger than Frank had expected for his age and rawboned frame.

The water was chilly, but not as cold as Ole had expected. Frank explained that along here the river was the product of many springs which fed into the canyon at a year-round temperature of sixty-eight degrees Fahrenheit.

They committed themselves to its current and let it sweep them across a deepish hole until they came to a broad sandy shallow. For more than a mile they traveled thus, alternately floating and wading, occasionally chuting through rock-walled narrows or picking their way over low natural dams of travertine—carbonates deposited from the river water. The men had felt good to begin with, floating the river; the farther they went, the better they felt. It seemed to Vic that this boded well, foreshadowing something good to come.

Frank, in the lead, finally stopped hip-deep in a broad pool, turning to grin at the others as they appeared around the corner of a huge rock. He pointed. A mound of travertine about twenty feet high stood beside the river, and together they waded to it. If there was a guardian here, Frank thought, it was without malice or threat.

Vic led them now, pausing momentarily at the foot of the mound, then they walked side by side to the top. At the top was a round hole about six feet across, widening below the lip. About six feet below the opening, a great spring of water filled the hole, rolling powerfully as if at a hard boil, although the water was not hot. It was rather like standing on a giant open-topped kettle, looking in. Swimming in it would be impossible, climbing out doubly so, and God knows, Diacono thought, where the bottom was.

"What do we do now?" he asked.

"We go through the gate," said Vic. "I'll go first."

"The gate," Frank echoed. "I hate to ask this, but where is the gate?"

"You're standing at the edge of it."

"That?" Frank pointed downward.

Vic nodded.

"Looks like suicide."

"It would be for most people, either way, whether they landed in the water or in the other side of reality. And it takes a pretty unusual self-awareness to come out sane; it can do some pretty wild things to your whole perceptual system. Two days ago I'm not sure even Ole could have pulled it off. It's like it was booby-trapped.

"That's one advantage of it looking so deadly: no one's likely to step into it on purpose unless he really feels sure of himself."

Frank's steady eyes met the equally steady eyes of Vic Merlin. "Vic," said Frank, "I don't like to disappoint you, but I don't feel that sure of myself."

"That's okay," Vic said, "you don't need to go. In fact, you shouldn't unless you feel ready, and you'll be helping just by being here on this side. When we come back out, we may not be in too good a shape, psychically or physically; we may be glad you're here to help us back to the truck."

Frank gestured with his head. "And you've been through it before?"

"Tory and I and Norm. Kelly stayed on this side in case we needed someone here."

"Did you? Need someone here?"

"No, as it turned out, we didn't. That was summertime, and we had sleeping bags with us. We just camped until we felt up to hiking back out."

"And two is enough on the other side?"

"It should be. I've learned a whole lot since the first time."

"And you just jumped in with no one to lead you?"

"We could shift reality and *see* the other side. We just walked down the stairs."

"Hmm. How about you, Ole?" Frank asked. "Do you see stairs?"

"Ya, but I can see through them. They look kind of airy, vith vater under them." He turned to Vic. "I'm ready v'en you are."

Vic nodded, and without saying anything more, winked at Frank, then stepped in. It wasn't clear to

Frank whether he fell in the water or not; it was as if he disappeared, or maybe as if the moment of falling had been deleted. But surely there had been no splash. A second later Ole followed, again with no splash.

Frank stared thin-lipped into the powerful surging roll of water. To him there appeared no faintest sign of stairs, nor of either older man. "What the hell," he muttered, and jumped.

It was not long before noon. Carol had crawled into the camper shell to take a nap. Jerry too had gotten suddenly drowsy and had lain down on the seat of the cab. Shortly afterward his body jerked once, then relaxed again. In back and at the same moment, Carol's did the same.

# < THIRTEEN >

A blind, two-footed jump isn't the best way to start down stairs. Diacono caught a heel on the edge of the fourth step and pitched forward heavily, brushing Ole as he hit. Fortunately, there were only two more steps to fall, and Frank was nothing if not durable.

"You okay?" asked Vic.

Frank got slowly to his knees and examined the heels of his hands, which were somewhat sore from the fall, then looked around. They were in a wide corridor lit by softly luminous walls and ceiling. The gate was not a round hole above them—not from this side—but a wide, recessed, vertical door, open into blackness. This side of reality seemed to have little to do with the terrain they had just left. The corridor's ceiling, about fifteen feet high, would have been well above the level of the canyon bottom on the other side.

Getting to his feet, Diacono rotated his shoulders. "Yeah, I'm fine. A lot better than if I'd landed in that spring." He turned to Ole. "Sorry I bumped into you."

The Icelander grinned at him. "That's okay. I'm

yust glad you didn't land on top of me." He looked at Vic, "V'at now?"

"We'll go this way." Vic pointed. "That's where we found the guardian before. He's the guardian, the commanding officer, and I don't know what else. We'll see what we can learn from him."

After about a hundred feet, the corridor turned. Ahead they could see several hundred feet farther to the next turn, the walls unmarked. "Are we underground," Frank asked, "or inside a building? There don't seem to be any windows."

"At one time it was camouflaged to look like a small mountain," Vic answered. "During the wizard wars. Actually, it was a fortress then. That was when people played their games and held their wars in this reality, a number of cycles back."

"Are ve illegal in here?" Ole asked. "Are ve likely to run into a security patrol?"

"As far as I know, if we can get in, we're okay. I'm pretty sure the guardian knew we were coming, at least as soon as we got close; I don't know how far out his sphere of detection goes. But if he didn't want us to get in, he'd probably have let us know before we tried the gate, or maybe bounced us back out."

Vic slowed, as if to finish talking before they arrived at wherever they were going. "There's hardly any staff in these places anymore," he continued. "They seem to pretty much run themselves. The big security forces that used to be necessary left a long time ago. They recycled into what Tory and I call the everyday side, to have something interesting to do. Forever is a long time to sit around twiddling your thumbs.

"And when they recycled, most of them forgot all about this place, as far as conscious memory is concerned. I've run into three of them on the everyday side, from one installation or another. Two of them were Noeties or ex-Noeties who were looking for a session and found me. That's how I learned about this particular gate: one of them remembered it in session."

"But othervise they don't remember?"

"Not usually. In the arcade universe—behind the curtain, where the being really is—it seems like we always know. But on the stage, the playground—in the video game itself—they almost never know.

"Now and then certain ones cycle back to the generator side of reality for a lifetime or so, and they remember while they're here, of course. They come back to tend the generator and help maintain the matrix—to keep reality going. But the technology that built the generator was tremendously advanced; their machinery apparently doesn't take much maintenance."

"How long has it been here?" Frank asked.

"Through quite a few cycles of reality; quite a few renewals."

They turned a corner; just ahead was an open door in one wall. "That's it," Vic said, and they went in.

Somehow, Frank realized, he'd carried around the idea that the guardian would be an Indian. Yet he was surprised to see what appeared to be a large, burly Indian looking at him across a desk with a computer terminal.

"Back again?" the Indian said to Vic. "You look like the trip through the gate was a lot easier on you this time."

Vic chuckled. "Like a walk in the park. I've learned a lot since the last time; it made quite a difference."

The guardian's eyes moved to Ole for a moment, and then to Frank. "You guys keep dangerous company," he said lightly. His shrewd eyes evaluated them, then he turned back to Vic. "What brought you back here?"

"I suppose you know how things are going on the other side," Vic replied.

"To hell in a handbasket."

"We think we know why. There's a surprise generator—or maybe chaos generator would be a better term—that's patched into the matrix generator somewhere, and it's accelerating. It's driving more and more people to do crazy things, pushing the whole system toward critical.

"So what we want to do is get it disconnected."

The big Indian leaned back in his chair. "You really *have* learned some things since last time! You can call me Gandy, incidentally." His attention focused inward for a moment, then back. "And you want the surprise generator disconnected."

"That's all right, isn't it?"

"Yeah, as far as I can see, if you can do it for yourselves. No one on staff will do anything partisan. What do you want to disconnect it for?"

"If we don't, the matrix is going to discontinue in about six months."

"If you do disconnect it," Gandy replied, "things are going to get pretty dull out there. Not as dull as this side, but pretty dull. I'll grant you that people might like that for a while, but they'd get tired of it before long.

"Besides, reality could use a good overhaul."

"Every overhaul I've looked at," Vic countered, "set up a new reality that turned out to be worse, and shorter-lived, than the one before.

"Every overhaul degrades the playing conditions a little more: Shut it down, put more restrictions into the program, crank it up again, and there we go, climbing for a while. Then *crash!*

"Every cycle, toward the end, starts to get it together—every one I've reviewed, anyway. Then things start to go to hell really fast, the system goes critical, and that's it."

Gandy eyed Vic appraisingly. "For someone from the other side," Gandy said, "you've come up with a hell of a lot of information. What you're suggesting is nothing but an overhaul of sorts itself."

"Not really," said Vic. "It's the removal of an unauthorized addition to the equipment. And I'll be surprised if it requires shutting down the matrix to do it. Apparently it got put *on* line without shutting it down." He paused, holding the guardian's eyes. "People out there might like the chance to upgrade things in the existing matrix—not have to go back to the cave and dig roots again, or transmigrate to other sectors."

Gandy leaned forward on his elbows, peering interestedly across at Vic. "The surprise generator may have been unauthorized when it was patched in," he said, "but it's been left on line through several overhauls. That amounts to de facto approval. And it's certainly added something valuable to the conditions of play."

Vic shook his head firmly. "The people who installed it got extradited back to wherever they came from, as too destructive to be loose. That ought to tell us something."

"Then you know who installed it."

"I know who must have. They've been sabotaging this universe almost from the beginning. They got pulled out of here nine years ago, all seven of them, and for the first time we've got a chance to get off this built-and-bust roller coaster."

The guardian leaned back, thick fingers laced over a generous abdomen. "I keep having to upgrade my opinion of you. So what do you want me to do—that I'm allowed to?"

"We'd like whoever's in charge to disconnect the surprise generator. He wouldn't be taking sides. The Seven have been extradited; there's really only one side left."

Gandy shook his head. "The Seven are gone, but they passed their game on to four lower-echelon people, so there are still two sides. That means I'm very limited in what I can do for you. Anyway, it's not at this station."

Ole spoke now before Vic could. "Okay then, so v'ere is it? Maybe ve can do the yob ourselves."

Gandy arched his eyebrows, then shrugged. "Your game, your choice. Okay, I can tell you where it is, all right: fourteen hundred miles from here in another hard-to-find place. Not as hard as it's been sometimes, though, when it was under a couple thousand feet of ice. Getting there alive may be the hard part."

Gandy's fingers moved over his computer keyboard. After a moment, one wall became a holographic field, showing a curved, three-dimensional map of central North America, while the room illumination dimmed for better contrast. A blinking red light, like a computer cursor, ran across it and stopped on a long island in Lake Superior. Isle Royale, Frank recognized, a wilderness park. The island grew until it occupied a large part of the wall, showing ridges and forests, like an idealized stratospheric view. The cursor now sat on one of the high points of the island's long central ridge—the gate location, Diacono realized. His eyes examined its surroundings for landmarks—a bay, streams, several inland lakes near the cursor.

"And that," said Gandy, "is all I can do for you on this." He waited a few seconds longer, letting them imprint the image; then switched off the holograph and grinned. "You guys have a real war on your hands. I'd say you have a chance—about one in, oh, call it one in ten. Maybe even one in four; I keep underestimating you. If the Seven were still around, that would be one in a trillion, but you've still got some pretty heavy-duty enemies.

"Now, I want you guys to get out of here before I say or do something I'm not allowed to, and get myself in trouble."

"Just one more thing," Vic said.

The Indian face scowled, then the scowl dissolved into a grin, which was replaced in turn by a laugh. "One more, then—maybe. Depending on what it is. Let's hear it."

"Are they limited to conventional weapons against us?" Vic asked. "So far it seems like it. And I include 'conventional paranormal' in conventional."

The grin changed to a closed-mouth smile. "If they attack you with anything that's not all right, they forfeit; that goes without saying. It would put them out of the picture immediately, and the result of their incorrect action would be corrected. But that leaves them plenty of legitimate means, including the use of, ah, certain quite sophisticated equipment that combines, um, felicitous combinations of components developed in this cycle—some things The Seven left them."

The eyes narrowed, glittering. "And that's all I'm going to say: Now *out!* You're straining my neutrality!"

Without knowing how they got there, they found themselves in the corridor. They started for the gate, talking as they walked.

"How did we do?" Frank asked. "Pretty well?"

"Real well," said Vic. "I'd hoped it would turn out that well, but I didn't know. The processes we used to get ready were really effective, and we found out where the surprise generator is." He nodded. "Yep. We did real well."

"Do you think the enemy—whoever that is—do you think they know ve been here?" Ole asked. "If they do, I'll bet they try to hit us going out. It vould be bad news if they made a bunch of rock fall on us in the canyon."

"Would that come under the heading of 'legitimate weapons?' " Frank put in.

"I don't know where the line is between okay and not okay," Vic admitted, "but considering what they were throwing at Ole when he was driving out from L.A., they could probably use a rock fall if it didn't require tractor or pressor beams or anything like that.

"But they may not know we're here. If they knew where we were going, it seems like they'd have tried to stop us coming in. I don't know."

"Maybe they thought the gate would stop us."

"Could be. Anyway, as far as rockfalls or anything else is concerned, we'll just have to handle things as they come up—the way Ole did driving out here."

"Ya," the Icelander said, "but I hope ve don't have to dodge no avalanche."

When they reached the gate, Frank followed Vic up the stairs with Ole bringing up the rear. There was nothing to it. Atop the mound of Sipapu, Frank too could see the steps leading down now, perhaps because they'd become real to him.

*All in all*, he told himself, *this wasn't bad at all, not half bad. I think I'm going to like this game.*

# < FOURTEEN >

A spur of sandstone, four hundred feet tall, stood out from the cliff, the rock of its narrow crest jointed and loose. Above it loomed five hundred feet of cliff, stepped back halfway to the top with a broad, slanting ledge. Millennia earlier, a mass of rock had broken from farther up, some of it embedding in the soil of the ledge. Since then, summer thunderstorms had washed away enough of the soil that several of the boulders were ready to move, needing only some small impulse to send them hurtling onto the spur below.

The base of the spur was in a shale slope, steep and narrow, where more old boulders from higher up lay precariously among spiny shrubs. The lip of the slope was weathered limestone that had not had a major fall for ten thousand years, and was ready.

On the plateau above the canyon and the spur, on the side inaccessible to the Navajo herds and hard against the National Park, a band of twenty-three antelope grazed. One of them, the herd leader, raised her head and looked around, confused for a moment. Others, catching the movement, looked up to watch, the movement spreading. The big doe took a tenta-

121

tive step, paused, then started to trot toward a point on the canyon rim two hundred yards away. Sheeplike, the others followed.

In a pickup truck four miles away, Jerry and Carol lay sleeping. In their sleep came something like a dream—one they would not remember when they awoke. Each of them faced a small band of antelope running toward the rim of a canyon. They threw fear bolts at the animals, trying to turn them back.

Sharon Van Wyk had been writing a letter when she was struck by a need to rest her head on her arms and close her eyes for a moment. She didn't argue with it, and fell asleep at once.

Bill Van Wyk had just finished discussing an equation with his students in Math 207. He looked at his watch; five minutes remained before the bell. Nonetheless, he dismissed the class and began absently to erase the blackboard. He would erase for three long minutes before he realized that the board was clean.

Frowning, Tory Merlin stood in her kitchen with oven mitts on her hands. In her mind she watched a small band of antelope running confusedly back and forth above a canyon. In the minds of the animals collectively, she placed the image of a great bear clambering up over the rim, onto the plateau top—an image complete with stench. It was a bear such as hadn't been seen in the district for nearly a century, a huge lumbering grizzly.

An antelope's fear of grizzlies does not require experience or training: It simply *knows* that a grizzly means death. Confusion was replaced by terror. The antelopes turned and sped away from the rim. Tory watched them go, then opened the oven door and removed the bread.

# < FIFTEEN >

Dusk was settling when Frank, Vic, and Ole hauled themselves over the headwall, out of Salt Canyon. Jerry and Carol saw them come out of the canyon into the draw, and met them halfway to the pickup. They were three thousand feet higher than the canyon bottom, and the temperature was plunging, a normal accompaniment of twilight in the high desert.

Ole and Vic were physically bushed, and crashed in the camper shell in two old sleeping bags, on bunk mattresses Frank had thrown there. Once on the highway, Frank answered Jerry's and Carol's questions, leaving them quiet and thoughtful. It was eleven o'clock when they reached the ranch house.

There they debriefed each other over sandwiches and hot chocolate. Nothing had happened on the road, and the others were surprised when Tory told them about the antelopes. Other people had been involved, she said. The animals had been driven by a command to run over the edge—she could feel it— and several other people were trying to turn them back. The antelopes had been running back and forth confusedly, so she had taken over. It had seemed that somehow a plunge by the animals would endanger the men in the canyon.

That, Vic explained to his novices, was the advantage of having people of power and awareness off the action site. They could often pick up and act on dangers before the targets did, especially tired targets. The advantage was greatest when the targets were under duress.

Tory had one other item for them. Later that afternoon, someone had tried psychically to "question" Sharon Van Wyk by stimulating a chain of recalls in her. Sharon, with her new awareness, had spotted the intrusion and called for help. The two of them had scorched whoever it was, and Sharon wouldn't need help in handling future psychic intrusions, even though she had probably cloaked the affair from herself afterward.

When the debriefing was done, they made their plans. It didn't take long because the plans were sketchy; they were in bed before one.

Tory didn't go to sleep at once. She wanted to know who their friends had been, and who their enemies were. She lay in the dimly moonlit bedroom with her eyes open, but it wasn't the shadowed ceiling she looked at. She saw instead the sunlit plateau above the Little Colorado, and the panicked antelopes. There had been six other attentions seeking to turn the animals away from the rim. Four of them she recognized now: Jerry and Carol, Sharon and Bill. The other two she could not identify, although she'd know if she felt them again. Both seemed female, both powerful enough to do what they had done. One of them felt—older, and light. The other, she sensed, had more power and less experience. Probably neither would consciously recall what had happened.

Only one being had been driving the animals, an

entity with a great deal of power and control. She got no particular sense of any other personal attributes— sex or age—but it was the same entity who had intruded on Sharon.

With the knowledge from Vic's debriefing, she knew who the entity must be, or rather, the group of which it must be a member. It was one of the four lower-echelon people whom Gandy said took over when the Terrible Seven had been hauled away: four in whom the cosmic fuzz had had no interest—who were outside their jurisdiction.

She had a rough sense of their operating style. They would be low-profile manipulators, operating mainly through money, position, and connections, with their advanced psychic power used mainly to lever, nudge, spy, and assassinate safely.

*It'll be interesting,* she thought, *to see if we can head them off.* Six months, that's what the fortune-teller had told Ole—six months, more or less, to save reality as they knew it.

But she felt no terrible urgency. To Tory Merlin, the reality behind reality was too real for her to feel threatened by the situation. This was simply an interesting challenge. If they blew it, there'd be a new reality soon after, and new games, as there'd been before. This *was* the reality cycle to carry it off in if they could, but the next would do if it had to: Sooner or later they'd get rid of or defuse the surprise generator, and with The Seven gone, they could create— who knew what?

It occurred to her that there might be something to that effect already in a master script somewhere. But even so, it was up to them to create the roles, scenes, and actions—to make it happen.

# < SIXTEEN >

Peter Shark's stony eyes were directed at the juncture of ceiling and wall, focusing on nothing in particular. He appeared to be alone, but in fact, three others were with him psychically—one of them actively, the other two as passive listeners. By their standards, it was turning into a long conference.

Shark popped another cigarette from the silver dispenser that his secretary filled twice daily on his desk. "So what happened then?" he asked silently.

Kurt Hardman's reply was likewise soundless, spoken flatly into his mind. "They hiked up out of the canyon and went back to Merlin's place in the desert. But remember: based on what I got out of the two ghosts, they definitely know about the chaos generator—they call it 'the surprise generator.' They know it's accelerating, and they know what's going to happen.

"So we know damn well why they went to the gate, even if I couldn't follow them in with the grid. They wanted more information. But now I can't tap any of them to find out what they learned there; they pick me up at first touch, and then Merlin or his wife jumps in, even from a distance."

Hardman's thoughts were rational enough, but the mind producing them was testy, even angry. "Those are the two most dangerous people on the planet," Hardman continued, "and we never even knew about them! It's hard to believe they just now crawled out of the woodwork."

Peter Shark frowned. Apparently these people had become what Leif Haller might have, if the Seven Lords hadn't stepped in and queered Haller and his operation. Now, with The Seven gone, it was up to the four of them. But it shouldn't be difficult. Merlin didn't have Haller's personnel, organization, or money.

"We need to know what they learned from the guardian," Shark said. "What have you done with the ghosts?"

Hardman replied with a sardonic mental chuckle. " I softened them up by zapping them back and forth between two terminals for a while before I questioned them. Before and after. Right now they're sort of smeared around inside a holding bottle, nice and apathetic. But I can revive them if we want them for anything."

Shark filed the information mentally. "You said that two of the group returned to their home in Flagstaff."

"That was *before* the others visited the gate; I already told you that. They seemed to pull out of the action, even though they're still connected."

Mentally Shark tried to examine that, but his attention just now was like an eye with a clouded membrane; it was hard to examine details. His mind swelled with irritation, and he shook it off; his special strength was his calmness and rationality.

"How would it work to just monitor their routine thoughts, without actually prodding around?"

"No damn way, Shark. They're like a lot of psychics—they've got a kind of automatic alarm against eavesdropping. I never could read Sigurdsson, and now that Merlin and his wife have worked on the others, none of them are accessible. When I tried to prod the woman in Flagstaff, just nice and light, she yelled, and she and Merlin's wife burned my ass. Clobbered me, actually. Later, when I only sniffed around her old man a little bit, Merlin jumped in. I was ready for that one, though, and bailed out quick.

"So I can't mindread them—can't safely contact their minds at all. If you want me to predict what the hell they're going to do, I'll have to actually watch them on the remote, analyze their movements, and extrapolate, which is going to tie me down; I need some help on this."

Shark scowled, his lips pursed. "The guardian may have told them where the generator is. He could probably interpret that as neutral information without getting nailed."

"Well, of course he did, if that's what they asked him. That's obvious, for chrissake! If they asked him, the sonofabitch told them."

Shark felt irritation surge. Hardman's surly response to everything he said wasn't helping his concentration. He reached deeper for self-control. "What makes you so sure he told them?"

"I checked him out with the idiot kid. The guardian's name is Gandy. The bastard worked cheek to cheek with Leif Haller in the early Noetie days, and when The Seven came down on Haller and his cronies, Gandy was one of them that got killed. He's only neutral because he has to be—and no more than he has to be."

So, thought Shark, there was little doubt that the guardian, this Gandy, had told Merlin where the chaos generator was—assuming Merlin was smart enough to ask; and it appeared that he was. On the other side of reality, Gandy might be above anger or vengefulness, but he'd still have enough emotional polarity to care who won.

Mentally, Shark backed away and examined the situation. What was needed now was effective action. If you struck effectively in present time, covering all the alternatives, you forestalled future problems. He would assume that Merlin knew about Isle Royale and would try to do something about it, so they'd kill him now. If they were wrong, that was Merlin's hard luck, not theirs.

This was nothing to fool around with. They could afford to take no chances. To continue as the proxies of The Seven during the next cycle, they had to ensure the on-schedule dissolution of the present cycle. That had been made clear, years ago, and till now it had seemed simple.

"There are direct and forceful actions you could take personally, today," he said to Hardman, "that would finalize this situation."

Kurt Hardman's emotional response was angry exasperation. "Jesus Christ, Shark! If I was dumb enough to jump Merlin, the rest of them would be all over me like a nest of fucking scorpions! I'd be a basket case for a month—maybe even dead! You'd still have the rest of them running loose, and no gridman."

Hardman, never stable, was really upset now. "If the grid makes you ten times as sensitive as otherwise, it damned well makes you ten times as vulnerable, too! You don't know what it's like, riding the grid on a job! That little training stint The Lords gave you wasn't even a sample; that was patty-cake. Try busting a witch sometime! If she has a chance to fight back, it's like a bout with the flu; a really tough one can be like dengue fever. It's bullshit like that that makes my body look sixty when it's forty-three.

"Tell you what, Shark," he went on sarcastically. "You come out here and ride the grid. I'll take me a vacation and you can be the gridman."

Shark's response was both conciliatory and vaguely sinister. "Sorry, Kurt. I won't try to make you do something that's too much for you. But consider my position: I have to see that this situation is handled. Each of us has his principal talent and consequent responsibilities. The Lords selected you to ride the booster grid. I'm not sure what I'll do with you if you can't function as needed."

"Nobody said anything about 'can't function,' for chrissake! The point is, why be stupid? All we need to do is set up an ambush near the gate. That's simple enough."

"Simple isn't the word for it, my friend. Gates and their surrounds are neutral ground."

"I'm not talking about shooting them *at* the gate, Shark! I'm talking about *near* the gate!"

"How near?"

"I don't know. How far away is neutral?"

"I don't know, either. That's part of the problem. We need to stop them along the way somewhere."

He's right about one thing, though, Shark thought privately. The situation could be handled by mundane methods and proxies without risk of losing their gridman. When all was said and done, connections, money, leverage, and unboosted psi were all the power they really needed for most actions. And they had plenty of those—those and professionalism. The booster grid could be damned useful and sometimes essential, but those were the basics.

And when this affair was over, maybe he'd see about finding a replacement for Hardman; the fat toad was losing his grip. Meanwhile, he'd have to make do with him.

Shark changed the subject. "If you were going to the island from Phoenix, how would you go?"

"From Phoenix?" Hardman shifted from combative to contemplative. "If I was Merlin? Hmm. The *quickest* way would be to fly—take a major airline to Chicago or Minneapolis, then a regional line to Duluth. From there I'd charter a small ski-mounted plane to the island."

"Do you think that's how they'd go, then?"

"If they're in a hurry—but they're probably not. And Merlin's no dummy; he'd know a plane would be easier to destroy, even if he or Sigurdsson flies it personally—which is unlikely, although I need to watch for something like that. No, what they'll probably do is drive to the lake."

"You weren't successful at stopping Sigurdsson when he drove to Arizona. Why was that?"

"Well *look* at it! I didn't know what we were up against then! I was using the equivalent of ballistic missiles on a mobile target evasively driven and of comparable speed. The old man dodged and the missiles didn't change course. I had no way of knowing the old fart was so alert!"

Hardman wondered momentarily if Shark had twigged on how he'd opened the tailgate—knew and just wasn't saying anything, saving it to hit him with later. He'd used grid-boosted TK—a small pressor beam, actually—to push the latch that allowed the office furniture to dump onto the freeway. That one small use of a pressor beam had set off alarms on the other side of reality, and instantly he'd felt a referee behind his shoulder. He didn't care to speculate on what might have happened to him if Sigurdsson hadn't dodged successfully.

"The way we need to go now," Hardman continued, "is to use intelligent, self-adjusting, target-seeking missiles: assassins, not accidents."

If there were just a way to use some of the ancient technology, Hardman thought to himself—technology from one of the wizard-war cycles, maybe. Even the Lords hadn't been able to get away with doing that, but it was nice to think about.

As Hardman privately thought this, an image formed in the mind of Peter Shark, an image of black night, enclosed by hills and reeking with archaic power. A tower stood on a hill, and from it, something utterly brutal watched. Inadvertently Shark's hackles raised, and Hardman chuckled sardonically.

"Looking at my mental pictures, eh?" Hardman said. "Heavy, huh? What you got there was the robot sentry I told you about, at the toll station—the one Sigurdsson got tangled up with. When the sentry activated, it rang a different alarm in the grid, one I never heard before, and probably a bunch more on the other side. That's what drew my attention to Sigurdsson in the first place. When he got out alive, I figured he might be a problem. Not that he powered his way out, but somehow or other it just didn't waste him. The robot mind—unpredictable if you don't know the program.

"Who knows? Sigurdsson might have been its master in some lifetime way to hell and gone back, when the rules were different. Maybe that's why it let him go. It doesn't make that much difference, because if he wasn't a powerful old sonofabitch in this life, he'd have been a grease spot right there, regardless. That thing is hot! As soon as I got a good whiff of it, I backed away and watched on remote.

"I was just wishing we had something like that; that's what pulled the picture out of my memory files."

Shark was glad they didn't need something like that. He'd known about the tollgate since back when he'd done *his* grid training, years ago—had known about it because when it took a car, its free-terminal tractor beam set off an alarm in the grid. He'd found it a bit amusing, and had wondered what legal loophole allowed it to persist. But this *sentry!* The tollgate was impersonal, while the sentry felt . . . evil. It gave him the creeps.

He pushed it out of his mind by shifting his attention to something else. "Speaking of relicts, Kurt, what about using elementals?"

There was a lag of seconds, then a plaintive, "Jesus, Shark, you've got to be kidding! Once you juice them up, they're impossible to control, and you know what kind of a job it is to get them suppressed again! And it's my job! The goddamn gridman's job!"

Shark could feel Hardman's emotion, something between outrage and grief. Maybe the fat toad would be more courteous next time.

"All right, Kurt, okay now. I'm not telling you to use elementals yet, but there may be a time when we'll need one. We may want a blizzard or tornado or earthquake somewhere before this is over.

"And as far as getting them suppressed again—if it takes too long, I'll cover for you with the referee. I'll take full responsibility."

*It'd almost be worth taking the heat,* Shark thought behind his psi screen. *I could say* mea culpa *all over the place and still make sure the blame fell on you.*

"You're right, though," Shark went on. "Ordinary means should be enough. I'm turning the Merlin group over to you to handle, and you do whatever it takes. I have to work pretty much full time on the Arab project, but I'll try to be available if you need me urgently. What resources do you need that you don't have?"

When Hardman answered, his hostility had disappeared, and he sounded almost docile. "Right now I'd like both Gracco and Sordom," he said, "to contact the muscle and supervise them as necessary. I'll stay here in Dallas on the grid, keeping track of things and coordinating."

Shark decided he didn't want Hardman too subdued; the man needed some spunk. "Fine, Kurt," he said. "And let me add that you've done very well in uncovering all this. Very well, indeed. I also appreciate that in some respects you have the most demanding job of any of us. So both John and Vincent are yours for this project."

Shark shifted his attention to the other two presences there. "Did you get that, Vincent? John?" he asked. "Any comments?"

They'd gotten it, and there weren't any comments. They were solid pros, and neither was a prima donna.

"Good," Shark said. "Do it."

# ⋖ SEVENTEEN ⋗

Coach Vern Barkum frowned up at Diacono from behind his desk. "Jesus, Frank, I can't give you next week off. You haven't given me enough notice."

"Yeah, I realize this is short notice, but we've got about as little pressure this time of year as we ever have." Frank delivered this very casually; his voice carried no insistence or urgency.

"*I* know that! What I'm saying is that I have to retain control here. I can't have my staff flying off in every damn direction on the spur of the moment."

Frank nodded. "Of course you can't. You're absolutely right. I'd feel that way too if I were you."

Barkum's reaction to his request had been expected. It wasn't that he was protective of his authority; his staff respected him, and he knew it. But he had a thing about order and schedules.

"Why don't we size up the whole leave situation," Frank went on. "August to Christmas week is out of the question, of course, and so are May and most of April. June is better than July, and March is better than February. But January is ordinarily okay, once the recruiting charts are done, and my work on them is. So we've got June as the best month, with March and the rest of January probably next.

"And I'd really a lot rather have the rest of January," he went on, "starting tomorrow."

Barkum grunted. *Ah well, why not?* he thought. He looked at Diacono, then grinned. "You got a girlfriend that wants to get away from the winter weather and visit Mexico City."

Frank shrugged.

"Okay, go ahead, but don't ask for an extension. I want you here in February so I can call on you to help close any kids we got hanging fire. You're the only big-name NFL veteran I've got."

Frank grinned. "I know," he said. The two men matched grips on it, then Frank turned and left, closing the door behind him.

Barkum stood looking at the closed door, still smiling, but rueful now. " 'I know,' " he mimicked. "Cheeky bastard." The man had to be in love, Barkum decided; he'd been bright-eyed and grinning all day, acting like the world was his oyster. And the line about Diacono's pickup breaking down had probably been pure bullshit.

Diacono strode down the hall to the training room, and to Lewis Quahu's office. Again the door was open, and again he closed it behind him.

"Hey, Lew," he said quietly.

"Yeah?"

"I want to thank you again for getting Vic Merlin's number for me. I spent the weekend with him and some other people, and we visited Sipapu.

"There really is a spirit there, you know."

"Is that right?" Quahu said solemnly, then unexpectedly grinned. Frank wasn't sure he'd ever seen Quahu really grin big before. He smiled lots of times, and he had great teeth, but grinning wasn't something he did much, at least in public.

"And the spirit really talked to us," Frank continued, "in words as clear and real as yours and mine here in this office. It made a fantastic weekend."

Quahu's eyes looked him over. "I believe you. You've changed. I could see you were different during staff meeting this morning. Talking with a kachina could do that."

Diacono nodded, pleased but suddenly a little self-conscious. "Anyway, I wanted to thank you and tell you how well it worked out. Oh, and don't mention this to anyone. I had to lie to the boss about why I wasn't here yesterday."

"Got it," said Quahu.

Frank opened the door, threw Quahu a salute, and went back out. He pulled his jacket on as he strode down the hall, then left the building. The most recent snow was slumping in the bright sunshine, and melting progressively back from the sidewalks. Getting into his pickup, Diacono backed out of his reserved parking slot.

He'd pick up a few hundred in cash at the bank, he decided. There were always places that wouldn't accept credit cards. After that he'd take care of a few things around the apartment and go give Bill and Sharon a quick update: he'd driven back in the pre-dawn hours and hadn't talked to them yet. Then he'd head back for the desert and the Merlins.

Miki Ludi stood on the sundeck in the night, the wooded slope falling away beneath. Marine air had moved in over the Los Angeles Basin, and the hills and low mountains that bordered it, making the air soft and moist, hiding the sky with low clouds. It was dark, for the city, with a feeling of privacy, but she also had a vague sense of something soon to happen.

Psychically she examined the vicinity and picked

up no intruding awareness. Without turning on a
light, she went back into her room, her eyes, catlike,
seeing as well as needed. She felt there was something she needed to know, but she had no inkling of
what.

She did, however, have an approach to finding
out. Opening a drawer, she took out a lighter and lit
a stout candle on her dressing table. That done, she
slipped out of her clothes and, lean-limbed, assumed
a lotus position on a small cushioned platform, fixing
her eyes on the flickering flame. They stayed there,
their only movement the flame reflected on them.
Anyone watching might have assumed she sought
*samadhi* in the manner of a yogin. Actually, Miki
Ludi had no interest in any universal oneness.
With basically ethical motives she sought psychic
power, and had made significant progress. She was
unorthodox in her search, and less eclectic than
experimental.

She had read widely, from Manley P. Hall to
Castaneda to Aleister Crowley, from Yogananda to
Leif Haller, and thence, briefly, to the various jour-
nals of parapsychology. But instead of choosing one
of the established approaches and following it, she
had experimented. That in itself was not so remarkable, but in most such cases, the approach fails to
produce much advancement. Miki Ludi was an exception; she seemed to be guided by something within
her, as if she already knew, as if she was an amne-
siac, her efforts simply an aid to remembering. And
if she still stood well short of what she wished to be,
she was nonetheless exceptional in more than her
beauty and business acumen.

Thus, after a minute or so her focus changed, her
attention open to whatever would come, yet aligned
with her intention, which was to know what had
been nudging her psyche this evening.

Results from this approach were seldom extravagant. Ordinarily she would remain semi-entranced—not until something dramatic or explicit happened, but until she felt that she was done. Later, perhaps next morning in the shower, or at the salon, she would find that she knew what she needed to know—or more often, did what she needed to do, perhaps for little or no apparent reason. In such instances, she was wise enough not to manufacture rationales. She seemed to know naturally that real wisdom is correct action, or the contemplation of it, and that knowledge and understanding are only substitutes, available for use in wisdom's absence, or backups to explain with.

But this evening before the flame, as sometimes happened, she also pulled in pictures and sensations. She saw her sister-in-law in a room with other people. The room they were in was fairly large, with a high ceiling, exposed beams, and a rough wooden floor partly covered with small rugs. The young police sergeant was there with a cast on his arm. She also recognized Olaf Sigurdsson's tall frame.

The others were strangers to her. One was a large man, heavily muscled and, to her, physically attractive. There was also an older man, wiry and bearded, and a small middle-aged woman, red-haired, with eyes that marked power.

There was no sound with this picture, although its people were talking and occasionally gesturing. She felt a certain communion with them, and wished she knew what was going on.

Miki was too wise to strain for more, though. Simply, she watched their conference—she knew this was more than ordinary conversation—and waited for whatever further might come to her. Then something began to pull her attention, and after a moment the room was gone and she was looking at semidarkness. She saw now a different room, lit only by something like a very large television screen. The screen showed the room and conference she had just watched—showed it clearly.

Watching the screen was a squat, fat, aging man, naked and of extraordinary ugliness. She could feel his power. The chair he sat on might have been plexiglass, and looked like some strange, transparent, molded circuit board. Its single arm made her think of a luxurious classroom desk, but it had a keyboard and control levers as well as a writing surface. The chair in turn stood on a low pedestal—a housing that gave no suggestion of its contents but had an insulated cable leading to the meter-wide viewscreen.

After a moment, it seemed to Miki that she was perceivable to this troll, should she catch his attention, and that that would be dangerous. Indeed, a central part of the experience was its sense of danger, as if she found herself in a grizzly's cage with the grizzly momentarily looking the other way. With that realization, the strange room was gone and she was back in her own. But somehow she knew that her act of disconnecting had been noticed, and that another visit might give her location away.

The emotion of fear was foreign to Miki Ludi, and rarely visited her, but her shiver now was not from cold. Unfolding her legs, she got up, snuffed out the candle, and in the darkness got ready for bed. This night's experiences were something she needed to sleep on. Tomorrow she might know what, if anything, to do as a follow up.

John Sordom liked it best when things were on the line—when it was time to handle hell out of something. Usually he found it exhilarating, but not this evening. As soon as Shark had assigned him to work with Hardman, he'd had a conference with the gridman. Immediately after that he'd phoned Manny Goldner in Casa Grande, Arizona, and made a verbal contract: Manny was to meet him at the airport in Winslow, Arizona, that same night, with all the material necessary.

It had taken a dozen rings to waken Manny, who'd been up all the night before, and through the day until evening, on a job south of the border. Sordom had made sure that Manny was awake enough to get the instructions accurately, and made him summarize it all before hanging up.

Manny was a good man who kept busy. He did a lot of commercial blasting for construction contractors, demolition contractors, oil drillers, and increasingly for revolutionaries of one stripe or another in Latin America—anything that required high-priced finesse with explosives. He'd worked for Sordom before.

This job didn't require that much finesse, but Sordom liked working with real pros. And besides having all the necessary materials on hand, Goldner kept an old Curtis Travelair around that would be just right for the job. It was unobtrusive and could maintain altitude at walking speed.

Sordom had never been to Winslow. He'd selected it because its airport could accommodate his light jet and because it was a small town only 130 air miles from Merlin's place. Before taking off, he'd called in Hardman to guide his pen in locating Merlin's place on one of the large-scale maps Sordom carried in his cockpit. There shouldn't be any problem locating it from the air; there weren't any other buildings around for miles, Hardman had assured him, and then had given him a mental image of Merlin's place.

Now the lights of Winslow appeared on the southwestern horizon. Sordom evaluated the country, what he could see of it by the light of a concave moon: high desert, barren as hell, with a little snow in arroyos and on steeper north slopes where the winter sun didn't get at it. The town didn't look like much, either—the asshole of the world, good place to test an H-bomb. He made his approach and landed, and as he taxied toward the parking area, saw a Travelair parked there. It had to be Manny's; there were damned few Travelairs left in the world anymore.

The little one-room terminal hunched dark and empty beneath the winter sky. The tin shed that housed airport services had a light in the window at one end—the office. A man in coveralls and heavy jacket was walking out to meet him, signalling with an arm where he wanted Sordom to park. Leaving the slim, poker-faced young Navajo to set the chocks and refuel the jet, Sordom walked to the shed, the relevant maps folded in the front of his jacket, and went into the little office.

Manny Goldner was inside, frowzy-headed and gray-faced, drinking coffee from a cup that read "Charlie" on the side.

"Change your name?" asked Sordom.

Goldner's broad features frowned in puzzlement.

"Your cup says Charlie on it."

Goldner looked at the name, then at Sordom. "The Indian lent it to me."

"You fit to fly? You look like hell."

"Yeah, I'm fit to fly," Goldner said truculently. "If you don't like my looks, I'll just find me a motel here and sleep for about twenty hours. The five hours you woke me out of, and three hours the night before last, is all the sleep I got for three days."

Sordom eyed him; the man was running on benzedrine. "You sure you're fit to fly?"

"I told you, didn't I? I just ain't fit to associate with, is all." He patted the pocket of his flight jacket. "You got cigarettes? I run out."

Sordom took an elegant, gold-plated cigarette case out of his own flight jacket and offered one of his Gauloises. The case always impressed the people he dealt with, even the drug kings with big money. It was partly that he handled it as if he was born to it. And if anyone ever decided to jump him for it, their education would be quick. It would also be terminal unless Sordom had some reason to spare them; he was enormously competent in matters like that— entirely aside from being virtually impossible to take by surprise. These traits had been the principal expression of his psi talent throughout his youth until the Seven Lords had worked on him: His actions almost always anticipated and negated what the enemy was going to try next.

He'd been highly trained and deadly before he left Nam. Under The Lords he'd become twice as deadly, and learned to associate with captains of commerce, governments, and the underworld without necessarily coming across as a killer.

Of course, The Seven had made a few other alterations in him, too—as few as necessary. Implanting was a limited technique with the technology allowed in the Tikh Cheki Matrix, even in hands as skilled as those of the Seven Lords. It commonly caused some irrational and unpredictable side responses, not so much to the implanted triggering phrases but to seemingly irrelevant words or situations.

So he'd been only sparingly tampered with, and had proven a very stable, rational, and ruthless operator. And loyal—that was the key. He believed implicitly that he, with Shark and Gracco and Hardman, would run this sector the next cycle, if they saw this one through successfully. And he would never reject the broad purposes imprinted on him by The Seven.

He watched Goldner take one of the cigarettes and light up. The man's hands were steady enough, and his eyes weren't that much too bright. He'd do, Sordom decided; he'd have to. And given his lack of sleep, he was probably more fit to fly with the bennies in him than without them.

"You ready to take off?" Sordom asked.

"Sure. I got my tanks topped off when I got here. You said twenty thou, right?"

"Right."

"I still ain't rich enough that I can say no to twenty thou just for a few hours' sleep. But when I get to bed next time, I'm going to unplug the fucking telephone." He raised his mug. "You going to have a cup before we take off?"

"No. We've got to get this job done *muy pronto*. Finish your coffee and let's get going. It's more than an hour's flight in that relic."

Goldner shrugged. Sordom shouldn't call the Travelair a relic; it was he who suggested they use it. Then, finishing the half-cold coffee with one movement, Goldner nodded, ready. The young Navajo came back in, logged the jet, received its keys from Sordom, and the three men walked out together.

Sordom stood with his shoulders hunched in the cold night while the Indian unfastened the tie-downs and Goldner started an abbreviated preflight check. The temperature couldn't be much above zero, Sordom thought; it was bullshit to have such cold weather in a desert. Deserts should be like Phoenix in the winter, or like early autumn in Chicago— maybe a little frosty now and then, but never really cold.

Then Goldner nodded to him, and the two of them got into the aircraft. Sordom's eyes took in the cabin, finding only a cardboard box with a parachute attached. "Is that the bomb?" he asked.

"That's him."

Sordom took a small pocket flashlight from his jacket and put its beam on the box. The cardboard was heavy, the box reinforced with wide bands of strapping tape.

"What's it doing with fuse on it?" he asked.

"I didn't have any impact detonators, so I rigged it with fuse."

"Shit, Manny! I didn't hire you to go out with some kind of half-assed mickey mouse bomb!"

"Look," said Goldner tiredly, "don't get your back up. You said this was a big rush job—you needed it done tonight. And it was a lot quicker to cut off forty seconds worth of fuse and fasten a cargo chute to the charge than to rig up a safe detonator. We'll drop it from seven hundred feet, and she'll blow about five seconds after she hits."

Why hadn't he just put a blasting cap on it and let that blow it on impact? Sordom wondered. But Manny knew what he was doing; he was one of the top professionals. Sordom eyed the bomb with that point of view and felt a little better about it. It was big— maybe eighty pounds. That ought to do the job with something to spare, even with adobe.

Then something else struck him about it. "That's not the color of fuse! Why didn't you use standard fuse?"

"It came with some goods I picked up in Honduras—French, they told me, but actually it's Russian. That's about all you can get down there unless you run into our own. That's standard color for Russian fuse; I've used it before."

Sordom contemplated it. It didn't feel good to him. But it was Soviet, all right; he recognized it now from Nam. He bent and looked more closely at it.

"Shit, John," said Goldner irritatedly, "there ain't

nothing wrong with that fuse; I know what the hell I'm doing. How the hell you think I lived this long if I wasn't careful about things like that? It'll work like a charm. All that'll be left of that ranch house is the cellar. Even if it never had a cellar."

Sordom was still pondering the fuse. "Look!" Goldner said, suddenly angry, "you want to do this tonight or not?"

Sordom straightened and nodded: Manny was the expert. "Let's go," he said.

They stepped into the cockpit and sat down. Goldner flipped the master switch, looked over the instruments, and turned the single engine over. She caught and roared into life. While she warmed up, Sordom went over the maps with him. Then they taxied out and took off.

They were flying about two thousand feet above the canyon as they approached the target. Goldner looked questioningly at Sordom. "Is that it?" he asked.

Mentally, Sordom had already called up the aerial viewpoint image that Hardman had given him. He wished the moon was brighter; it was in the fourth quarter, less than half a disk. He was going to have to call Hardman in to be sure. This was no situation for guessing, and Hardman would be on the grid tonight, even if he was napping.

"Circle," he ordered. Then mentally he called to Hardman and asked the question. The gridman had been awake; it occurred to Sordom, not for the first time, that he would not want Hardman's job. The answer came quickly; the buildings below were the Merlin place.

"That's it," he told the pilot. "Seven hundred feet, you said."

Goldner nodded. Their eyes met. Manny was doing

fine, Sordom told himself, just fine, but he'd take over the controls when the job was done and let the man sleep on the way back to Winslow. He gave Goldner the high sign, then, crouching, went back to the bomb.

He had donned a parachute; now he tightened its straps. He'd be leaning out the door on the bombing run. Sordom opened the door and fastened it back, then attached the static line of the cargo chute to a cable overhead.

The long banking turn took them well out over the desert basin again. When they had straightened, they were aimed up the canyon at what appeared to be about seven hundred feet. Goldner cut their speed to about eighty miles an hour, and Sordom slid the heavy box to the wind-whipped opening in the plane's side.

Leaning out, the cold air snatching at his face, Sordom saw the cluster of buildings and box elders farther up the canyon. It would be pointless to make a drift chute pass, he decided. They were lower than the ridges that walled the canyon, down out of any crosswinds, and Manny had told him the wind was negligible anyway.

He picked up the little plunger on the fuse's end that would ignite it. The buildings rushed toward them, and Manny cut back the throttle, the airspeed dropping to sixty-five or seventy. Sordom's eyes were glued to the buildings. He pushed the plunger, and for just a split second, as the "fuse" snapped angrily into life, he knew what was wrong with it: it was primacord!

The plane blew apart in a tremendous explosion. Back in Dallas, Kurt Hardman screamed. It even wakened Shark in New York. John Sordom's psyche was too shocked to do anything as his body disintegrated; it would be days or weeks before he regained a disembodied awareness. Manny Goldner was just as dead but far less devastated, because for him there was not that awful instant of trying to stop the passage of time, that terrible, futile effort to hold away the explosion.

It woke up everyone in the ranch house and broke every window in the place, but that was the extent of the real damage. The CIA agent who had craftily introduced primacord, disguised as Russian fuse, into the terrorist channels of revolutionary Central America would never have imagined this particular scenario.

## < EIGHTEEN >

The explosion had brought everyone in the ranch house bolt upright in their beds as glass rained from the windows. This was followed seconds later by a loud bang as a piece of metal from the aircraft struck the corrugated iron machine shed close by. Within two minutes they had all pulled on clothes and gathered in the kitchen—the Merlin family plus Ole, Jerry, Carol, and Frank. Tory already had coffee on—coffee for fellowship, she said.

The clock showed four-seventeen.

Carol was the next-to-last in. "What was it?" she asked.

"An airplane blew up," answered Ole. "Yust up there."

He pointed upward toward the southeast, then concentrated. "A small vun, vith—I get two people in it."

"How the heck could a small plane make an explosion like that?" Jerry asked. "Even if the gas tanks blew?"

Vic had come in while Ole was talking. "They had a bomb they were getting ready to drop on us," Vic said, "and it blew up before they could push it out. The gas tanks blew too then."

Tory looked around, counting heads. "Looks like nobody got cut," she commented, then looked at her two sons. "Somebody's going to have to figure out what glass we need to get before the boys go into town this morning. Any volunteers?"

The dark, compact Kelly looked at his lanky, red-haired brother. "I'll do the measuring," he said, "if you'll get the glass at noon."

"Okay," Norm answered nonchalantly. "I'll go on back to bed and get another hour's sleep." Both young men left the kitchen. Jerry couldn't help but think of the argument there'd have been among him and his brothers over a matter like that.

Vic looked around at the others. "We were going to get up at six anyway. Suppose we just stay up now and get an early start. We can get through Phoenix ahead of the real rush-hour traffic."

"If y'all are going to do that," said Tory, "I guess I'd better fix breakfast. I'm getting low on eggs, so unless somebody won't eat pancakes, that's what we'll have."

"Sounds good to me," said Frank. The others added their agreement and dispersed. Ole and Jerry went outside, to lessen the demands on the single bathroom. Without speaking, they walked side by side to the shadows below the box elders and stood a few feet apart facing downhill.

"Well," Jerry said, "things seem to be going pretty well."

"O-oh?"

"It seems as if everything the enemy tries blows back in their faces."

"Ya, ve ain't doing bad at all. But I ain't going to get too cocky. It looks like they got more than psychic powers, and if they can send people out vith airplanes and bombs, ve don't know v'at the hell they'll try to do next. But you're right: ve're still alive and doing good, and at least a couple of them ain't."

They stood quiet then for a moment, until they had finished. "My arm feels a lot better," Jerry commented as he zipped his fly. "The doctor said six weeks in the cast, but I don't think it'll be that long. It's not just that it doesn't hurt; somehow it feels as if it's healing really fast. And don't ask me how I know; it just feels that way."

"Good," Ole said. "Ve can stop along the vay somev'ere and get it x-rayed. The cast can probably come off early. That Noetie stuff helps things heal faster, and this stuff of Vic's could be speeding it up more yet."

They sauntered back toward the ranch house, slowly, as if there was more to say. "You know," Jerry said thoughtfully, "this stuff that Vic's come up with—it still seems unreal to me when I stop to think about it. If I didn't see and feel the results for myself—see the effects in the rest of you and feel it in me—I *wouldn't* believe it. But I wish to hell I'd gone through the gate with you guys. That would have *really* made it real for me."

"Ya," Ole said, "that vas something else—the vildest thing I ever done. And I done some vild stuff. Probably you can go through the next gate v'en ve get there." He stopped and faced the younger man. "You know, if they're going for us vith things like bombs and guns, that revolver of yours yust might come in handy yet."

Jerry grinned. "Yeah. So far I've been along mainly for the ride, although according to Tory, I had something to do with holding back an antelope stampede. I really don't have any idea of what that was like; I wish I could consciously remember it."

"Maybe you vill—v'en Vic or Tory has time to vork vith us some more. Meanv'ile, yust enyoy feeling good; most people in this situation vould be too nervous to spit. They'd be blibbering their lips. You're doing great."

Jerry nodded, then pushed his stong hand out to the Icelander. Ole met it with his own, larger one. "You're darn right I'm doing great," said Jerry, "and it started when I got mixed up with you. I'll tell you what else, too. You said 'enjoy feeling good'; well, that's just what the heck I'm doing. Life has never felt this good to me before, even though somebody just tried to bomb me out of existence."

His grin widened. "And here we are, faced with the end of the world. I guess the key is, we know it won't be the end of *us*, or of anybody, even if we don't get it stopped." The grin lessened to a small smile. "Although I don't know how I'd like doing the caveman bit. Maybe we wouldn't have to start out like that, though, eh? I suppose whoever reprograms the reality generator could set things up the way they want to. Now that would be an interesting job!

"But this is the time to do—whatever it is we've been working toward all this time."

The grin flashed back again. "Enough of this cerebral bullshit. We've got us a game, Ole. We've got us a game."

# < NINETEEN >

"Shark!"

"Yes?"

Hardman's thoughts came heavy and hard. "Merlin's group is on the road, in two vehicles: a white Cadillac sedan and a black Ford four-wheel-drive pickup with a camper shell and big, off-road tires."

"What route?"

"I'm coming to that, goddamn it! Lemme finish!" Mentally Hardman glared. "They've turned south on I-17. That probably means they're going to take I-10 by way of Tucson, but they could take US 60 through Globe."

*Good,* Shark thought to himself, *Hardman's surly again.* And hard; he'd never sensed such hard determination in the gridman before. Shark had wondered how Hardman would do after Sordom's fiasco last night. John Sordom had been the one of the four that each of the others could talk to as a friend. And Hardman, with his strange, confined, and necessarily reclusive life, had often, Shark knew, held private psi conversations with Sordom through the grid.

Sordom had been crouched over the bomb when it went off, and Hardman had been monitoring his

153

mind at the time. It must have been a hell of a shock for the gridman. Shark decided that Hardman was tougher than he'd given him credit for, to have come around so strongly and so soon.

Shark looked at the clock on his office wall. Nine-twelve. Arizona was on Pacific—no, Mountain Time; it would be seven-twelve there. And eight-twelve in St. Louis, where Gracco was unless he'd already left for Minneapolis.

He put his attention on Vincent Gracco and got something that was part concept and part picture. He could see Gracco's face and a hand-held telephone, and knew it was the mobile phone in Gracco's car. He was probably driving to the airport and setting up meetings while he drove. When Gracco was off the phone, Hardman could give him the information on cars and routes.

Shark himself already missed John Sordom. Among the other three, Sordom had been the most nearly like himself, with broad interests and knowledge. But to handle the necessary negotiations in this short-term situation, Gracco was better suited; he'd grown up connected to the Mafia and spoke the language of the big-time rackets. If he'd had to lose one man, Sordom had probably been the one whose loss would prove the least injurious in the short-run.

And that's what there was: a short-run. There were no long-term situations left in this cycle. Even the Arab project was irrelevant now, really, something challenging and enjoyable to play with, to fill the time while waiting. But within a few months . . .

Briefly, Shark considered jumping into the Merlin project himself, but rejected the idea. The mental eavesdropping and nudging that he did so superbly in financial and governmental circles were not of much use where he didn't know who to snoop on and nudge. He'd already told both Hardman and Gracco

to call on him if they needed him. For now, he'd
keep hands off.

Vincent Gracco's dark eyes looked through the
windshield of the Cessna Citation at the snowy ex-
panse of farmland and subdivisions on the approach
to Minneapolis. Busy with his thoughts, he ignored
the radio exchanges between air traffic control and
his pilot. He was going to have to work his ass off,
trying to handle two men's work by himself.

According to Shark and Hardman, Merlin and his
people were coming north to try for the Isle Royale
gate; his job was to see they didn't make it. He
would set things up here this morning, then fly to
Kansas City, Oklahoma City, Denver, and Omaha.
That would cover the main highway routes, and
the odds were that the Merlin gang would never get
this far.

Minneapolis filled his view as they continued to
lose elevation toward Wold Chamberlain Field. He'd
be picked up there by the people he was coming to
see. They'd talk at one of the airport hotels while his
pilot had lunch, then he'd head out again. It never
even occurred to him that he might fail to get full
cooperation here—not with the money he could of-
fer, and not with the way he could nudge their
heads.

*Minneapolis. A weird place,* he told himself, *to
have a capo named Olson.* Manoukian in K.C. and
Martinez in Denver weren't Sicilian either, or even
Italian, but their names didn't sound as strange as
*Olson,* for chrissake. But then, Gracco was only half
Sicilian, he reminded himself; his mother was Irish
and Polish.

He smiled. *A hundred percent American, that's
me, an equal opportunity employer. Choose 'em by
reputation and record, and maybe by what I get out
of their heads, not by where their last name comes*

*from*. According to the computer, Olson owned at least a dozen city and county attorneys and was the boss as far north as Duluth; north of Duluth there wasn't enough money to bother with. He'd been indicted for racketeering, extortion, narcotics, murder, and conspiracy to commit murder, to name some major charges, but he'd never been convicted since serving time as a juvenile for mayhem and arson. It added up to tough, smart, and effective.

*Maybe he can take them alive,* Gracco thought. *Some of them, anyway. Be interesting to question them.* But he decided not to mention it to the people he was contracting with. For practical purposes it would be better just to kill them.

The private jet took the runway without a bump. He'd be talking to Olson in only minutes now.

# < TWENTY >

Southwest forecasters were taken by surprise, not for the first time. The storm had been expected to pass to the north, with only intermittent light showers for southern Arizona, and that not till later in the morning.

Sometimes weather seems to have a mind of its own.

By the time the Caddy and the pickup reached Eloy, fifty miles south of Phoenix, clouds totally covered the sky. The two vehicles were passing the stone fang of Picacho Peak when the rain began. It built quickly in intensity, and in an hour was coming down hard as far south as the Sierra de la Madera and as far east as Silver City, pouring hardest in the mountains, falling with opaque density on the forty inches of snow in the high Chiricahuas around Rustler Park.

Riding the grid in his Texas home, Kurt Hardman watched his quarry tool eastward through Tucson, their tires splashing water. If they thought this was rain, he told himself, they hadn't seen anything yet.

Usually bone dry, Cienaga Wash surged with angry brown water where it passed beneath the Inter-state.

"I thought this was supposed to be desert," said Frank Diacono.

"It can rain really hard on the desert, especially in summer thunderstorms," Vic replied. "Summer and early fall. But I never saw it rain this hard here in the winter."

The wipers beat furiously across the streaming windshield.

"Do you think it'll last long?"

"I sure don't know. You hardly ever see it rain hard down here for more than a few minutes, except sometimes in September or October. But I suppose this could be one of those once-in-a-century exceptions."

Vic looked at Frank. "Any time you want a break," he added, "I'll be glad to drive."

"I'm doing fine. I like to drive and I like storms. Maybe after our sandwich break in Benson." Frank pulled out to pass an eighteen wheeler, the wash from its tires momentarily inundating his windshield as he moved up. "How far is Benson?" Frank asked. "About ten or twelve miles?"

"Something like that."

"I wonder where Ole is? When I travel with another car, I like to stay in sight of it. But he drives like Mario Andretti."

"Right. But we won't lose him. He'll be pulled off at some eating place up there."

*Yeah,* thought Frank, *I don't suppose you guys could lose each other.*

Shortly afterward, as they approached the 302 exit, they saw the tall signs of gas stations and a restaurant. "That's where they are," Vic said, "at that *Benny's*. Turn off here."

Frank didn't question; he slowed and took the exit. The rain fell relentlessly. When they turned into the restaurant lot, they saw the white Caddy parked almost at the building's entrance. There was a parking space next to it, and Frank took it. Jumping out, they slammed the doors behind them and dashed into the restaurant.

Ole, Carol, and Jerry were in a large corner booth, drinking coffee. Ole waved a greeting, and the other two turned to look, then slid around to make room for the newcomers.

"Kind of vet out there," Ole greeted them.

"Just a little bit," Frank answered. He eyed Ole meaningfully. "If it wasn't for Vic here, I don't know if I would have found you."

"Ya, but you did. It's kind of handy sometimes to have somevun around that knows like he knows."

And that, Frank thought to himself, takes care of that subject.

It was between breakfast and lunch, and the place was mostly empty. The waitress came over and filled their cups, then waited while they looked at menus and ordered. When she had left, Ole looked at Vic.

"Yerry vas saying he feels like his arm is healing fast. He'd like to get an x-ray, and find out v'en he can get the cast off. How vould it be if ve stopped at a doctor here in Benson and got it x-rayed?"

"Sounds fine to me." Vic looked at the others. "How does it sound to the rest of you?"

"Wait a minute," Carol said. "Less than a week ago he broke his . . ." She looked to Jerry, then at Ole. "It's the ulna, right? I thought that took about six weeks to heal. He told me you took the pain away, but do you mean it could be healed already, too?"

"I've seen things like that heal in two or three veeks vith Noetie techniques," Ole answered. "I don't know v'at might come out of Vic's stuff. It vould be interesting to check it out."

Frank got up from the table and went to the phone booth by the entryway. He was back in a couple of minutes. "There's a hospital in Benson," he said, and showed a pocket notepad. "I got the address. It should be easy to find in a town as small as this."

It took longer than they'd expected. There was only one doctor on duty, and he wasn't certified to take x-rays. The doctor who was certified had just left for an early lunch and would be back in about an hour. After a brief conference they decided to wait; an hour and a half later he returned.

Jerry, lying, told him the accident had been fifteen or twenty days earlier. The doctor looked at the x-ray and congratulated him on the remarkable progress; in about a week the cast could be removed.

Jerry paid and they left. Outside they clustered for a minute on the covered porch, watching the downpour, for the first time hearing thunder, dull in the distance. "Do they get floods around here?" Carol asked. "If they do, this could be one of the times."

"I've never heard of any flood problems on I-10," Vic answered. "But I never heard of it raining this hard around here for four hours at a time, either."

"You still want to drive?" Frank asked him.

"Yeah, if that's all right, I'd like to drive for a while."

Frank took a ring of keys from a belt clip, handing them to Vic. Lowering their heads then, all five dashed for the vehicles, jumping in and slamming the doors behind them. Together they drove to the east ramp, Vic leading now, and pulled under the canopy of a Chevron station to fill up with gas. An attendant came out and began to service them. Ole and his riders, and Frank, dug into luggage for rain gear. A massive Indian, as big as Frank but seeming older, stood under a corner of the canopy wearing a camouflage poncho. Vic was standing by the cab, and the Indian started toward him.

"I'm looking for a ride," he said.

"I figured you were," Vic said, then gestured at

Frank, who had just backed out of the camper. "It's fine with me, but you better ask him. It's his truck." The Indian turned to Frank, and Vic nodded affirmatively to Diacono as the Indian repeated his question.

"Okay," Frank said, looking the man over, then turned to Vic. "I'm going to try to get a little shuteye in the back. Any time you want to switch off driving again, just stop. Or if you need me for anything," he added meaningfully.

"Sure thing," said Vic.

When the tank was filled, they got back in and hit the interstate. The Indian said nothing, looking straight ahead.

"You been waiting there long?" Vic asked.

"About two hours."

"I guess maybe you were supposed to ride with us." Vic turned on the heater without the fan. "You heading for Oklahoma?"

This time the Indian turned to look at him. "Yeah. How did you know?"

"You didn't look like one of the Arizona tribes. You looked more like Oklahoma, or maybe the Dakotas."

"Huh! Not many white men would know the difference. You from Oklahoma?"

"No. I started out in Texas, lived back east for a while, and then came out here. What have you been doing in Arizona?"

"Passing through." He paused as if evaluating whether he could talk to this white man. "I was at a native religions conference up in Oregon," he added, then turned his eyes to the rainswept desert.

They'd left the station ahead of Ole, who seemed content to follow for now. Vic could see the Caddy in the outside mirror, obscured by the water drops on the glass. About a dozen miles northeastward down the freeway, a police cruiser was stopping cars at the Dragoon exit. Vic pulled up and stopped. A patrolman in a slicker walked over, and Vic rolled down his window. Frank came around from the camper wearing a poncho.

"Willcox Playa has flooded the highway up ahead," the patrolman said. His face was wet and red from the cold rain. "The only way east from here is the unsurfaced road through Dragoon to Route 666, then south to Douglas. From there you'd have to take US 80 back northeast to the interstate. All told, that adds about ninety miles of distance. Or you can go back twelve miles to Benson and wait for the water to go down."

Thunder muttered distantly.

"If we go back," Frank said, "how long do you think it'll be before the interstate is open?"

"Hard to say. Ordinarily the water goes down pretty quick after the rain stops. But apparently it's raining up in the Cherry Cow Mountains, instead of snowing, and the rain is melting the snowpack up there. That's one reason the water's so high. So it may take a while after the rain quits, depending on whether it turns cold or not."

Frank nodded. "Thanks, officer. I'll talk to my friends and see what they think." He gestured toward Ole's car close behind. "The Caddy's with us."

The officer peered intently at Diacono, as if trying to place him. "Do I look familiar?" Frank asked. "I'm Frank Diacono—used to play for the Denver Broncos. I've been on a few TV commercials."

The wet face grinned at that. "That's it, sure enough. Have a good trip, Mr. Diacono." Another car was slowing to stop, and he turned away to meet it.

"What do you want to do, Vic?" Frank asked.

Vic replied without hesitation. "Go south on 666 and then back north from Douglas."

"Right." Frank walked back and talked briefly with Ole, then returned to the pickup, opening the off-side door of the cab. He pulled off the wet poncho and shoved it behind the seat before jumping in and slamming the door behind him. "I might as well ride up here," he said. "I'm not sleepy anymore, and I can see better." He presented his hand to the Indian. "I'm Frank, Frank Diacono."

The big Indian received the hand and shook it. "My name is Paul," the Indian said. "Paul David."

Vic shifted gears and turned onto the exit ramp, east off the highway. It seemed to him that the rain was a little lighter than it had been, but it was still a steady downpour.

Kurt Hardman had tried to contact Vincent Gracco psychically as soon as he saw the Caddy and pickup turn southeast from Phoenix on I-10 instead of taking Route 60 east toward Globe. But Gracco hadn't picked up the psychic reach then; he was the least sensitive of the Four, now Three.

Hardman had finally gotten his attention in a washroom after the luncheon conference with Olson and his lieutenants. Gracco had immediately phoned the capo in Tucson, Joey Adrano. Adrano, however, was out of town, and it had taken a while to find someone there who'd consider making a verbal contract with someone they didn't know personally. Then Adrano's son, Johnny, had phoned Big Eddy Bocatto in St. Louis for a reference. It had taken a while to reach Bocatto, too.

A car with three gunmen finally left the Adrano mansion near Tucson about the time the doctor was returning from lunch, forty miles east in Benson.

After some twelve miles of gravel road, the Caddy and the big pickup reached the narrow blacktop of Route 666. Just north of the junction, the playa had drowned 666 as well, its waters spreading northeastward as far as they could see. To the east of them too it had almost reached the pavement. Willcox Playa that afternoon was by far the widest body of water in the state; that morning it had been only a broad flat saline plain. Vic turned south, and after a few miles left the playa behind.

Before long they met a still narrower blacktop from the east. Vic turned off on it and stopped. The rain had intensified again, and the thunder was louder, nearer.

"What is it?" Frank asked.

"It feels like we ought to take this road. D'you have a road map?"

Frank opened the glove compartment and took one out, unfolding it between them on Paul's lap. "Okay," Frank said when he'd found their location, "I know this area; I've hiked the mountains up ahead, the Chiricahuas, but I've only been in from this direction once. This road will take us up a canyon into the mountains—Pinery Canyon, I think it's called—then over a steep pass, and out a canyon on the other side. But I don't know if the canyons are passable now; the streams have got to be way out of their banks. And Onion Pass may be blocked with snow."

All three men peered eastward, where dimly they could see the rain-curtained bulk of the Chiricahuas— what the patrolman had called the Cherry Cows. Frank turned his eyes to Vic's profile, where there seemed a moment of emptiness, of absence, before Vic looked at him and spoke.

"It feels to me like this is the way to go. I don't have a lot of certainty on it, which probably means there's no guarantee, and I wasn't able to see the pass, but it feels like the best bet. I'm just not picking things up very well now."

Frank nodded. They heard a car door slam, and Ole came striding over, wearing a slicker. Vic rolled down his window. "V'at's going on?" asked Ole.

"Vic has the feeling we ought to go this way," said Frank.

"Good. Then let's go this vay." Ole raised his head to look eastward toward the mountains, almost as if he were sniffing the air. They rumbled at him. Then he turned his face northwestward for a few seconds. "East is the vay to go all right. Somevun is coming after us back there somev'ere. Vith guns."

"With guns! How far back?" Frank asked.

"Hell, I don't know. Not a hell of a long vay; they're on narrow blacktop."

Frank's jaw tightened, and he put his hand on the door handle. "East it is, then; maybe that will lose them. Trade places, Vic. I know this vehicle and I know the roads."

Frank and Vic each got out, scuttling around to the opposite doors. After restarting the engine, Frank looked at Paul David, who had remained sitting in the middle without noticeable change of expression.

"I hate to say this," Frank told him, "but you might be better off to get out here, rain or no rain. There are some guys after us. If you get soaked, you can always dry out. But if you stay with us, you could end up shot."

The Indian face looked stolidly at him. "I'll stay with you."

Frank shrugged, and saying nothing more, shifted gears, starting east down the new road. *Why not?* he thought. *Tory talked about scripts. Maybe the Indian's got a role in this play, too.*

Minutes later, the black Chrysler Fifth Avenue stopped at the same junction, of Route 666 and the lesser blacktop with the Arizona 181 sign. The driver looked at the man on his right. "Which way now, Johnny?" he asked. "Keep going south?"

Johnny Adrano took the mobile phone receiver from its recessed cradle atop the dashboard. The thing still worked back where they'd left I-10, he thought; maybe it would work from here, too.

He dialed the confidential number he'd been given, then waited. It took a few seconds to get a ring. On the fourth ring, the phone was picked up at the other end.

"Vincent Gracco," a voice said.

"Gracco, this is Johnny Adrano. We're out here in the middle of nowhere, and a fish just swam past the windshield. We come to a fucking fork in the road, and I don't know whether to go straight or turn left."

"Got it. I'll check with the satellite and see which way they went. Then I'll call you back."

"Johnny," murmured the man in the Chrysler's back seat, "that is bullshit. How the fuck is some satellite out in space going to see one fucking little car and pickup down here? Especially through all these clouds."

"I ain't no fucking spaceman; I don't know those things. How do they do any of that stuff? The money is right, that's what counts."

"We ain't seen none of that money. All we seen is rain."

"The Bocatto family is one of the best. And Eddy Bocatto is an honorable man; I've heard my old man say it himself. And Bocatto says this Gracco is a man of his word. We'll see the money."

"I still think it's . . ."

"Shut up! I'll tell you when to think."

In the cabin of his jet en route from Kansas City to Oklahoma City, Vincent Gracco drummed his fingers on the desktop next to his keyboard. The large, high-resolution screen displayed a map of the Middle East. Gracco wasn't involved with Shark's Arab project; it was a role-playing game he'd been passing time with when Adrano had called. Gracco had immediately sent a psychic call to the gridman; Hardman had sent him a pulse of acknowledgement but hadn't withdrawn from whatever he was doing.

Finally, after twenty or thirty seconds, Hardman was with him, and Gracco told him the situation. "I told him you were a satellite in orbit that could see the whole scene," he added, grinning.

Hardman's reply was impatient, unamused. "Tell them to go east. East about ten miles they come to a gravel road that goes up . . ." The gridman paused, as if checking place names. "A gravel road that goes up Turkey Canyon. But your hit team doesn't. They stay out of Turkey Canyon. The blacktop turns north there, and they just keep following the blacktop for a ways. After another ten miles or so they'll have to check in again. There's another fork there, but Merlin hasn't come to it yet. I'll let you know which one Merlin takes as soon as he gets there."

"Got it." Gracco didn't trouble to repeat the directions; he could copy things mentally that were much more complicated than that. "I'll keep a feeler out for you," he added, "and I'll tell them to stay on the phone."

He felt Hardman disconnect. He wished the gridman could guide the hit team directly, to save the time and inconvenience of passing things on. But if Hardman could get through to them, they'd only freak out. Gracco, finger stabbing, dialed the black Chrysler.

Frank continued east eleven miles to the Turkey Canyon Road, then north, then east once more to the mouth of Pinery Canyon. There the blacktop turned north again, to cross Cave Creek on a bridge, but Frank continued east, on gravel now.

The rain had intensified again, and through its pervasive drumming and occasional thunders, they could hear the mountain torrent that yesterday had been little more than a brook. Through the trees of the lower canyon's woodland they could see brown waters raging well out of their banks.

Frank recognized anxious stomach: He couldn't remember whether there were any fords to cross or not. If they tried to ford anything like that, they'd be carried away like an empty can. Yet turning back seemed out of the question, with gunmen following them. And staying on the blacktop would only have taken them to a dead end at the Chiricahua National Monument, almost surely abandoned at this season; they'd committed themselves irreversibly when they'd left 666.

Of course, their pursuers might have missed the turn and continued on 666 south toward Douglas. When that possibility occurred to him, Diacono felt a little better.

The Chrysler didn't pause when it came to the Pinery Canyon Road, it simply slowed somewhat for the rough gravel surface. Johnny Adrano had become increasingly wound up by the chase, and at his insistence, the driver had been pushing at up to eighty miles an hour on the irregular, rain-slicked blacktop.

Only three or four minutes before they came to the Pinery Canyon Road, they'd been told that their targets had just gotten there and gone east on the gravel. They were closing fast.

Frank Diacono rounded a curve and found a Chihuahua pine, uprooted from the soggy soil, lying across the road. He stopped, set the hand brake, released the winch, and jumped out, not pausing now to put on his poncho.

But Victor Merlin was out even more quickly. Grabbing the hook on the winch cable, he ran to the prostrate pine and hooked the cable around its upper trunk. When Diacono saw what Vic was doing, he climbed back into the cab. Vic stepped over the trunk to the other side, out of the way, and signalled; Frank threw the winch into gear and began to pull. The tree, about a foot thick at the base, began to move.

"Lucky it's not one of those big Apache pines or Douglas-firs we'll come to farther up the canyon," he muttered to Paul. When he'd pulled it far enough to drive through, Diacono opened his door and waved Ole through ahead of him.

Ole pulled even with him and stopped while his front window rolled down. "How come you vant me through first?"

"I'm going to pull the tree back across the road after I go through. Stop on the other side and I'll take the lead again."

Ole grinned, bobbed his head in approval, and drove through. Vic backed through behind him and winched the tree back across the road. Then Vic unhooked the cable and they drove on.

The Chrysler was going too fast for the road conditions. When it rounded the curve and he saw the fallen tree, the driver jammed down on the brake pedal and the heavy car skidded, taking the shallow, water-filled ditch with the front end. Adrano cursed angrily; they'd had enough room to stop without locking the brakes. Then they sat there silently for a few seconds, the driver's face flushed from Adrano's curses.

Adrano would have been even angrier if he'd known that the target vehicles had driven away less than a minute earlier.

"What the hell do we do now?" asked the man in the back seat.

Adrano glared at the driver. "First the moron behind the wheel is going to see if he can back us out," he said.

The car had stalled; now the driver started it again

and shifted into reverse. The rear tires spun in place. Johnny Adrano looked out the window, scanning the woods.

"Next," he said, "you guys are going out there and find some pieces of wood you can pry with. I ain't going to sit out here in this fucking canyon for maybe two or three days without nothing to eat."

Ole Sigurdsson thought he'd never seen it rain that hard before; in fact, he was sure of it. The farther they went into the mountains, the harder it seemed to pour. Thunder rolled through the clouds almost incessantly here. The road had left the canyon and was climbing Onion Pass on a series of switchbacks. It had been semidark most of the day; now it was getting darker as evening moved in, and Ole turned the Caddy's headlights on.

They reached an elevation where the ground beneath the denser evergreens was still covered with snow: gray, wet, and shrinking fast. Another gravel road branched off to the right, its Forest Service sign announcing, *Rustler Park 5 miles*. A little farther on, the pickup stopped ahead of him, and Ole pulled up behind it.

Another tree lay across the road, this one much larger than the first. Frank, Vic, and Paul got out of the truck, and after a moment of staring reluctantly through the streaming windshield, Ole got out, too, with his passengers. Frank came around to the rear of the pickup and climbed into the camper shell. There was a long tool chest inside, used for a bench and to house things like a shovel and crowbar. From it he dug a double-bitted ax. Climbing back out, he took off the sheath and felt the cutting edges thoughtfully.

"I was going to sharpen it a few weeks ago and forgot," he said. "But it's not too bad."

Paul reached out his hand for it. Diacono looked at him. "Bus fare," the Indian said.

Diacono nodded. "Let me know when you need a break; there's plenty of tree there for both of us. Douglas fir is harder than pine, and we need to cut through her twice. We need to cut out a section about ten or twelve feet wide that I can pull with the winch."

While the others clustered beside the pickup cab, Paul set to work limbing the part of the trunk that lay in the road. They stood watching in the rain, not concerned now about keeping dry. Vic and Frank wore ponchos, and Carol and Jerry hooded rain jackets, but Ole was bare-headed, the downpour plastering his lank hair wetly to his skull. Rain streaming off their rain gear had already soaked their pants from knees to cuffs; it would work its way higher by capillarity.

Thunder boomed and banged at them.

"Did you ever see it rain this hard before?" Jerry asked no one in particular.

"Maybe, for a few minutes at a time," Carol answered. "In Chicago."

"We'll be lucky if a bridge or culvert hasn't washed out up ahead somewhere," Frank said. "We might have to try driving up to Rustler Park and breaking into one of the Forest Service buildings there for shelter—assuming that road's open." He paused then and added, "You don't suppose the world's going to end with a rerun of the biblical flood, do you?"

"Are you serious?" Jerry asked.

Frank had to look at that. After all, the world was due to end soon. "Not really," he said. "If that much water got pulled out of the oceans to make rain, then the sea level would drop, and that's the base level to flood from. There's only so much water on the planet, and it either occupies the lowest places—the oceans— or it's on its way there." He turned to Vic. "Right?"

Vic nodded absently, as if his attention was else-where. Behind him the ax began to thunk into the trunk of the Douglas fir.

Johnny Adrano sat in the car with the telephone in his hand. He was soaking wet from shoes to thighs; all three of them were. When it had come down to it, he'd gotten out to help in the effort to get the heavy car unstuck. The only result was muddy pants, broken pry sticks, and anger. His two henchmen stood by the open door, listening to Adrano's half of the phone conversation. Rain drummed on the thin metal roof, a counterpoint to the thunder.

Adrano held the phone away from him for a mo-ment, staring angrily at it, then put it to his ear again. "I don't give a gnat's ass if they are struck a few miles up the road. I've had it with this goddamn job. What do you mean, agreement? Don't give me that bullshit about agreement! There ain't no binding agreement until one or the other of us delivers, and I ain't seen any money yet . . .

"I don't *give* a fuck about the goddamn fifty thou! I ain't walking no two or three miles in this fucking storm . . . No, not even for an extra fifty thou . . . An extra what? A quarter million total if we get them tonight?"

He looked out at the other two; they were as impressed as he was.

Paul hated to stop short of a complete cut through the tree, but after several minutes of nonstop chop-ping, his cold wet hands were too fatigued to grip the ax any longer. He'd attacked the task too strenu-ously, not pacing himself; the result was a rough vee-shaped cut in the trunk, about a foot and a half wide and nearly as deep. Another ten inches would see the first cut through.

He put down the ax, leaning it against a branch,

flexed his beefy fists, and looked at Diacono. Diacono nodded acknowledgement, then turned back to the others. "We can have this out of the way in another fifteen minutes or so, and we're at least an hour's hike from back where we left the road blocked behind us. I don't think we have anything to worry about unless we run into something ahead that stops us completely, like a bridge or culvert washed out."

He turned then and walked over to pick up the ax. Hefting it, he addressed the incomplete cut and began to swing, a little more slowly than the Indian had. Again the chips began to fly.

Squinting, Paul looked upward, the tireless rain beating on his dark face. "I think the rain god is mad at us."

Vic looked startled.

"You said it," said Jerry. "I think he's mad at the whole state of Arizona, at least."

"No," Paul said thoughtfully, "I think he's mad at *us*."

With the Indian's rejoinder, Ole picked up Vic's mental response. "V'at is it?" he asked.

"He's right," Vic said. "I should have spotted it earlier. There's more behind this storm than atmospheric physics. There's an intention—an awareness and an intention. There's a being up there somewhere dumping all this water on us. Call him a rain god."

An angry rain god? Despite all that had happened over the past week, Jerry and Carol found this statement hard to accept.

"If there is a rain god, why would he do that?" Jerry asked.

Vic shrugged. "I sure don't know. Maybe someone told him lies about us."

"I hope he doesn't decide to snow on us," Carol said, half joking. "If this was snow instead of rain, we'd really be in trouble."

"Maybe he's working within some kind of limitations," Vic said, "like what weather elements were handy on short notice. Or maybe he just feels like raining. I never looked into how elementals operate."

"Elementals?" Carol asked. "What's an elemental?"

"A rain god is one kind of elemental." He looked around at the others, while a few yards off, Frank continued his steady chopping. "Now look," Vic went on, "here's something I want each of us do. Put your attention on the rain god and tell him hello." He looked at Jerry. "Even if you're not sure he really exists. You don't have to say it out loud, but just send him a hello, and then tell him okay. When you've told him hello, then think an okay at him, with a lot of admiration in it for making the greatest rainstorm ever. Don't worry if this doesn't make sense to you, and close your eyes to do it if it makes it any easier."

*This*, thought Jerry, *is nuts*. He closed his eyes. "Hello!" he called mentally. "Hellooh rain god!"

The now-familiar rush of chills flowed over him, having nothing to do with cold rain, and suddenly he found himself grinning, his eyes open. "Hellooh! Okay!" he sent out silently. "Hellooh! Okay! *Fantastic* up there; you've been making the wettest damn rainstorm I ever imagined! You're the greatest rain god there's ever been on this planet! You're *incredible!*"

He looked around at the others. They all wore grins; Ole's threatened to split his face. Carol's eyes were shining as she turned them to Vic.

"He heard us!" she said. "He really really heard us!"

"He sure did," said Vic. "I figured the hellos and okays would do something, but I hadn't expected that sort of a backflow. When do you suppose was the last time he got that much admiration communicated to him? I wouldn't be surprised if the rain eased up a whole lot now, and pretty quick, too."

Paul David's eyes still were closed, but he nodded. "He's still there," he said, "and he's getting ready to do something. I don't know what it is, but he's concentrating on something." He opened his eyes. "I never knew any whites like you before. I sensed you were different when I first saw you, but you still surprised me." He turned to Vic. "And I never heard that prayer before. You're some kind of medicine chief!"

Nearby, Frank smote one last ax stroke, the last small bridge of wood broke at the bottom of the cut, and the big fir slumped. He stepped back from it. "That's one," he said, and walked over to them, the ax in his right hand. "One more to go." He looked around. "Hey! You know, I think the storm is letting up a little. It's not raining as hard."

Suddenly he tensed, half crouching. They all felt it, a growing tension in the air, and as one person they hit the wet and gravelly road. There was an indescribable *Blam!*—an overwhelming crash of sound accompanied by an intense flash. Pieces of wood struck the pickup and thudded and plopped on the ground around them. Stunned, no one moved for several seconds. It was Vic who raised his head first.

"Take a look at your tree, Frank," he said.

Diacono raised his head. "Holy Jesus!" he muttered. Lightning had struck the fallen fir—had somehow darted down between the standing trees around them and hit it at the other shoulder of the road, tearing it in two there. One by one they got up, staring at the severed trunk.

"You can put the ax away, Frank," said Carol slowly. "The rain god did it for you."

It took two minutes to hook up the section of the tree which lay in the road and winch it out of the way. Then they got into their vehicles and started on again.

Thirty minutes later they emerged from the mountains on the other side, at what purported to be a town but consisted of a store, a pair of visible houses, and a Forest Service guard station. There were lights in one of the houses, but no other sign of life there, and they rolled on through.

It was only a couple of miles now to a paved road, Frank knew. Then it should be a clear run to the Interstate, with the mountains between them and Willcox Playa. They could stop for supper in Lordsburg and either stay overnight there or continue to Deming or even Las Cruces.

When they trudged at last to the fallen Douglas fir and found no Caddy, no pickup, Adrano and his men were too tired and sodden to be more than disgusted. In pique, they emptied the magazines of their submachine guns randomly into the surroundings and started back down to their car. At least the rain had stopped, or nearly so. Little more than the drip from the trees fell on them in their trek back.

It was after midnight when a tow truck arrived from Douglas, Arizona, sent by Gracco, and the hit team returned, famished and sneezing, to Tucson. Gracco ended up wiring Adrano twenty thou, to salvage as much good will and silence as he could from the fiasco. The Four could easily afford it.

# < TWENTY-ONE >

Frantic, Hardman sat on the grid in his darkened room. He'd lost them. After only about seven hours sleep in the previous sixty, he'd fallen asleep in spite of himself, fallen asleep on the grid.

He could have maintained a direct psychic contact at least through a doze, and dozing was the heaviest he'd ever slept before while riding the grid. But this contact had been visual only, to avoid psychic assault. And he'd been sleeping too little, staying awake on Coca Cola, caffeine tablets, and determination. So when sleep had captured him, it had been for more than an hour and a half, and he'd awakened with a horrible start, momentarily weak with fear.

He should have slept longer than three hours the night before. But he couldn't know, when the Merlin group stopped at the motel in Deming, that they wouldn't get up at 2 A.M. and hit the road again. They could have; it would have been just like Merlin. So he'd laid down on the bed in the grid room, after setting the wake-up for midnight. At 1 A.M. he'd gotten back on the grid and waited—waited for something to happen. Nothing had, until Merlin and his crew had gotten up at four-thirty.

Hardman had wanted to be gridman from the first, from the time The Lords had selected and recruited him, fifteen years earlier, and acquainted him with their operation. Gridman! The power had seemed almost godlike, and as soon as he knew of it, Kurt Hardman, known since childhood as "the toad," had wanted that more than anything in the world.

He'd ridden the grid for almost that long, first as trainee, then as gridman, and loved it. And while The Lords had been in the world, it had been a leisurely post. Since they'd been taken away, with Shark left in charge, his work load had been way up. But even then, only occasionally had he felt really overloaded. The hardest part had been handling certain troublesome psychics that previously The Lords would have taken care of.

Riding the grid, he'd discovered, was hard on one, aging the body, but mostly it was worth it for the marvelous power . . . depending on what one did, or what one ran into.

Actually, most of his serious trouble had been when he'd been riding the grid for fun and games instead of business. He'd found and interfered with several witches who hadn't been impinging on group activities at all, and one of them had nearly killed him. Since then he'd been much less venturesome.

Now, with the Merlin group lost, he was too shaken, his adrenalin level too high, to go to sleep again very soon. He had no idea where they were, and he'd be in serious trouble if Shark found out what had happened. That was one of the bad things about being the gridman: it made him so damned vulnerable to Shark. Shark could punish him.

Hardman's hand touched the keys that accessed highway maps to the screen; he'd isolate the more probable routes and put sniffers out. If that didn't work, he'd go for direct psychic contact, just long enough to locate them, although even that would be dangerous with these people.

Ole didn't feel well at all; something was going on, but he didn't know what.

Before they'd left Deming, New Mexico that morning, the group had decided to leave the interstate at Las Cruces, in favor of lesser highways. It seemed obvious that someone was monitoring them somehow: That was the only explanation for gunmen having been able to follow them the day before. He and Vic had also concluded that the monitoring must somehow be visual, via machine. They'd have felt any direct connection to their selves—their psyches.

Jerry had come up with the next suggestion: If someone was monitoring them by machine, and if the someone was in a human body, he probably needed to eat and sleep and go to the bathroom. Maybe he left them now and then, and found them afterward by scanning ahead from where he'd left them.

But if they repeatedly changed roads, maybe sooner or later they'd lose their monitor. At least that might make it harder and more exhausting for him. Or her.

There were all kinds of assumptions in that, none of which anyone felt certain of. But all of them now, not only Vic and Ole, recognized the value of hunches, especially the hunches of a psychic. And at the least, changing routes would make them harder to ambush.

So from Las Cruces they'd taken US 82 northeast to Alamagordo, then 54 north to Tularosa, then 70 east through Mescalero, and so on. After they'd left 380 at Tatum, Ole could feel the difference: It had worked. For a while, things had felt cleaner than at any time for days. But for the last three hours . . . Apparently they had their monitor back.

Sigurdsson's Caddy topped a rise, and a half mile ahead he could see a cafe, its illuminated sign the only bright spot in the night. A road sign in his headlights told him further that County Road D was just ahead. He glanced in his rearview mirror; the pickup was out of sight. It might simply be cut off by the rise behind him or it might have fallen a mile or more behind. He knew he was careless of things like that, especially where Vic was involved, but he could connect when the need arose.

Now it was time to talk about what to do next. Ole slowed and turned off the highway to park by the cafe.

"What's happening?" Carol asked beside him. In the back seat, Jerry sat up and raised a sleepy head to look out.

"Ve going to take a break; ve need to talk."

They got out of the car and went inside to wait for the others.

Vic had dozed off between the two larger men. Paul too dozed, off and on. Frank was considering waking one of them to replace him at the wheel; it wasn't that he felt sleepy, but he was getting a little glassy-eyed.

He topped a rise and saw a cafe ahead. He'd like to stop for coffee, but he didn't want to fall too far behind the others. Idly he wished again that Ole would stay in sight.

They should reach McMurtree in under half an hour, though. Ole would be waiting for them there outside the first eating place, and they'd decide whether to drive on or stop for the night. He sped by the cafe without paying it any attention.

*     *     *

"Sher'ff, this is Depitty Two. One of the suspect vehicles just passed us here at the Range Line Road stakeout—a black four-wheel-drive Ford pickup with Arizona plates. But there weren't no white Cadillac sedan ahead of it, and it ain't come in sight behind it yet, either."

Sheriff Bill Johnson's face showed no change as he pressed the transmit switch on his microphone. "How long since he went by you?"

"About half a minute; he ought to be gettin' to you in three, four minutes."

"All right. You let me know the minute you see the Caddy. When he's gone by you a quarter mile, you'll come on out and follow him, but don't use your flasher and don't close up on him. You understand, Ray John? I don't want him to know anything's happenin' till he sees the roadblock. *Then* I want you to come up on the double.

"And shoot if they try to double back on you, because we don't want these people to escape. They're communist agents, and it's up to us to see they get stopped, but otherwise we want 'em alive."

"Yessir, sher'ff, I'll let you know the minute it comes by, then be right out after 'em as soon as they get a quarter mile ahead. No siren, no flasher, and they ain't no way I'll let 'em get back by me. It oughtn't be long now. Depitty Two out."

Sheriff Johnson switched to transmit again, to talk to Deputy One, the patrol car parked on the other side of the road. "Okay, boys, there's going to be a Chevy Camaro and a Toyota sedan coming through in about a minute. Soon as they're on by, I want you to block the bridge. The next thing along after them is the pickup we want. Y'all get out then and have your guns ready. Shoot to kill at the first sign of trouble, but *do not* shoot if you don't need to."

*     *     *

"What do you think, Ole?" Jerry said. "They should have been along by now. Do you suppose something happened to them? Maybe they drove by and missed us."

"Vic wouldn't do that. Would he, Ole?" Carol asked.

Ole stared thoughtfully, sipping his coffee, then nodded. "That's v'at happened," he said, "I'm pretty sure. They vent right by and never saw us. Vic must have gone to sleep, and I didn't pick it up."

"Hadn't we better get going again, then?" asked Jerry.

Again Ole nodded, but for a moment made no move to get up.

"What's going on?" Jerry asked.

"I ain't sure." After half a minute more, the Icelander slid his long frame from the booth without saying anything further; the others followed, uncertain. The puzzled waitress met them at the cash register, and Ole gave her two ones. They walked out to the car and got in.

Ole started the engine and left the curving driveway, not back onto the highway but onto the county road which crossed it, driving north.

"Uh, Ole," Jerry began.

"Ya, I know. This ain't the same road. But something's wrong up ahead, I ain't sure v'at. And if ve follow them, it's yust going to make things vorse."

"If something's wrong, shouldn't we go help them?"

"It von't help if ve follow them into a trap."

He drove three miles farther, turned east on the next crossroad, then stopped, his brow furrowed. Neither of the others spoke.

"Okay," he said at length, "I know v'at happened now. I got the picture. There vas a roadblock, and they got picked up."

"Picked up! What for?" Carol asked.

"Somebody made it vorth somebody's v'ile, I suppose." He shifted into reverse, backed out into the intersection, and turned north again on County Road D.

"Where are we going?" asked Carol.

"North. Out of this county. Look in the map book and see how far the county line is from the highvay back there."

"Shouldn't we try to help them?" Jerry repeated.

"Ve vill; ve are. The vorst thing ve can do now is get caught by the same people that caught them. And v'en they decide ve ain't coming along behind, they'll probably be looking for us. That's v'y ve need to get out of this county."

Jerry didn't question Ole's clairvoyance. For just a moment longer, though, he felt the need to go back. Then the impulse evaporated, as if he'd tuned in at some subliminal level to the event Ole had picked up, and knew for himself that Ole's response was right.

"It's about fifteen miles to the next county," Carol said. "About twenty to a town." She looked from the map to Ole. "Can you tell us anything more?"

"It vas a roadblock, like I said. Yerry, you're a policeman. V'y don't you explain?"

Jerry glanced at the nighted countryside flashing by; Ole wasn't worrying about the speed limit just then. "Well," he started slowly, "out in the country like that, on a secondary highway, it would ordinarily be the county sheriff's department that set up the roadblock. So the danger is probably restricted to this county."

"I see," said Carol. "And if our route was known, they would only have notified the sheriff's department of one county!"

"Right. Maybe a sheriff that they—whoever "they" are—knew was on the take. And if they were expecting two cars and only get one, they're going to be worried. They're less apt to, uh, shoot someone if we're still loose."

"Do you really think they might do such a thing?"

"I really don't know. Things can happen in some rural counties that would be darn near unthinkable in L.A. or with a state organization. But with us running loose out here, we're a big unknown and unpredictable factor. It gets a lot harder for them to pretend, say, that there'd never been such a road-block or such an arrest, or such people as Vic and Frank and Paul.

"Besides that, they can't know why we didn't come on through. We're a mystery, and their attention is going to stick on us. That's what mysteries can do. It's going to make it hard for them to plan anything or dispose of anyone."

He turned to Ole. "Is that the same way you figured it?"

Sigurdsson didn't take his eyes off the road. "You did a good yob. But I didn't figure it out, any more than you did. Ve yust knew it. V'at you called figuring there, that vas yust you fishing up the reasons and putting them into vords. That helps sometimes v'en you're not used to operating as a psychic."

He said nothing more then, and they sped silently down the road in the wake of their headlights.


"What now, sher'ff?"

Deputy Jack Boyd was the night dispatcher and jailkeeper. He was also the least talkative man on Sheriff Johnson's staff, and the deputy whose ethical plasticity the sheriff felt most confident of. The sheriff had his other on-duty deputies out on the road. Two men in Deputy Two were still at the junction with the Range Line Road, watching for the white Cadillac, while two others in Deputy One were back at the roadblock location at Kiowa Creek Bridge. The hope was that the white Cadillac had been delayed on the road somewhere and would be along soon.

The sheriff had been trying to convince himself that this was indeed the case, but he had a premonition that it wasn't. Which gave him a problem. His Dallas contact had offered him $40,000 to turn these people over dead or alive. As far as Sheriff Johnson was concerned, alive was better. He didn't like the idea of killing, short of self-defense, and there could be a problem in covering up a shooting.

Rinaldi had said he'd send some men to pick them up. His people would have CIA credentials or what would pass for CIA credentials; people would believe anything about the CIA. They'd pick up the prisoners or their bodies, tell any deputies involved to keep the whole thing quiet on the basis of national security, and privately leave the $40,000 with the sheriff in hundred dollar bills.

It was to have been as simple as that.

But if Rinaldi wasn't interested in half a catch, then the sheriff would be stuck with three prisoners arrested, without any charge he could make stick. If he charged them with something phony and held them, he'd have to allow them a lawyer, and they'd be out quicker than shit through a goose. Judge Schoenert was a sharp, hard-nosed old sonofabitch; couldn't nobody lie to him and get away with it.

While if he let them go, them suckers'd probably sue his ass dry. No, Rinaldi would either have to take them, or he'd . . . what? All the sheriff could think of was to shoot them attempting to escape, and that wouldn't work at all: The state attorney general's office would look into anything like that too damn close. It wouldn't be like shooting them at a roadblock for resisting arrest.

*Shit,* he told himself irritably, *I'm worryin' about nothin'. Rinaldi'll take 'em, and I'll have myself $20,000*

*for half a catch. All I got to worry about is how to
spend it without nobody wonderin' about it.*

He answered his jailkeeper's question. "What now
is, I call them guvmint boys and tell them to come
pick up their prisoners."

He went to his desk and dialed the phone. Deputy
Jack Boyd watched him for a moment, then wandered back to the high-security cell to peer through
the small window at their catch. They'd come in
peaceful enough, and there weren't none of 'em had
any foreign accent, although one of the two big ones
did look eye-talian. But they hadn't acted scared, nor
mad either, like you'd expect if they was innocent.

The prisoners saw him looking at them through
the small square of reinforced glass in the door, and
the older man with the whiskers smiled at him as if
the two of them shared some secret joke. Boyd
stepped away, uncomfortable.

Back in the office, he found the sheriff just hanging up the phone. "When they gettin' here, sher'ff?"
asked Boyd.

"About an hour and a half." The sheriff looked as if
a weight had been lifted from him. "They'll be flyin'
in to Jim Vance Airport, and we'll pick 'em up there.
They'll take custody of the prisoners, and we'll haul
'em out to their plane in the van."

He looked meaningfully at his jailkeeper. "And
remember, none of this ever happened. This is a
national security matter, and those CIA boys play for
keeps. Anybody leaks this, we'll likely find his hide
on a bob-wire fence somewhere."

Boyd nodded. He wasn't prepared to totally disbe-
lieve, but somehow or other the whole business
sounded phony to him. The sheriff would not make a
good poker player. Not that it made any difference to
Boyd, one way or the other. He could have it either
way, real or phony, and he wasn't the kind to gossip
about business.

He'd be damned interested though to see those "CIA boys" and see what he thought of them.

The sheriff had just walked over to the coffee maker when the phone rang. Boyd picked it up.

"Buffalo County Sher'ff's Department, Depitty Boyd."

The voice at the other end sounded cool and professional. "Deputy Boyd, this is Lieutenant Parmeter of the Federal Bureau of Investigation in Albuquerque. Let me speak with the senior watch officer, please."

Boyd's eyebrows arched. "Just a minute," he said, and putting a hand over the mouthpiece, turned to the sheriff. "It's for you. F.B.I."

A fleeting pang hit the sheriff, leaving a residue in the pit of his stomach. He came over and took the phone. "This is Sher'ff Johnson. What can I do for you?"

"I'm Lt. Joseph Parmeter of the Special Narcotics Strike Force of the F.B.I., in Albuquerque. It's been reported to us that you are holding in custody three of our agents, arrested in a black four-wheel-drive Ford pickup truck with Arizona plates. These agents, as a matter of security, carry no Bureau identification. They are using the following identities: Victor Merlin, Frank Diacono, and Paul David.

"I am prepared to fly agents to McMurtree tonight to arrange the release of these people, and in the meantime I hope you'll make them comfortable. But if the charges against them are misdemeanors, or if formal charges haven't yet been filed, the Bureau would feel deeply obligated to you if you would release them tonight. That would allow them to complete their very important mission, and it would save both funds and man-hours at this end. Could you do that for us, Sheriff Johnson?"

Bill Johnson's strong, high-cheekboned face had gone wooden. Gentle Jesus! This could be somebody from the white Cadillac, or he might be talking to an actual F.B.I. lieutenant. It could even be some racketeering operation in competition with Rinaldi! But the voice sounded genuine; it sounded like a fed.

"Who am I talkin' to again?"

"Lt. Joseph Parmeter—that is *P* as in "papa"; *A* as in "alpha"; *R* as in . . ."

"All right, all right, I got it now: Parmeter."

Bill Johnson's mind worked feverishly. Somebody had to have let this story out. It could have been somebody of Rinaldi's, or it could even have been one of his own men; no telling where the F.B.I. had infiltrated or had a tap—if it was the F.B.I.

"And what was that office again that you're with?" asked the sheriff.

"The Special Narcotics Strike Force of the Federal Bureau of Investigation," came the patient reply.

*The sonofabitch sounds so goddamn official!* he told himself. *There weren't none of them hoods could sound like that. And that would explain why them fellas in the high-security cell back there hadn't put up any fuss when they'd been picked up, or even when they'd been* locked *up. It was like they knew someone would straighten it all out.*

*Shi-it!* "And what did you say they were doin', comin' through here?" Johnson asked.

The sheriff was stalling now, trying to think.

"I'm not at liberty to divulge that information, sheriff. All I need to know, at this time, is whether you can release them now to go on their way, or whether I have to send agents to arrange their release." The lieutenant sounded slightly impatient now.

*If I keep them,* Johnson thought, *Rinaldi'll be by to pick them up. And sure as flies in shit, I can't give them to him now. If I give them up, there'll be hell to pay when the feds get here. There'll be hell enough to pay if the feds have to come after them at all, 'cause they'll sure as hell want to know what their people were charged with.*

"Sheriff? Are you still there?"

"Yeah, yeah. I got one of my men checkin' on somethin'."

*Maybe I could tell him I'm turning them loose, and then give them to Rinaldi instead. But hell, if I turn them loose and they don't call right in to Albuquerque, that Parminter or whatever his name is will know sure as shit something's wrong.* The sheriff could see $40,000 flying away—$20,000 at least.

"Lieutenant," he said, "I'll tell you what I'm gonna do. As a fellow officer, I don't want to put you-all to no needless trouble or expense. So I'll just let 'em out now and they can be on their way." He said it as if it were his own idea.

"Thank you, sheriff. We certainly appreciate your generous cooperation, and our letter of thanks will be on its way tomorrow."

They hung up. *Letter of thanks,* thought Johnson. *With a letter of thanks and a dollar-twenty I can buy a box of Skoal.* He turned to Deputy Boyd. "I'm lettin' those three new prisoners out," he said. "It was all a mistake. Get their valuables out of the cabinet for 'em."

Boyd stared at him. "What you goin' to tell them CIA fellas when they get here?"

"God damn it, don't argue! Jesus Christ! All I get is arguments around here!"

The deputy shrugged and watched the sheriff stomp into the hall toward the high-security cell. Bill didn't hardly ever get that mad, Boyd thought as he went to the padlocked cabinet.

Johnson unlocked the heavy cell door and swung it open. The three men inside looked up. "Y'all are free to go now. Lieutenant Parminter just called from Albuquerque and told us who you are."

Diacono nodded curtly. "Of course," he said. He turned to Vic and Paul, nodded again, and without saying anything more, they followed the sheriff down the hall. Nor did they speak when they picked up their wallets, checked the contents, and received the keys to the pickup. They didn't even say anything when they went out the door. They were afraid to: They didn't want to risk queering whatever had happened to set them free.

Sheriff Bill Johnson watched the door close behind them. It occurred to him that what had really happened was, they had some kind of concealed radio in the pickup cab, and had gotten off a call as they'd stopped for the roadblock.

Rinaldi was going to be madder than hell. Well, Rinaldi could go fuck himself.

Diacono drove east out of town about two miles and took a left on the next north-south road, which was graveled. If anything happened to change their minds again back there, he wanted to be off the highway and hard to find.

The next objective was to get out of Buffalo County.

"Does anyone have any idea at all what the hell happened back there?" he asked.

"Not yet," said Vic. "But whatever it was, I expect we'll find out before long. I'm pretty sure one of the others had something to do with us getting out."

"How are we going to find them again?"

"I don't know yet. We'll just have to wait and see."

On the right side of the cab, Paul David looked out across the moonless plain. Houses and lights were far between out here; it was lonely country at night. But this pickup didn't feel lonely. He liked these people he'd hooked up with; they felt right to him.

And he did not think of them as dangerous to be around, not even tonight.

there outside he'd broken up with Slim, but that risk to him.

And he didn't much mind going camping out, to be truthful, once in a while.

# < TWENTY-TWO >

Eventually the gravel road met a secondary highway, and Frank turned east on it. Before long they passed a *Reduce Speed* sign. Frank slowed, and his headlights picked up another sign: *Speed Limit 35,* and then *Swabia, pop. 805.*

"Maybe there'll be a place to eat here," he said. "It's been a long time since lunch."

Paul said nothing; he was almost broke and only a few hundred miles from home now. He could hold out.

"That'd be fine with me," said Vic. "I'm hungry enough to eat the rear end out of a skunk."

Ahead, a Texaco sign stood in its own lights. Next to the station was a small cafe with a sign that read "Eats." Frank slowed further. "As a matter of general principle," he said, "I don't go into places with a sign that says 'Eats,' but this time . . ."

Before he could finish, they saw the white Caddy parked beside the place. Frank pulled up in front. "Go on in," he said. "I'm going to fill my tank, in case the gas station's getting ready to close. I'll be in in a minute."

Vic and Paul went into the cafe, where Ole, Carol,

and Jerry were sitting in the large corner booth, grinning at their entry. Jerry stood up as the new-comers walked over to them.

"Ole said we'd better take the big booth," said Carol. "He said you'd be along."

"It's your fault," Ole said to Vic, "you and those processes you run on me. I didn't used to be vorth a damn for knowing the future. Now I could go into competition vith Madame Tanya."

The waitress came over with three hamburgers and a pair of menus. Vic and Paul both declined a menu. "Just give me two hamburgers," Vic said, "with french fries and coffee. I really feel hungry."

"I don't want anything," said Paul.

"Are you sure?" Ole asked. "I'm buying. I don't do that very often, so everybody better take advantage of it."

"Okay, I'll have a burger and coffee."

"And bring a coffee for another guy," Vic added. "He'll be in in a couple of minutes."

"What's Frank doing?" Jerry asked.

"Gassing up."

Vic looked at Ole. "What happened to you guys?"

"I stopped at a eating place, and after a few min-utes, v'en you guys didn't come in, I figured you'd vent on by. And then I got this idea that you vas in trouble vith the police, at a roadblock, and that ve vould be too if ve followed you. So ve bypassed."

Vic grinned. "You sure called that one right." He began to tell them what had happened, as far as he knew it. Their coffee arrived, and then Frank came in and gave his order.

"I'm not entirely sure what happened to make them let us go," Vic finished, "but I've got half an idea. Something about a lieutenant in Albuquerque." He looked at Jerry. "I don't suppose you know any-thing about that."

Jerry grinned. "My psychic powers tell me it was a

Lieutenant Joseph Parmeter of the Federal Bureau of Investigation."

"Jesus!" Diacono said. "They let us out on the basis of a phony telephone call? That's about as miraculous as lightning hitting that fallen tree!"

"That's right," said Carol. "Jerry, that puts you in the same class as rain gods."

"V'y not?" Ole said. He looked around then, and somehow each of them gave him their full attention. "It vas a good thing ve veren't together. Maybe that's the vay ve should travel: separate. If there is only vun person monitoring us, he's going to have a hell of a time if ve're on two different routes."

"Sounds like a good idea to me," Vic said. "How will we split up? The same way we've been?" He looked around at the others. "How does this seem to the rest of you?"

"It makes sense," said Jerry. "Somehow I don't like it, but I think we ought to do it, if we can figure out a way to get together at the other end."

"Carol?" asked Vic.

She nodded soberly. "As long as there's someone with each group who can do what's needed when we get to Isle Royale. Otherwise, we need to stay together." She looked at Ole. "Can you do it? Jerry and I haven't been through a gate; I'm afraid I wouldn't even recognize one."

"Ya, I feel like ve could pull it off alone if ve needed to. V'at I'm looking at is improving the odds that at least vun set of us gets there, although the vay ve been going, I'd say ve'll all probably get there." He paused then and looked at Paul. "Except our hitchhiker, of course, who's only going partvay. You're velcome to stay vith us to Oklahoma if you vant, but novun here vill blame you if you decide to split now. Ve ain't the safest people to be vith."

Paul matched eyes with Ole. "Could I be any use to you if I stayed with you all the way up north? I'm not needed in Oklahoma right away. There's not that much to do on the farm till March." His eyes made the circuit of faces. "But maybe I ought to know what you're doing."

"It's a wild story," Jerry said, and looked at Vic before turning back to Paul. "Most people would say we're crazy if we told them."

The Indian grunted. "Most people would think I was crazy if they knew what I'd believe."

They paused then as the waitress brought the rest of the burgers. Vic looked at his. "Boy, I think my mouth was bigger than my appetite. I can't eat all this. Can anyone help me?"

He looked at Paul, who knew then why Vic had ordered two burgers instead of one. "I'd be obliged if you'd eat one of these for me," Vic went on. "You're enough bigger to hold two, and besides, you and me need to have a long talk tonight, and it'll work out better if you don't have an empty stomach. There's a lot I need to tell you if you're thinking about going up north with us."

As they ate, they agreed to separate when they left. They'd meet again at Duluth on the evening of January 24. None of them had ever been in Duluth before, so no place was specified except that it would be near the airport. Vic and Ole seemed content that this was planning enough, and the others, if less than comfortable with the arrangements, were willing to accept their casual confidence as sufficient grounds to go for it.

After an exchange of hugs, Ole left with Jerry and Carol. They'd turn north on Route 277. Frank and Vic, with Paul, finished their suppers and lingered briefly over pie and coffee before they left. Frank said he'd have no trouble staying awake at the wheel.

Vic and Paul climbed into the camper shell and bundled up. Vic would give Paul a session sufficient to make it all at least semi-real to him, and then a brief rundown on their mission.

The big Indian was perhaps the readiest of anyone Vic had ever worked with, except Ole. They didn't quit until well after midnight, when Frank pulled off on the shoulder for a break.

Vic relieved Frank at the wheel then, and Paul and Frank settled down in the camper to sleep. In the few minutes it took Frank to drift off, it occurred to him that the older man was a marvel. He had no doubt that Vic would drive on until breakfast with no difficulty at all.

Then Frank was asleep, and as he slept he dreamed of a beautiful woman, her raven hair worn bobbed.

# < TWENTY-THREE >

"Vincent, what the hell is going on out there?" Shark demanded. "You are supposed to eliminate just *five* people—*five people*—perhaps none of them armed. Kurt tells me that they are a man with a broken arm, another that looks like a wrestler, a young female, and two elderly psychics.

"You have virtually unlimited funds. You have a resource—Kurt on his grid—that gives you an advantage beyond the imagination of governments, that lets you follow and predict the movements of those people. You have access to a network of professional collaborators, available and ready.

"So tell me, if you please, why the hell this ragtag group is still alive and running around loose."

Shark was using the videophone because Gracco couldn't carry on an explicit and detailed telepathic communication except with or through the gridman. Now Gracco fixed him with his eyes.

"Shark," Gracco answered, "don't give me that sarcastic bullshit. I'm not one of your flunkies; you didn't hire me. I was chosen by The Lords, the same as you, and I don't squirm or embarrass worth a shit. I know as well as you do that I'm the best.

"And something else: the only sonofabitch as good as me at what I do blew himself up a few nights ago, messing with those same five people. So if you're looking for apologies or alibis, look somewhere else; I don't even need to give you any explanations. If you want information, *that* I give to you."

Hardman, on the grid, was also listening, keeping awake on speed now. Watching the black pickup tool through the Texas night did not require close attention.

Gracco, he told himself, could afford to stand up to Shark; Gracco wasn't susceptible to the kind of psychic punishment that Shark could deal a gridman.

"We're dealing with some high-powered psychics," Gracco went on. "You know that as well as me. If they were easy, I wouldn't have even heard of them. Hardman would've taken care of them days ago with some nice little accident."

Gracco smiled cold-eyed into the video pickup on the phone, a smile with neither humor nor hostility. "Just so we understand each other," he added.

"Now, what I've been doing is setting up a network of booby traps for them, like a fucking mine field, and they're just getting into the perimeter of it. With people like them, the odds of any one of the mines getting them aren't all that high, but the odds of them getting through the whole mine field, you can stick in your ass and never even notice it.

"You already know that the organizations out of Oklahoma City, Kansas City, and the Twin Cities are laying for them. And those people run the rackets in other places, from Wichita to Des Moines to Duluth, so we got good coverage. If they'd taken the western route north, I had that covered, too. And Rinaldi, in Dallas, was ready if they went across farther south.

"Now I've done something else. The capos all have a lot of influence outside the organizations. A lot of people owe them, and a lot more want to be on their good side, so I got them pulling in all the favors they've got coming. It's costing us plenty, but you said don't worry about the cost.

"On top of that, I told them that Merlin and his people have been working on a new superdrug, that they're heading for Canada to sell it to a pharmaceutical company there, but they don't have it written down. They're going to deliver it from memory, and each one of them knows the whole formula.

"This drug gives a high, but it's not addictive and it doesn't hurt anyone, so governments will let drugstores sell it over the counter cheap. It'll put everyone else out of the drug business.

"I know that doesn't make sense if you really look at it, but it's got these guys worried, and they're not taking any chances. They're spreading the word to every two-bit local boss from Oklahoma to the Canadian border. The odds of Merlin and his people getting as far as Minnesota are shit.

"That's the story I told everyone but Olson. I didn't tell him anything I didn't need to, but what I've told him is about eighty percent true.

"Anyway, I've got all these people watching for them, and that includes some fuzz on the take. And meanwhile, we've got Kurt. Right, Kurt? He keeps me informed, and I pass the word along to whoever I think can do anything with it.

"And if they get through *that*, some way or other, they've still got to get to the island. Olson tells me it's about twenty miles out to it from the nearest place on the north shore, and like maybe eighty or a hundred from the south shore. They get storms out there that can sink ships, and winter is the big storm season on Lake Superior, which is likely to turn them off all by itself. The harbors and shore lines are frozen over, and a small boat is all they could drag out to open water. And, of course, a grenade will sink anything small.

"So they aren't likely to try a boat.

"And if they fly, they'll be sitting ducks; Olson's got a couple of planes that can shoot them out of the air. Kurt shouldn't have to do anything but keep track of them."

He smiled at Shark again, a smile like ice. "There's no way they'll get to the gate; you'll never get a safer bet than that on anything."

Shark smiled at Gracco's refusal to propitiate or even alibi. "Thank you for the report, Vincent; it does sound reassuring. Keep me informed of any developments. And now, unless you have something more for me, I'm sure each of us has things to do."

"You got it, Shark," Gracco said, "you got it."

With that, Gracco disconnected, turning the phone screen blank. Shark stared thoughtfully at it. "Kurt," he said silently to the gridman, "how does it look to you now?"

"Gracco's right," Hardman replied. "There are too many different obstacles for them to find their way through. But meanwhile, like I told you, they've separated, and I can't monitor both vehicles. I've stayed with the vehicle that Merlin's in because he seems to be the most dangerous. As soon as he's been taken care of, I'll find Sigurdsson, even though I'll have to do it with a direct psychic reach. If I'm quick enough, I should be able to find him, make the monitor connection, and get free before they know what's happening and jump me. Then I'll stay with him visually until he's been eliminated."

Shark nodded mentally. "Thank you, Kurt. And how are you doing personally just now? I realize that you're operating on virtually no rest."

*Fuck you*, Hardman thought privately, *You're afraid I'll break down and won't be able to continue; otherwise, you wouldn't give a shit*. "This type of monitoring isn't that hard," he transmitted mentally. "It's just so damned continuous. I'm using a little chemical help to keep going, but I can stand that. When this operation is over, I'll take a few days off the grid and be okay."

"Good. Let me know at once when there's been a successful strike on any of Merlin's people, or if any problems come up. And now, I'll let you give your full attention to our quarry."

Shark let the psychic line drop. Despite himself and despite all that Gracco was doing, he was worried. Not extremely worried, but he felt some concern. Sordom had been within a minute of eliminating the whole nest of them—had actually lit the fuse— and failed. Then Rinaldi had Merlin himself captive in a Texas jail, and somehow Merlin managed to get himself freed. Now they had separated, which suggested that they knew they were being monitored. Merlin, at least, was dangerous. Sigurdsson apparently was, too. The others were unknown quantities, but they must have significant ability; otherwise, why would Merlin take them along?

If Hardman burned out and lost his visual connection, that would really be a setback. Perhaps, through Hardman, he should establish his own psychic connection to Merlin—just a quick touch, sufficient that he could reconnect if he had to fly to Dallas and ride the grid himself.

But not now. Hardman's challenge to him to ride the grid himself had been rhetoric; the gridman was jealous of his prerogative. It was best to let the toad get a little more exhausted, more willing to let someone else move into his area of responsibility.

## ‹ TWENTY-FOUR ›

Miki Ludi woke up restless and scanned around the dark room. Nothing. It seemed to her that she'd wakened to do something, whatever that might be. Silently she got up and lit the candle on her dressing table, then assumed the lotus posture on the cushioned platform.

She was able to focus on her unseen intention more quickly than usual, and abruptly her viewpoint was above a nightbound plain, perhaps five hundred feet up. It meant nothing to her—starlit darkling emptiness with an occasional yardlight at one of the scattered farmhouses. Below was the light cone of a vehicle—a pickup truck—hurrying down a minor highway.

She found herself drawn to it, and in an instant was in its cab. She recognized the driver—a wiry bearded man; she'd seen him once before in a trance, in a room with Carol and Sigurdsson and Sergeant Connor, and others whom she hadn't known. As she looked at him, his face turned, his eyes on the spot where her viewpoint was located.

*And he could see her!* Afterward she would wonder, briefly, why she hadn't instantly disconnected and left. It was what she might have expected to do. But no threat flowed from him, only admiration for what she had done, and a thought: "Howdy. My name is Vic. Is it all right for you to tell me yours?"

She didn't answer. Instead, her awareness took in still another presence with them, one which she realized now had been there before her, and which, like hers, had no body with it there. Warily she examined this second one: female, she realized. Again warily, she sought an image of the person to whom it belonged.

Without any feeling of abruptness, yet with no apparent lapse of time, she was looking down again, but now on a small desert canyon, with shadowed buildings and trees below her. This she knew was where the second presence emanated from.

But that was not all of it, for now something else impinged as well: a faint sense of startled surprise that was not hers. And further, she somehow knew it was not of that moment; it was a persisting brief instant stuck in that place from sometime before.

Again the night changed. Although the desert location remained the same, there was a moon now, half a disk low in the sky, marking a different hour, a different night. Not far away she saw a softly glowing golden sphere, which transformed almost at that instant into a small oily cloud, an ugliness which flicked away, repelling her back to the moonless dark of present time.

And the other female presence was with her again, questioning wordlessly, a presence strong enough that Miki reflexively shied away from it. Instantly the desert was gone. She was in her room again, the Los Angeles night and its diffused city glow soft around her. Her body shivered once, slightly; slowly she got up and went back to her bed. She wondered what this had been about, what it meant. As she lay down, it occurred to her that when she had slept and wakened again, she might remember none of it, at least not right away, though there at least would be a vague sense of having done something.

It took no longer than a minute for her to fall asleep. And while she slept, the presence of Tory Merlin came silently to her. There was a period of psychic query, of silent communication, then her visitor was gone.

Tory returned to that place above the canyon, to view the earlier night to which Miki had drawn her attention. More skilled than Miki, stronger and more sure of herself, Tory viewed the whole event— the two ghosts drawn to the golden sphere, and their entrapment. From that time-place she shot forward with them, up their time track to the present, compressing the intervening days into scant minutes, pausing to witness their interrogation.

Then once more she was with Vic on the Texas road, and he pulled onto the shoulder. Leaving his body to nap, together they visited the holding bottle that contained the ghosts, questioning them—again, a matter of a minute or so. After that they gave each of them a session, a swift flow of subliminal thoughts, of naked concepts unencumbered with words, taking only minutes. When they separated, Vic wakened his body, getting out of the cab into the frosty blackness, walking around the truck, stretching.

The back of the camper shell opened and Frank put out his head. "Anything wrong?" he asked softly.

"No, everything's fine. I just needed a stretch."

Vic got back into the cab and restarted the engine. *So that's what had happened to the two ghosts! Give them some time for their sessions to soak in, and do a little more work with them, and they'd be something else again.*

He grinned, engaged the clutch, and drove on.

Ole and his riders spent six hours at a motel. It

seemed perfectly safe; he was sure they were not being monitored. In midmorning he stopped at Vernon, Texas, before crossing into Oklahoma. When they left Vernon, two hours later, he was driving a sky-blue Ford van.

Vic, Frank, and Paul were deep in Oklahoma when dawn dissolved the night, and they stopped at a truck stop outside Clinton, Oklahoma for breakfast. Vic studied their highway atlas while they waited for their food.

"It's time for us to zig again," he said. "If we go east on the interstate about six miles, there's an exit that'll put us on a country road north." The others followed his finger on the map. "Then we can either jog west to 183 or go northeast on this road and cross the Canadian River here." He looked up at Paul. "How does that seem to you? You're familiar with this country."

Paul nodded. "Looks okay."

"And you feel as if someone is really following us around with some kind of monitor?" Frank asked.

"How does it seem to you?"

"Well . . . That would account for our friend the sheriff. And it's no stranger than Sipapu and Gandy, or lightning hitting that fallen tree in the road. Can you actually *feel* someone watching us?"

"In a way. But it's not like he's watching us directly. It seems like he's watching us *through* something—some sort of viewer."

"He. It's a man, then?"

"That's how it feels."

Something had been bothering Frank about this; now he spotted it. "Well, if he can see us, can't he hear us, too? Or read our minds?"

"Seems like he ought to, but it feels like he can't. What I get is that he's monitoring us with some kind of device that only picks up sight." Vic shrugged.

"Anyway, that's how it seems to work; our jackrabbiting seems to be keeping them off us."

"He's fat," Paul put in, surprising both of the others, who turned to him. "Short and fat," he added. "And he sits in a seat something like a school desk, looking at something like a big television."

"You can see him?" Vic asked.

"I don't really see him. I just got a sort of picture while you were talking."

"Great! What else do you get on him?"

"Nothing. Except he talks to certain people with his mind."

"Can you get what he tells them? Or what they tell him?"

"No, I don't get anything on that. I don't even have the picture anymore."

With a wicked grin, Frank looked off to one side toward the ceiling and made twisting movements with his big fists, as if wringing water out of something. The other two looked curiously at him.

"Just showing him what I'll do if I ever get hold of him."

Vic grinned. "That's neat. I'll bet he got it, too."

"What good does it do him to watch us?" Frank asked. "Do you think he'll set us up for some crooked sheriff again, or what?"

"I guess he might," Vic said, "if we get into the right county. Or the wrong county, from our point of view. I think probably he's one of 'The Four' that Gandy mentioned, and they've probably got connections to the Mafia; that's probably how they'd find out what sheriffs might do something like that. But it really doesn't feel important to know, as long as we keep doing the right things."

It wasn't until the outskirts of Wichita, Kansas that they stopped again. They were sitting in a *Benny's*, by a window; from there they could see the pickup.

A gray van drove into the parking lot, and paused briefly behind the pickup as if examining it. Two men were visible in the van, which had a mobile phone antenna. Then it drove on and parked, backing into a slot on the opposite side of the driveway. From there the two men could see anyone leaving the restaurant or approaching the pickup. Neither got out; they sat as if waiting.

"What do you think?" Frank asked.

"Either of you guys got a knife?" Vic asked. Frank's eyebrows raised at the question; Paul reached into a pocket and brought out a stout-bladed Buck folding knife.

"Good. Paul, what I'd like for you to do is go over behind that old Dodge sedan over there, as if you were going to look in the trunk. They probably won't pay much attention to you after they see you crossing to that side of the parking lot, and they're less likely to have a description of you than of Frank or me.

"Frank and I will be just inside the door. When you get to the back of the sedan, I'll go out, walk over to the pickup, and get in. If they get out and come over my way, you slip over behind their van and slash their rear tires. Then, if you have a chance, take their ignition key.

"Frank, if they don't come over when I go out, I'm going to start the pickup and drive away. If they don't come after me then, they probably aren't what we think they are. If they follow me out, they probably are. I'll try to come back and get you guys, but if I don't make it, you'll be on your own.

"Is that all right with both of you?"

Paul nodded. Frank frowned.

"Don't you *know* if they're after us?" Frank asked.

"Not in this universe I don't," Vic said. "Not with any certainty. But it kind of feels like it."

"What do I do while you and Paul are putting your asses on the line?"

"Whatever seems right to you, Frank. I hope they turn out to be innocent."

"They can see this window from there," Frank said. "They can see us sitting here together and see us get up to leave."

Vic shook his head. "It's dark in here, and the window's in the shade, while the parking lot's in the sun. They don't see much but the reflections of cars."

"Okay," Frank said after a moment, and slid out of the booth. "Let's do it, then."

The two men in the van waited restlessly, the engine idling. The driver sat with the phone to his ear, listening to nothing. The other reached for the radio. "Let it be," said the driver. "The last thing I need now is fucking noise."

The hand drew back.

A man came out of the restaurant, large and burly. Two of their targets fitted that description. But instead of heading for the pickup, he turned in their direction, walking around to the rear of a sedan three cars down, and their attention left him.

The phone spoke into the driver's ear. "They're getting out of the booth! They're heading for the door!"

Fleetingly, the driver felt spooky. How in the hell did Bobby know that? "Heads up!" he said to his partner. "They're coming!" He put down the phone and reached inside his jacket.

At that moment, Vic came out and walked briskly toward the pickup. The driver's left hand touched the door handle nervously, his right closing on the butt of his .38 special. His partner's, suddenly clammy, tightened on the old M-1 automatic carbine. Their eyes stayed on Vic until he got into the truck, then moved to the restaurant entrance. "Where's the other two?" the driver muttered.

They saw condensation eject from the pickup's tailpipe. "Let's get him," said the rifleman urgently.

"No!" the driver said sharply. "Wait for the other

two; they're probably taking a leak. He's just warming up the motor."

Even as he said it, they saw the pickup move, begin to back out. His foot touched the gas pedal, his hand moving to the shift lever. In their intensity, they didn't notice the angry hiss as a knife slammed into the sidewall of their right rear tire, nor feel the sag at that corner as they started out of their slot.

The pickup backed sharply right, then jerked forward toward the far exit of the parking lot, the van jumping after it. As the van went by the restaurant entrance, Frank darted out, intending to grab the rear door handles and ride the bumper, but it moved too quickly, and as he watched, there was Paul clinging to the perch he'd intended for himself. Diacono stood futilely, watching first one vehicle and then the other turn left out of the lot and speed away.

Vic sped toward one of the service stations nearby, circled it with the van close behind, and headed back for the restaurant lot. The chase vehicle was followed by a stink of flapping, burning rubber, its driver cursing but otherwise ignoring it. The van's sharp left turn back into the restaurant lot dismounted the flat and fuming tire, and he skidded, the right rear side of the van hitting a decorative entry post.

Somehow, Paul held too tightly to be thrown off. Ahead, Vic slammed on the brakes; Frank darted out to him, jerked open the door, and jumped in. Quickly then, the pickup shot out again as the driver of the van straightened his vehicle and started after them once more, the bare wheel rim singing on the pavement. As the van passed the restaurant entrance, Paul dropped off, rolled, and watched it as far as the other lot exit, then moved quickly to the restaurant entrance as the driver made the turn.

Blowing a gusty sigh of release, he waited. Either they'd swing around again and pick him up, or he'd have to hitchhike home. Without examining his reasons, he hoped they'd pick him up.

Hardly a minute passed before he knew. Across a weedy field, he saw the pickup turn left at the corner, left again at the next, then back toward the lot once more. The van, giving up the chase, limped into one of the service stations. Frank pushed open the door and Paul clambered in. This time they turned right when they left the lot, and sped away.

Frank looked sober as they tooled east on US 54. Vic, on the other hand, was grinning broadly. "That was a mighty good job you did back there, Paul," he said. "It sure slowed them down. I'll admit I got a little worried when Frank told me you were riding on their rear bumper, but I figured you'd get off so we could pick you up."

"I hope to hell we don't have to go through bullshit like that all the way to Duluth," Frank said.

Vic nodded agreement. "We're about halfway now, and they've already made three tries that we know about. We'll just have to keep going and figure we'll make it."

"What do we do if our luck runs out?"

"If luck is a flow instead of a pool, it doesn't have to run out—like the magic pitcher in the fairy story."

Frank didn't answer immediately; he was looking at Vic's words. *Magic. Fairy story. I've been living them the last week,* he told himself.

"I just hope no one cuts off the flow, then," he said.

"Where does the luck flow come from?" Vic asked.

"Right," Frank said, seeing where Vic was leading him. "I guess we'll just have to keep on creating it."

# ⟨ TWENTY-FIVE ⟩

A few miles after they turned north off US 54, Vic pulled over and stopped. "What's going on?" Frank asked him.

"I feel dopey. I need one of you to drive a while."

Frank looked at Paul. "Have you got a driver's license?"

The Indian nodded. He got out and went around to the driver's side. Vic went around to the off-side.

"Don't you want to get in the back?" asked Frank.

"Maybe later. Just now, though, it's not so much needing the rest. It feels like there's something I need to do that takes more attention than I can give it when I'm driving."

Frank nodded. "Got it," he said.

Paul shifted into gear and they started out again. Vic leaned back, closed his eyes, and let his head sag. Within seconds he became aware of a presence with his: Tory's. They weren't in the cab together, or on the ranch, or anywhere in particular, but in that limbo of no location, no space, no time, outside of any universe. There was no thought there, but only being, and there was continuance in a static *now*

211

without time. They were there while five minutes passed in the Tikh Cheki Matrix.

It was rejuvenative, but they did not continue longer there because they had committed themselves to intentions, and wished to persist in those intentions. So after five minutes they returned to the matrix at a place called Dallas—in a suburb called Irving, actually—in the state of Texas. The man in the heavily curtained west room had the power to perceive their presence, but they were in the basement, and he was not alert to the possibility of intruders.

Here, with the ghosts, they continued their activity of the night before, and when they were done, the entities that once had worn the identities Lefty Nagel and Leo Hochman were no longer confined. And though also freed of any hostility or grudge toward Kurt Hardman, they were nonetheless agreeable to playing a game which might have been called "Foil the Four."

Hardman's home was now haunted, but covertly.

Vic and Tory weren't done, though; there was someone else who was ready—more than ready. Tory put her attention on an entity who happened to be at a matrix coordinate known as the Studio City Fitness Salon.

Miki Ludi had just finished showering after leading a class in dance aerobics, and now sat down in her office. Since her sister-in-law had left, she'd been attempting to handle accounts herself—billing, logging in payments received, cutting checks to creditors—the essential minima of Carol's work. Her violet-blue eyes looked distastefully at the stack awaiting her; if she did not hear from Carol today, saying she'd be back inside a week, she would hire a temporary.

Right now though, she felt—sleepy. Unusual. She

was trying to avoid the piled-up pending-basket, she decided, and took the top item off the stack. Pacific Bell Telephone; that was a simple one, easy to start with.

But it was foolish to try to function, as sleepy as she was. And she could hardly sleep too long sitting at her desk. She got up and locked her door, sat back down, and rested her head on her crossed arms. For just a few minutes, she told herself.

She awoke smoothly and looked at her wall clock: twelve minutes. Without even looking at the pending-basket, she got up and went to the Nautilus room, where Donni, her right-hand girl, was supervising exercises. She drew her aside.

"I'm taking the rest of the day off," she said. "I'm getting so stale, I can't stand myself." It wasn't the truth, but it was something Donni could understand; she used the "getting stale" bit herself. "You're in charge until I get back."

Donni nodded, and Miki left, getting into her Corvette and starting for home.

Ole Sigurdsson turned over the wheel to Carol and got in the back. They were no longer being elusive; he no longer felt any need for it. They were on Interstate 40 now, headed for Oklahoma City and Interstate 35.

The blue Ford van didn't provide him with the sense of possession the Caddy had, but it was roomy and comfortable. He lay down in back and went to sleep.

Hardman had become a part of the grid—more specifically, part of its viewscreen—operating almost robotically. He had neglected his body for years, except sexually, and been under the influence of amphetamines continually for almost twenty-four hours. His eyes were bloodshot, his pulse rate 109;

his blood pressure, had anyone taken it, would have read 175/115. When his body felt too squirmy to bear, he signalled his housekeeper; Maria would come in and give him a light massage without distracting him from the screen. He was in frequent telepathic touch with Gracco, who was getting increasingly tired and grouchy.

Through the gridman, Gracco was following the progress of the black pickup on a highway atlas, hampered somewhat because some of the minor roads taken were not on its pages. Occasionally he contacted one of the network that Milazzo and Manoukian had provided, to give a predicted, reachable hit location. But the goddamn truck kept changing routes. At least twice, prior to Wichita, he'd apparently had people within three miles of interception, but mostly they were out of contact—were without mobile phones—and none had sighted their quarry.

In the Wichita area he'd had three hits squads out—one of them with a mobile phone. How close could you get and still miss? Gracco's urbane confidence had evaporated after the fiasco outside *Benny's*. This Merlin was the luckiest sonofabitch on the continent, if not the entire planet, and Gracco was psychic enough to know that luck wasn't something you fell into. You created it. Ergo, Merlin was even more able than he'd expected—dangerously able.

Gracco was beginning to think of his arrangements with Olson as more than just an exercise in emergency backup planning. Minnesota, even Duluth, could easily prove to be where it would finally happen—or fail to happen.

He rejected the last thought as defeatist, and refused to acknowledge it further. When Merlin escaped Wichita, Gracco had left word with Moller there to send someone speeding north up I-135 to Newton and hit the side roads from there. Two more cars were speeding southwest from Topeka, and one each had been dispatched from Salina and Junction City. They all had CB radios, but only one from Topeka and the car from Salina had phones; the others he could only get directions to through intermediaries, via their CB radios. It was hard to coordinate an operation like that—hard even to get information accurately relayed. But with a little luck . . . And there was that word again.

When he saw Merlin replaced behind the wheel by the hitchhiker, Hardman had roused from robotism and felt briefly hopeful. It did not occur to the gridman that psychic alertness might be effortless. For him it was tiring; prolonged, it was grueling. So it seemed to him that the exercise of psychic powers must have worn down Merlin and his brawny jock henchman. And though somehow they'd roped the hitchhiker into their game—his part in the Wichita melee had shown that—the Indian could hardly have the psychically directed evasiveness they'd shown.

That had been forty minutes ago. Since then the pursuit car from Wichita, closing fast, had been forced into a long detour when a cattle truck had broken down ahead of it on a narrow county bridge. The cars from Topeka, on I-70 and US 56, were still some distance away, though closing. The cars from Junction City and Salina were jockeying for intercepting positions, but only one of them had direct contact with Gracco. It seemed to Hardman that success there was quite uncertain.

And he was not sure how much longer he could continue to ride the grid—ten or twelve hours at most. He hadn't slept at all since the day before— about the time Merlin had left New Mexico—and once he crashed, he wouldn't be much good for at least a day. This, it seemed to him, was the time to finish Merlin's ass, whatever it took, which meant it was chance-taking time.

Merlin had avoided the broad, rolling rangeland of the Flint Hills, keeping to well-settled prairie farm-land where roads at one-mile intervals laid their own grid on the country. Now Hardman decided he needed to see not only the pickup and its immediate sur-roundings, but as much of the local road network as possible, so he moved his viewpoint to an altitude of 3,000 feet local.

The pickup looked larger from there than he might have thought, and he could see a large stretch of farmland—dark-gray soil with a tinge of green where winter wheat had sprouted, shades of tawny where stubble still marked last year's fields of wheat, sor-ghum, corn.

While keeping track of the pickup, he asked Gracco for a description of the nearest two hit cars, and to keep him apprised of their approximate locations. Gracco told him to go fuck himself, he had no time for that, but a minute or two later told him what the cars looked like and approximately where they were. After another five minutes, apparently both cars were within three minutes of Merlin, and closing. The hit cars from Topeka were eight and twelve miles away, the one from Wichita farther still.

Hardman drew his viewpoint back to 4,500 feet; from there the black pickup was tiny but still recog-nizable. A minute later he could see a car which a quick zoom identified as the Salina car, and shortly, the car from Junction City. The pickup turned east onto a gravel road, on a course that intersected with the road the Junction City car had taken, but the Junction City car would have to speed up to get to the crossroads first. Hastily, he told all this to Gracco.

On the screen, Hardman could see both of the chase cars speed up. He was sweating now, tending to hold his breath till he felt suffocated. He zoomed his viewpoint down to about one thousand feet. The pickup was less than a half mile from the crossing when the Junction City car arrived there and turned toward them.

The pickup braked abruptly, as if its driver *knew* what car that was; he jockeyed quickly around on the narrow right of way and sped back the way he had come, only to see the Salina car reach the crossroad in that direction.

The pickup never paused. There was a tightly grown osage-orange windbreak along the north side of the road, with a gap that allowed farm machinery in and out of the field. Paul whipped the pickup through the gap and started across a field of corn stubble; it bounced violently as it crossed the rows. The Junction City car sped after it, the Salina car following, both cars slamming hard on springs and shocks never meant for off-road stresses.

The pursuers were keeping pace. A man in the lead car was leaning out a window, squeezing off shots with an automatic pistol, but the car lurched and bounced too wildly to allow accurate fire. In a moment of sudden determination, Hardman projected his psyche into the pickup itself, striking at the driver's mind. Paul bellowed, jerked the wheel as if fighting with it, and the pickup careened, almost rolled, before Hardman recoiled, momentarily blinded, from the response that struck him.

Meanwhile, the pistol fire had stopped; in the bouncing car, the gunman had banged his temple against the front edge of the window while leaning out, and for a moment almost lost consciousness. Halfway across the mile to the next road, the pickup went from stubble into new winter wheat, where the ground had been disked in the fall. It was soft, and there was no time to get out and set the hubs for four-wheel drive. Paul shifted down, the big tires throwing dirt and young wheat sprouts. Now the truck bounced less, but still bounced, and briefly its lead shrank. Then the first sedan reached the wheat, where the car quickly bogged.

A man jumped out with a rifle, cursing, and threw a wild fusillade of bullets after the pickup. The second sedan stopped before it reached the wheat, one of its men getting out with an automatic carbine, adding its firepower to the rifle's.

Paul, his jaw clenched, kept the truck moving, his meaty fists gripping the steering wheel tightly, and they gained speed. Bullets ripped through the tailgate, the camper shell, slammed into the cab body, pierced the rear window. One passed between Paul and Vic to slam into the dashboard, another scored the roof; two more, somewhat flattened and spent, made holes in the windshield, surrounded by patterns of cracks. The outside mirror shattered on the driver's side.

Frank and Vic had bent forward to lower their profiles, and in scant seconds there was another break in the shooting. "Changing clips," said Frank, grunting the words out as they jounced. No one answered; he looked at Vic and saw that his eyes were closed, in pain or concentration.

The break was longer than he'd expected. The gunmen had had to get replacement clips from the cars, thus the range was more than four hundred yards and widening when the next flurry of bullets was loosed. Paul felt something strike his lower back, but neither stopped nor flinched. More glass fell in on them from behind, and another network of cracks appeared in the windshield, superimposed over one of the others.

Then there was only the sound of the overwound engine, and of their breathing. In scant seconds they were out of the wheat field and on a farm machine lane, then careening through a gap in the multiple tree-rows of a shelterbelt and out onto a blacktop road.

Vic straightened. "Paul, that sure was good driving. We're lucky none of us got hit, or any of our tires." He looked at Paul then. "Are you all right, Paul?"

"Yeah." Paul's voice was hoarse and raspy. "Something hit me in the back, but it doesn't hurt and I don't feel any blood running. Probably a spent bullet, went through too much steel."

"Good." They were approaching the next crossroad. "We lost our monitor," Vic added. "Just keep on straight till the road after this one and turn north. Then Frank will take a turn at the wheel and I'll look at your back."

Hardman had sat doubled over for a minute, his face gray with shock, before jerking his eyes to the screen again. The pickup sped through the wheat field throwing two low rooster tails of loam behind it. His skull felt split, his ears rang intensely, and he was nauseated, but he would not quit now. He gathered his power again and opened himself as he poised to strike.

Then a savage dart struck his mind. He knew his assailant and turned on her, but before he could focus, he was stabbed on another vector, and another, and then a fourth, and more. He struck about wildly, his psyche staggering, but he was battered from every side by lances of fiery intention. He screamed once in pain and rage, then slumped, dead weight.

His housekeeper heard the scream and came running from the kitchen to find him sagging heavily across the console arm. The screen was a meaningless flickering pattern of zigzags. Briefly, she tried to rouse him, talking sharply at him in her Spanish, then hurried to call the gatehouse and tell the guard.

The guard, when he got there, sought a pulse in the fat wrist but wasn't sure whether he was feeling in the right place. He peered beneath a lid, then left the room to phone Peter Shark.

Shark already knew; he'd felt it, been rocked by it. Kurt Hardman had died in the skirmish, his heart already weakened by neglect, amphetamines, and general self-abuse. Shark instructed the guard, then grimly called for his pilot; he'd have to fly to Dallas at once and ride the grid himself. He didn't have a lot of experience on it, but The Lords had made sure he could use it.

# < TWENTY-SIX >

Vic sat a while with Paul in the camper, handling the mental trauma from Hardman's attack. Meanwhile, Diacono zigzagged generally westward. Westward wasn't the way to Minnesota, but it removed them from the immediate war zone, the area where they might expect to encounter an enemy. After a while he crossed I-135 and drove into a town, where a sign announced "Lindsborg, pop. 3,155." There Diacono pulled into a small garage marked "Knutson's Automotive Repairs and Body Shop," and the three of them got out.

A large blocky man walked over, wiping his hands on a rag and eyeing the ravaged windshield. Probably Knutson, Diacono decided.

"Lemme see if I can figure out what you want," Knutson said.

Frank nodded. "Right—new windshield. Also a new back window, new outside mirror, and patch some bullet holes."

Knutson circled the truck, then whistled softly. "What the hell happened? Looks like you drove through the opening day of deer season."

"We don't actually know. We were at a motel in

221

Oklahoma last night—at some Interstate exit out in the country—and when we went out to the truck this morning . . ." He shrugged. "Some drunk with a gun in his pickup decided to take target practice, I guess; people do strange things anymore. But we decided we'd better just keep going and get it fixed in Lincoln, so we wouldn't be late. We're supposed to meet with the Nebraska coaching staff tomorrow noon."

Frank looked at his watch. "There's an extra fifty dollars in it if you can get it done inside of four hours."

While Frank talked, it occurred to Knutson that the story might be less than true, and a frown of suspicion touched his grease-smudged brow. Opening the driver's door, he leaned inside. Then his eyes picked up the bullet hole low in the back of the driver's seat, and the absence of any blood, there or elsewhere. His suspicion evaporated, and he turned back to Diacono.

"You're lucky nobody was inside; he'd have been hit sure as hell. If you can give me five hours, I'll fix her up for you. The filler's got to have time to dry. But there's no way the paint job can be ready today, even if you just want a touchup. That'll have to wait till Lincoln."

"Fine. I'll worry about the paint job later. Just put primer on the patches."

When Frank had signed the job order, they went outside. There was a bank down the street, and he turned in that direction; he needed to cash a check. This trip, he told himself, was getting expensive.

"Well," he said, "what next? Can we drive the Interstates, now that we've lost our monitor? Or do you think he'll pick us up again?"

"I'm pretty sure he's dead," said Vic. The others looked sharply at him. "I think he blew a fuse back in that wheat field. He threw a whammy on Paul back there; that's when Paul lost control for a minute. Then I attacked him, but I wasn't the only one. There was Tory and several others. We've got friends in this.

"And about what we do next—what we'd better do is get hold of some license plates somehow or other that don't say Arizona on them. There seems to be a lot of people looking for a big black pickup with Arizona plates."

"Gracco!"

Vincent Gracco had been sleeping heavily after too many hours awake; it had taken Shark a full minute of psychic prodding to waken him.

"Yeah? What is it, Shark?" he mumbled thickly.

"Unh! You're on the grid already!" Gracco, in pajamas, sluggishly swung his legs off the bed and put his feet on the carpet. "What's happening?"

"Who knows? We seem to have two carloads of psychics running around somewhere in the middle of the country headed for Lake Superior, and I don't know where they are. If they've got any brains at all, they've changed vehicles by now so they'll be impossible to spot. We're in trouble, Gracco; we need to talk about this."

Gracco considered saying something to the effect that if he didn't get more sleep, they'd be in worse trouble, but somehow he didn't. "Okay, I'm listening."

"We can't depend on cancelling them along the road somewhere now, the way we thought we could. We could get lucky—we're about due—but we can't depend on it. And I just took a look at Lake Superior from way up. There are practically no clouds, and there's ice with snow on it around almost the entire shore. In some places it extends out for miles. The whole west end is frozen over for maybe twenty or thirty miles out from Duluth.

"Given those conditions, if you were Merlin, how

would you try to reach the island if you were somewhere up around Lake Superior?"

"They've almost got to fly," Gracco said. "They could hire a tractor to haul a boat out near the edge of the ice—a small boat they could push the rest of the way by hand—but they'd have to be nuts to do something like that. The tractor could break through when they got close to the edge, or they could swamp trying to cross open water . . ." *But we're not monitoring them now*, Gracco reminded himself. *They'd be hard to spot on all that water.* "What kind of beaches are there on the island, if they tried a boat and got that far?"

"There's an ice shelf along the whole south side of the island, but the north side is partly open, probably from wave action. All the bays and inlets are frozen over, and mostly where it's open, it's cliffy."

Gracco shook his head. "It's fifty to one they'd fly and come down on one of the little lakes on the island. Olson tells me there are a lot of little lakes out there."

"Dozens of them," Shark agreed, "all frozen over and covered with snow. There's one they could use that's only two or three miles from the gate."

"Okay," said Gracco, "here's what I'll do." He squinted at the clock by his bed. "It's four-thirty in the morning here. I'll get on the horn to Olson and let him know we've lost track of Merlin. We've already talked about what we'd do if that happened.

"We can't cover all the airports in this part of the country, but we'll contact every charter company as far south as the Twin Cities to let us know if they come around, because they could hire any plane with skis to fly out there.

"There's something else we need to look at, though," Gracco continued relentlessly. "They could stay lucky and make it to the island. To the gate. We need somebody out there to waylay them. I know it's dangerous, because we don't know how far out the neutral zone goes. But we could decide on a hundred feet or a hundred yards or a mile, and take our chances—blow them away if they show up out there. If we cut them down earlier, no harm done. But if they get that far, we got nothing more to lose."

Shark didn't reply, and the absence of disagreement encouraged Gracco. "I told Olson that Merlin thinks some escaped Nazis stashed a big cache of gold and jewels out there after World War Two in an old prospector's hole. When he asked me why we don't just ambush him on the island, I told him Merlin might decide to cool it before he got that far, and we needed to hit him along the way if we could. I told him Merlin might be crazy, but he's also a genius, and a slippery sonofabitch.

"It wasn't the greatest story in the world, and Olson didn't totally buy it, but with the money I'm waving around, he settled for it.

"Now, the island is a national park and wilderness area. I was talking to a guy that flies dope for Olson, and he says there's a law against landing a plane out there, or even flying over the island below 9,000 feet, without special authorization. It's even against the law to be on the island at all in the winter; they think it bothers the wolves or some dumb shit like that. So I suppose if the Park thinks someone's out there, or hears a plane, they get on the horn and call the Coast Guard or the Michigan State Police or somebody—I don't know who.

"Anyway, we need to play it cool and not get noticed. So what I'll do is get some guys together that know their way around the woods in the winter, and dress them in camouflage whites. Then I'll fly out there with them at night—come around out of the northwest, where there's no ranger station to hear the plane. We can land on some lake near the gate and go there on snowshoes.

"But I'll need you to show me where the gate is. You're riding the grid, and I doubt if I can find the gate just by flying around feeling for it."

Shark nodded mentally; setting an ambush was the necessary final safeguard. "Get a big map of the island and call me back," he said. "I'll show you the gate on it."

A big map of Isle Royale—where could he get one on short notice? The U. of M. library would have one, Gracco decided; a place like that had everything. Shark could guide his pen psychically, right there in the library. Then he'd fold up the map, put it in his shirt, and it was his.

"Will do," Gracco said. "I'll whistle you up on that later today."

They disconnected. *So fucking much to do*, Gracco thought, *I need three of me. When this is all over, I'm going to have me a nice long sleep and then take a vacation in Monte Carlo*.

< TWENTY-SEVEN >

The date was January 24, and at five-thirty it was fully night. Diacono had pulled the pickup over against the snowplow bank; the engine was idling, the sound of the heater fan a blurred and unobtrusive whir. Enclosed together in the warm cab, the three of them looked out across the Duluth airport as if there was something there to see besides snow, lights, a few buildings and parked cars. Frank had turned on the radio, the volume low.

"And now the KDAL weather," it was saying. "Don't forget to plug in your engine heater tonight, or fire up the stove in your garage, or whatever it is you need to do to start your car in the morning. Because if you've been looking for a break in the arctic weather, you'll have to keep on waiting. The forecast low for the Lakehead again tonight is minus twenty-eight, with the high tomorrow another minus five. For those of you listening from up in the Range, Hibbing will reach forty below again tonight and climb only to about fifteen below tomorrow. International Falls will have minus forty with minus eighteen the high. Right now the temperature at KDAL is a chilly, and I mean *co-old*—minus fourteen. And if any of you want those temperatures in Celsius, you can have them; Dr. Fahrenheit and I are packing our tennis rackets and swim trunks, and taking off for . . ."

Frank turned it off. "It picked a great time for a cold wave," he said. "They should have put the surprise generator in Yucatan." He turned to Vic. "Where now? If we're going to find Ole, tonight's got to be the night."

"Why don't we check in at that TraveLodge we passed back there?" Vic said. "Then we can find a restaurant and eat supper, and if we haven't run into Ole's crew, we can check out the terminal and see if they're there."

"Right," said Frank and shifted gears. The simplicity of Vic's mental processes would have bothered him once, he realized. Now he admired them and found his own becoming more and more like them. It occurred to him that that simplicity grew out of self-trust—or was it the other way around?

Just ahead was a median crossing, where he turned east and headed for the TraveLodge Vic had mentioned. Briefly, he wondered why they didn't stop at the nearer motel they passed on the way; it looked suitably economical. But Vic would have his reasons, even if he might not himself know what they were. Frank had learned a great deal about the nature of intuition lately.

While the desk clerk checked them in, Frank looked over a small flyer on the desk, advertising Terbovitch's Steak House.

"Is Terbovitch's a good place to eat?" he asked, holding up the flyer.

The clerk looked up. "Real good," she said. "That's where my husband usually takes me when we eat out."

Frank looked at Vic and Paul. "Might be a nice change from truck stops," he suggested. They took their bags to their large room, took turns in the bathroom, then went back out to the truck, slamming the doors against the cold.

"How're we going to start the pickup in the morning?" asked Paul.

"I'll take the battery out and bring it in the room with us," Frank said. "That ought to do it."

They reached Terbovitch's early enough that the hostess led them into the dining room with no wait at all. "How about that big one?" Vic asked her, pointing to a large table near the front window. "We're expecting some friends to come in, and we'd like to have them sit with us."

Frank raised his eyebrows at Vic as the hostess took them there. When she'd gone he asked, "Do you really think they'll show up in here like that?"

Vic grinned. "I wouldn't be surprised. Why else did you choose this place?"

They'd just gotten their coffee when Frank looked out the window to see Ole, Jerry, and Carol crossing the parking lot. In turn, Ole spotted them the moment he came in, and a minute later they were sitting together.

"We thought we recognized that pickup when we drove in," said Carol. "And Ole said it was yours, even if it does have Kansas plates."

"I don't suppose there's a story behind how you got those plates," Jerry said wryly.

"They came off a pickup parked by a shed, with the hood up and the engine removed; I doubt if anyone will miss them very soon. And meanwhile, the brownies pushed three twenty-dollar bills under the shed door."

The waitress brought menus for the newcomers. As they looked them over, Vic asked, "What happened to your cast, Jerry? Did you lose it somewhere?"

"We got it removed at a town called Faribault this morning. The x-rays showed complete healing." He flexed the arm and fingers, studying their movement. "Feels pretty good; I feel like I'm on sick leave on a false pretense." He looked at Frank. "Where are you guys staying?"

"The TraveLodge just up the road."

"So are we!" Carol said. "What rooms?"

"We're all in one-nineteen—their only room with three beds."

She laughed. "We've got one-twelve and one-sixteen. I guess you got in just after we did. Do you have your winter clothes and equipment yet?"

"We bought it in Duluth," Vic said. "About a hundred pounds of it, plus snowshoes. You-all have anything interesting happen along the way?"

"Not since ve left Texas," Ole said. "It's been yust like a holiday. And ve got snowshoes and stuff, too. Oh! And I traded in my v'ite Caddy for a blue Ford van. That's probably v'y you didn't notice us at the motel."

He eyed Paul. "So you decided not to stay in Oklahoma."

Paul smiled. "This was getting too interesting. Besides, I'm never going to find a stronger medicine chief than Vic. He gives me a medicine session every night. Pretty soon I'm going to walk on water."

"That would be easy on a night like this," Carol said. "Have you heard the weather forecast?"

Frank made a face. "Twenty-eight below." Then, talking quietly for privacy, he and Vic told the story of the melee at Wichita, the shooting scene in the wheat field, and the apparent demise of the monitor.

"This could be the most dangerous part of the whole trip, coming up," said Jerry. "Now that we're getting so close to the goal."

"How so?" asked Frank. "They lost their monitor—whoever 'they' are."

"Well, but they must know where we're going. Otherwise, why all that effort to stop us?"

"Good qvestion," said Ole. "I think you're probably right." He looked at Vic, who nodded.

"But that doesn't make sense," Frank objected. "If they knew where we're going, why try to kill us along the way? Why not just wait for us out on the island, and ambush us at the gate? It seems to me . . . Hell, I don't know. Why *did* they make all that effort to stop us, unless they knew where we're going?"

"That don't make no difference to v'at ve do next," said Ole. "Ve ain't got that many choices. Ve fly out to the island, land on some lake that's close to the gate, and go there."

"Do we all agree that that's what we do next?" Vic said. "Hire a plane and go?"

*And there it is,* thought Frank, *the moment of truth, staring us in the face.* Carol was nodding soberly; Jerry followed suit; Paul simply watched calmly. "Well," Frank said, "that seems like the best way to do it. And considering what we've already come through, without serious damage . . ."

He didn't feel as confident as he sounded.

When they'd finished eating, they lingered over drinks. Frank got up and borrowed a phone book, bringing it to the table.

"Let's see now." Opening it, he thumbed the yellow pages. "Aircraft Rentals and Charters . . . Here we are: 'Ojibwa Charters.'" He looked up. "How does that sound? I got into this operation through an Indian spirit, got in touch with Vic through two Hopis, and we learned about the Isle Royale gate from the guardian of Sipapu. Then we got help from a rain god in the Chiricahuas, and Paul saved our ass in Wichita, not to mention getting a big bullet bruise in his back piloting the pickup. Ojibwa Charters sounds just right to me."

Vic grinned through his beard. "Sounds good to me, too." He looked around the table, his eyes stopping on Ole, who sat for a moment with a faraway look in his eye before nodding.

"What did you see just then, Ole?" Vic asked.

"Nothing. I almost saw something, but then it vas gone."

The helicopter came in low from the north, from a Canadian lake, carrying eleven armed men, including Gracco. The hour was 3 A.M. It landed four of them, in camouflage white, at the east edge of Isle Royale's Chickenbone Lake. Before it left, it hovered, its rotor blast obscuring their tracks and its own. From there the four gunmen hiked through the forest to the west end of the lake and set up a winter tent under the cover of some spruce, banking it with snow.

Meanwhile, the chopper crossed the hills to Hatchet Lake and put down four more men. Then it flew in to Lake Harvey, away from any trail, to lurk at the forest edge as an air assault force. It left only once, before dawn, when Shark, on the grid, showed Gracco the exact location of the gate.

According to the schedule board on the wall, Ojibwa Charters had two planes. The man in the office was about fifty, and wore a green and black checkered wool shirt. His brown Indian face had a yellowish tinge, as if he used atabrine or had jaundice. His winter cap, its fur earlaps turned up, was shoved back to show medium brown hair. He looked up as they entered, taking them in, and the slightly oriental eyes that stopped on Paul were pale blue.

"What can I do for you?" the man asked. His slight accent reminded Sigurdsson of Finns he'd known during his years in Kitliak, Washington.

It was Ole who answered; he was their agreed-upon spokesman. "Ve need somevun to fly us out to Isle Royale," he said.

"It's against the law to fly out there without authorization, and I ain't got authorization."

"Right. V'at are your rates?"

The eyes went to Paul again before returning to Ole. "They're whatever I say. I been known to fly for nothing when I want to, and there's people I wouldn't work for for a thousand dollars an hour. What you want to go to Isle Royale for?"

Paul answered before Ole had a chance to. "That's hard to talk about," he said. The blue eyes went to him again, suspicious. "It has to do with Indian spirits. Many people would scorn it; some Indians would. We wouldn't talk about it to people like that."

The man didn't answer at once, just looked at Paul.

"My name is Alex Lampi," he said at last, and it was to Paul that he spoke. "I'm half Finn. My mother is Chippewa, from up by Grand Marais. Her family wasn't on no reservation, so they didn't have no preachers working on them to turn Christian. They just trapped, and fished for trout and whitefish and herring. Sometimes they logged." He looked at the others. "Why don't you people go have coffee somewhere? Him and me need to talk."

Ole nodded slowly, then looked around at the others. "Maybe ve should go find a restaurant somev'ere. It don't feel like a good idea to hang around the terminal together." Turning back to Paul he said. "Ve'll phone back in tventy minutes or so."

Paul nodded. "Right," he said, and watched them leave. Then he turned to Lampi, but before he could say anything, Lampi spoke again.

"You know, I could have told you guys 'sure, come back in two hours, and I'll take you.' Then I could have made a phone call to a guy and got $5,000 for letting him know." Lampi held up a slip of paper with a telephone number on it. "He said he was C.I.A., but he smelled to me like Mafia or something. Well, I don't need that kind of money. I'll either take you or I'll tell you to get lost. Now what's this all about?"

"Do you believe in the spirits?" asked Paul.

"Not especially. My mother did, and her family, and the other Chippewa families that lived around us. They all believed, more or less. Like I said, we didn't live on no reservation, so we didn't have no church trying to shame us out of it.

"But me—I'm more like my old man. He was friendly to Indian spirits, but he didn't believe in them. One time—more than one time—he told me he liked the Chippewa gods better than the white man's God. And he told me about the old Finn gods and spirits—stories a lot like the ones my mother's people told.

"So what is this about the spirits? And what's it got to do do with Isle Royale?"

Paul thought briefly before he began to talk. "I wasn't in this at the start," he said, "so the first part is hearsay. But I'll tell you what I heard and then what I saw. And any time you want to tell me to get lost, that's okay, because it's a strange story, especially to someone who doesn't believe in the spirits."

It was more than thirty minutes later when Ole phoned; at twenty minutes he'd felt it wasn't the right time. Lampi answered.

"Is it time for us to come back yet?" Ole asked.

"Stay away from here," said Lampi. "There was a guy in here looking for you just a few minutes ago that I don't think you want to see. I told him I ain't seen you." Lampi chuckled. "Paul was sitting right here and the guy hardly looked at him. I started talking Chippewa as soon as I saw him coming to the door, and he thought it was just two Indians shooting the shit.

"But it ain't a good idea for you to come around here anymore. So drive west on US 53 about ten miles to a little place called Twig. There's a store there. On the south side of the highway there's a lake, Grand Lake. You can probably drive down to it; the ice fishermen should have a road plowed in there.

"I'll pick you up on the ice in a De Haviland Beaver about four-thirty; it's a single-engine job. I'll bring Paul so you don't have to come here after him. And don't forget to bring a light ax—a cruiser's ax. Where you're going, you could freeze to death without an ax and matches. I'll fly you up the north shore, across the Canadian border, and then down to the island in the dark. Nobody ought to hear us if we come in from the north, and I'll have my running lights off.

"It'll cost you $400 to take you there and $400 more each time I got to go out there afterward; that's for me and my plane, cash in advance. And I don't mind telling you it makes my stomach feel bad, because that's a bad-looking guy that's after you."

When they'd hung up, Ole went back to the table and ran it by the others. "What will we do between now and four-thirty?" Carol asked.

Vic grinned. "Whatever we want. We can go into town and see a movie if you'd like. Then we can eat a late lunch, dress up in our winter woods clothes, and start."

"Just a minute," Frank said. His eyes went briefly to Carol. "I don't think we should leave a vehicle unattended out by a lake somewhere when we take off for the island. We need someone to drive back to the motel and watch out for the vehicles—safeguard our transportation home. It shouldn't take all six of us to do . . . whatever it is we end up doing out there."

For a moment the restaurant booth was very quiet; a feeling of electricity built, then faded. "Who,"

Carol asked quietly, "do you have in mind to baby-sit the cars?"

Diacono didn't answer for several long seconds, then said, "Frankly, I was thinking of you."

"I think *you* should be the one," she said pleasantly. "It's your truck. And you're the heaviest: The plane ought to fly better if you stay behind."

Frank looked at her thoughtfully. "I appreciate how you feel about this," he answered. "And I'm not going to make a big issue of it. But it *would* be a good idea for someone to stay with the vehicles. And as far as I know, I'm the one of us who's most experienced in the woods; probably the only one of us who's experienced on snowshoes. And Vic and Ole are the ones most likely to know what to do when we go through the gate.

"And Carol—honest to God, snowshoeing in hills and virgin forest is pretty damn strenuous. There'll be blown-down timber and probably brush to hike through with thirty-inch bearpaws strapped on your feet. I know I'm sounding like a male chauvinist . . ."

Her hand moved to his on the table, and he paused, uncertain of what was about to happen. "You may sound like a male chauvinist," she said, "but I know you better than that. Now let me give you my viewpoint. I work for my sister-in-law in her fitness salon, and she's had me on a strenuous exercise regimen for months. I may be as fit as you are, even if you are stronger. On top of that"—her voice got harder now—"I didn't get to go through the gate at Sipapu, and there is no way I'll agree to be left behind this time." She patted his big paw. "Just so there's no misunderstanding."

He shook his head ruefully, flexing his hand, and looked at Jerry. "I don't suppose there are any volunteers."

"Don't look at me," Jerry said. "I think it's a good idea for somebody to stay with the vehicles too, and

I don't like cold weather. But I didn't go through the gate at Sipapu either. Besides, I'm the only one here with a gun, and the only one who's familiar with it."

No one said anything for a while then; they just sipped their coffee. Finally Jerry broke the silence. "Do you think we're really going to get away with this?" he asked conversationally. "They could be waiting for us out there."

"I sure don't know," Vic answered. "We've done pretty well so far though. Anyway, for me it would be more fun to lose my body trying than to lose it waiting. But I don't figure to get beat on this. It feels like a winner to me."

The De Haviland cruised through the night at about three thousand feet, over a panorama of broad forests broken with the irregular white patches of bogs, lakes, and occasional cutovers. Lampi and Vic sat in the cockpit; the others were in the cabin behind them. All of them were looking out the windows.

Off to their right spread Lake Superior. The west end had been white with snow-covered ice to well beyond Two Harbors. Now, except for shelf ice, the great lake spread black to the invisible night horizon.

Lampi pointed. "That black out there ain't all open water," he said. "It froze farther out since this cold wave, and the new ice ain't got snow on it yet. This could turn out to be one of those winters so cold that she freezes all the way over. I only seen it happen three times. You can get forty inches of ice on inland lakes and Superior will still be open."

Vic peered in that direction. "Do you think it's frozen out to Isle Royale now?"

"Could be. It ain't so rare to freeze out to the island from the north shore, and it's the right kind of winter. We'll see when we get there."

Vic sat back and closed his eyes. A moment later

his body went slack, staying like that for two or three minutes; Lampi eyed it uncertainly several times. Then it straightened and the eyes opened.

"You said you've got relatives at Grand Marais," Vic said.

"Actually, they live farther up the shore, up toward Hovland. My next younger brother lives there, and my sister and her family, and my mother."

"Have they got snowmobiles we could rent?"

"Snowmobiles?" Lampi stared at him for a long minute. "You went out there and looked at the ice, didn't you? You went out in the spirit and checked it out. Paul told me about you—that you're a real medicine chief, and the place you guys are going is a spirit gate."

Smiling, Vic nodded, his eyes seeming somehow to glint, perhaps reflecting the instrument lights. "It's frozen all the way out from the north shore to the island," he said, "and the places I checked, it's eight or ten inches thick."

"Yeah, as cold as it's been . . ." Lampi frowned thoughtfully. "My brother-in-law's got two Ski-Doos— one for himself and one for his oldest boy—and my brother's got one. Probably all his neighbors got a snowmobile of some kind; you wouldn't have any trouble renting two or three. But you'd have to go seventy or eighty miles on bare ice, and that's a long way by snowmobile in weather like this."

When Frank had bought their gear at a wilderness outfitter's in Duluth, he'd also bought a large topographic map of the island, and they'd marked the approximate location of the gate. When Lampi had met them at Grand Lake, Vic had shown him where they were going. Now Vic took the map from his pocket and unfolded it on his lap. "Let's look at it," he said.

Lampi turned on the cockpit light. "That's McCargo Cove," he said, pointing. "From there, you'd have to

go all the way along here." His finger followed broken lines that marked trails. "And I doubt to beat
hell that the trails will take a snowmobile. They tell
me the trails out there are really narrow, a lot of
places. You'd have to ride for several hours on the
ice, colder than a sonofabitch, and then you'd probably end up needing to snowshoe five or ten miles
after that, which is harder than maybe you think, for
people that ain't used to it.

"So the best thing is for me to fly you in to
Hatchet Lake. Then you only got about three miles
to hike."

Vic nodded. "If you knew right where we were
going," he said, "and you wanted to ambush us,
where would you do it?"

"Umm. Right at the spirit gate. You couldn't slip
around me then."

"But suppose you couldn't do that; suppose the
spirits wouldn't let you harm us anywhere around
the gate, and you knew that. Then where would you
set up the ambush?"

Lampi pursed his lips. "Here . . . and here." His
finger touched the map twice. "On Hatchet Lake
and Harvey Lake. But I'd land over here at Chickenbone Lake so I wouldn't leave any tracks on the ice
at the other two to scare you off. Then I'd send guys
out to Harvey and Hatchet, around by the north trail
so they wouldn't leave tracks where you'd see them.
I'd set my main ambush on the south side of Hatchet,
where the trail starts up to the spirit gate, because
Hatchet is easy the best place to get to the gate
from." The finger traced routes.

"And if I had them, I'd send guys up from
Chickenbone to this trail junction here, in case you
landed on any of those other lakes. They're all pretty
far from the gate, but I'd do that anyway, to not take
any chances."

Lampi glanced at Vic to see his reaction, then

continued. "Look, I'll tell you what, and this is the best we can do. I'll come in low over the ice so the sound don't carry far, with no lights, land three or four miles out, and taxi right up McCargo Cove to the head of it. We can be pretty quiet that way; they won't see or hear us unless they're practically right there waiting." Lampi's face went solemn then as he folded the map and returned it to Vic. "But from there you'll have to play it by ear."

Vic nodded acceptance; that's how they'd do it.

# < TWENTY-EIGHT >

Once they'd crossed the Canadian border, Lampi reduced their altitude. Then, over a section of shore away from any road or habitation, he turned off the De Haviland's running lights and swung eastward over Lake Superior. Soon he was flying at less than a hundred feet, the ice beneath them transparent over night-black water, looking as if it could not possibly stand the weight of a landing plane.

Jerry Connor peered out a cabin window and sorted his responses to the situation. He felt alert and intense, yet calm. His body, overall, felt excitement, anticipation. There seemed to be no fear—not as he'd known fear in the past. His stomach and bowels were reasonably calm.

For a while they flew almost parallel to the island at what Jerry decided must be a distance of eight or ten miles. Then the plane banked, dropped lower, and briefly flew straight at it before Lampi cut back the engine and landed smoothly on the ice. For the next fifteen minutes they taxied, Lampi reducing their speed and sound as they drew nearer to the island, which now loomed as a fronting ridge, darkened with forest.

241

To Jerry the term *cove* meant a small bay with a wide opening to the sea. McCargo Cove, however, resembled a great ax cut through the fronting ridge, a narrow cleft between rocky bluffs. In the cove, the ice was old and snow-covered. As they taxied slowly up the cove's two-mile length, he watched for whatever might be seen, but especially for any sign of watchers—the embers of a fire, the spark of a cigarette, a movement among the trees. There were none of these. Finally he saw a concrete dock ahead, jutting out from the beach, its snowcap showing the depth of snow here. It lay about three feet thick, he judged.

A short distance past it, at the head of the cove, Lampi stopped the plane, came back through the cabin, and undogged the door. "This is it," he told them, and stood waiting. Frank and Paul jumped out, sinking crotch-deep, and tramped down a small patch of snow for a place to unload gear. The others handed the packs out, along with the snowshoes, then got out themselves. Lampi got out last, his face sober.

It didn't seem terribly cold, but Jerry could feel his nostril-hairs stiffen as they froze, tugging slightly at his nasal membranes.

"Look," said Lampi, "I ain't going back to Duluth tonight. It's too damn far, and I'm worried for you guys. I'd stay right here, but I'd be a sitting duck—no good to anyone except for a target. So I'll wait at Grand Portage, half an hour from here. If everything goes okay, radio me when you're ready to start back, and I'll meet you right here. But if you get in trouble and got to run for it, you might want to head south through the bush, down Greenstone Ridge, and follow the creek down to Siskiwit Lake. I can be there before you are, and pick you up."

"Right," said Vic, then surprised the Finn-Indian with a hug.

*And he's grinning*, Jerry thought, observing the psychic. *Is he that confident?* Faking seemed out of character for Vic, and it occurred then to Jerry that it was neither confidence nor a front. The man would go all out to win, but *he could have it either way, win or lose!* He really could.

And it occurred further to Jerry that *he* didn't feel all that heavy about it either—which he found remarkable, considering what they were trying to accomplish and what might easily be waiting for them.

Lampi was hugged by each of them in turn, then they watched him get back in the De Haviland and taxi slowly away. It was reassuring that the plane was so quiet at that speed.

The cold was beginning to penetrate their heavy clothes; it was time to start moving. Diacono knelt, putting on first his snowshoes, then his pack, the others following his example. When they were ready, Frank led off. Even though he wore forty-inch trail shoes, he sank halfway to his knees, breaking trail for the others. He carried the biggest pack, too, a bulky Duluth pack with Vic's sleeping gear and the radio Lampi had rented them, along with his own stuff.

The night was perfectly still, and they walked through a cloud of their own breath. Jerry brushed at his eyes with a thick mitten, then realized that what he was brushing at was moisture from his breath, frozen on his eyelashes. He turned to look back at Vic, following him; the man's bristly brows were frosted, his grizzled black beard already coated white with rime. This was, Jerry decided, something to tell his grandchildren about—if he lived to have any.

The trail left the cove, plunging into forest, paralleling a strip of brushy swamp where a snow-covered creek could be glimpsed, with occasional small beaver ponds. After a bit they passed through a dense alder swamp on a trail consisting of planks laid end to end on low trestles, so narrow it was difficult even to snowshoe across. Snowshoeing at all had been awkward at first, but not as difficult as he'd thought it might be. His body, even his hands, had warmed with the exertion, and before long the showshoe stride became automatic, invigorating, the feel of the silent forest strange and beautiful. He decided he'd like to do this in the future, as sport—assuming they salvaged the present reality.

Jerry's sense of time became strange: Subjectively, much or little could have passed, though he suspected it might have been an hour when Chickenbone Lake came into sight ahead on their left. They all looked at it as they mushed along, but no one spoke. Then, near where the trail left the lake, Frank stopped them with a gesture, and pointed. Jerry's gaze followed the pointing arm to a low, white, domelike tent, about fifteen feet in diameter, humped among birch trees beside the trail, perhaps a hundred and fifty feet ahead.

Together they gazed at it, hardly breathing. Its unobtrusive presence carried a sense of silent threat, and without a word, Frank led them from the trail to circle past it out of sight.

Yet even the feeling of threat had not sparked strong fear in Jerry Connor, or, Jerry sensed, in any of them. But there *was* alarm: Their mission was to disconnect the surprise generator, and here was threat of failure.

And he could sense other feelings there, which he sorted among as he snowshoed between tall slender aspens. Part of what he sensed, he realized—part of what he felt as threat—was the varied emotions of their intended murderers, of men waiting to kill who had not even created a rationale for their act. It was a subtle psychic miasma blended of apathy and hostility, with an overlay of glee.

Correctly identified, it lost what effect it had had on Jerry Connor, became a datum.

In silent unity, the six threaded their way among trees, around sapling thickets, through brush, each alert, feeling the night. Shortly, Frank led them back to the trail, and almost at once it began to climb.

Gracco had worked furiously, contracting with a suitably criminal chopper contractor, selecting suitable personnel from the men Olson referred him to, then getting everyone equipped and briefed for the ambush. The men were a mixed lot—some good, some only adequate. One requirement was experience on snowshoes, which drastically reduced the supply of eligibles, for most young hoods known to the Olson machine were city-bred.

Shark had been riding the grid. At that stage there was nothing to monitor, of course, but he was available and on watch. Mostly he chewed his nails, figuratively, reviewing his mistakes, fearful that Merlin would still somehow make it. As the gridman now, he would know instantly if the surprise generator was taken off-line; he would feel it psychically through the matrix.

Finally, the preparations had been complete. Gracco had landed his ambush parties, and still the surprise generator was emitting its pulses of chaos. It became possible then for Gracco, and especially for Shark, to take a deep breath; the odds seemed heavily in their favor again.

But Merlin had fooled them too often, and neither Gracco nor Shark had relaxed. Gracco stayed at Lake Harvey with the mobile strike force, while Shark, riding the grid, had spent the last eighteen hours with his viewpoint 500 feet above Greenstone Ridge, at a point a mile east of the gate. From there he would be able to see a plane miles away, approaching any of the feasible, or even unfeasible landing lakes from any direction. And if he could not hear with his own ears, he remained psychically attuned to the hearing of Gracco, even when Gracco was asleep, alert for any sound of a plane.

For eighteen hours Shark had watched, and nothing had happened. It was hard to stay awake and alert, and twice he had dozed, for moments only, wakening with a start and a thudding heart. Caffeine tablets had been of little avail. If something didn't happen soon, he might have to try Hardman's amphetamines, something he hated to do because they impaired the judgment.

He paused in his orderly scanning of the night to look at the distant lights of Thunder Bay, Ontario, some thirty miles north. That wild Canadian shore seemed to him a strange place for a city of a hundred thousand. But minerals and natural harbors were wherever the matrix put them, he reminded himself, and man was hungry for both. The business of minerals was itself a major game for beings to play, with many roles, as well as being a necessary background element for most other games on the Tikh Cheki Matrix.

Shark resumed his scanning then, rotating his viewpoint clockwise away from Thunder Bay, around to the east, the south, the west, with nothing to see in any of those directions except night and nature. No sign of man, no plane, no lights except the silent stars in a sky from which all moisture had been frozen.

What caused him to direct his viewpoint downward then, he did not know, but look downward he did. And below him in the starlight he saw what had not been there before—tracks, the tracks of snowshoes along one of the windswept openings that make up much of the crest of Greenstone Ridge. For a moment his heart seemed to stop, as fear gripped within his chest. Then his intention kicked in, and he swept his viewpoint westward along the trail while his panicked mind trumpeted an alarm to Gracco.

*   *   *

The six were in a wooded saddle when they felt it, though only Vic and Ole knew at once what they felt. Just ahead was another stretch of open crest.

"We've been found," Vic said quietly. "Or our tracks have. Not by someone on the ground; it's our monitor again."

"Vic," said Ole, "you know best v'at to do inside the gate. You sving down through the voods vith Frank and Paul. The rest of us vill go ahead on the trail v'ere he can see us easier. Maybe he'll vatch us and von't see you."

No one argued. Ole's group went on, Jerry leading them, breaking trail out into the opening, hoping that night and the leafless crowns of birch and aspen would hide the other group from above. Meanwhile, it couldn't be too much farther to the gate, and on the open crest, the windslab let them walk faster.

Shark saw the three move into the open and felt a surge of exultation. This find too he called to Gracco. But there should be two or three more down there somewhere. There had to be, and they too had to be stopped. So he reached to find them, not just looking with the remote viewpoint but reaching out himself, psychically.

In that act of reaching, he was vulnerable, and they hit him, those invisible enemies he had not known of, and at that moment he realized what had happened to Hardman. Shark was stronger than Hardman had been, and lashed back violently, but they were too many, coming at him on too many vectors. For several seconds he fought, then jumped from the grid seat to sprawl wet and shaking on the floor.

With Shark's first psychic yell, Gracco had shouted, waking his men, who'd been sleeping fully clothed in their arctic tent. The pilot and copilot scurried out and started their engine, already warmed electrically by a gas-powered generator. They made a swift pre-flight check while Gracco and his two gunners secured for flight. Then the machine swung up from the snow cover on Lake Harvey's edge. Meanwhile, the second call had come from Shark, and immediately afterward a confusion of psychic violence that had driven Gracco's attention back; after that, Shark's presence had been gone.

"Where to?" said the pilot as they lifted.

"They're on top of Greenstone Ridge," Gracco said. "East of point zero. They got by us somehow; I guess my observer never saw their plane."

But how? Gracco wondered. He'd had a sound pickup outside the tent on a tree trunk. They should have heard.

He directed the pilot toward the location of the second call, a location which the call had psychically imprinted on him. It took only three minutes to get a sighting—of three figures half running along the ridge crest, somewhat strung out. Gracco didn't know whether they were in the neutral zone or not, but he didn't hesitate. The two gunners were already leaning out the doors in their safety harnesses, grotesque in bulky arctic coveralls, their masks and gloves electrically heated, heavy automatic rifles in their hands. He ordered them to shoot.

The chopper swung across the snowshoers' path and paused, the sound of an automatic rifle a counterpoint to the racket of engine and vanes. Bullets churned the snow around the targets, and Gracco craned in the cockpit, trying to see the results. The graceless craft pivoted almost in place, rotating to let the gunner on the other side fire his magazine, then pivoted again.

Below, all three figures were down. The one who'd been in the lead tried briefly to get up, then fell back. Gracco ordered his gunners to continue, none-theless; this time he would not be outfoxed.

Frank had led Vic and Paul some distance down the ridge into forest, curving through soft powdery snow and a patchy undergrowth of young conifers, making considerably less speed than the three on the crest. They heard the chopper, then the firing, after-ward dimly glimpsing the machine, like some un-gainly Jurassic reptile flying through the night. Frank did not need to ask Vic. He knew. Ole was dead, and Carol, and Jerry; he could feel it. And despite knowing what he'd come to know about the nature of death, he felt loss, and momentary anger.

He slowed only long enough to shed his pack, the others following his example, then lowered his head and snowshoed on as fast as he was able, leaving Vic and Paul to keep up as best they could. Paul was very strong and almost heedless of fatigue, but in mediocre condition. Vic was lean and wiry, but he was more than fifty, and a smoker. Both had tired severely over the miles. Now they dug in, pushing themselves in the wake of Diacono's powerfully driv-ing legs.

Gracco strained as if effort could enable him to see better. The ones they'd killed must have been a lead group; there were no tracks ahead of them. The others must have fallen behind. He backtracked a mile before he realized what had happened, and ordered the pilot to turn west again. Along here the south slope was the gentlest, the side the others had probably taken, and they flew along it at low speed. Gracco told the gunners what they were looking for, and all eyes sought to penetrate the shadows of the leafless canopy.

And they might indeed have sighted them, had it

not been for the numerous young firs and spruces standing black beneath the naked aspen and birch.

The chopper flew as far as the gate, then swung back. In a glade, Gracco spied the quarry's snowshoe trail, called for another turn, and told the gunners to fire at random into the woods.

Frank heard the renewed firing and looked back toward Vic and Paul. They were in sight, not far behind; Vic paused and waved Frank on. The chopper made its next turn just ahead, and again the blind firing on the return swing was behind them, but near enough that they could hear slugs clipping branches, hitting tree trunks. Frank lowered his head and continued. Twenty seconds later the chopper came back again; there was more gunfire, but now Vic was waving him to go *up* the ridge.

Angling toward the crest, Diacono broke heedlessly out of cover into an opening with only scattered scrub birch and young spruce. He was seen almost at once, and once more the chopper swung around, coming at him low. Again the guns played their drumbeat of death, but no bullet struck him, though the snow churned all around. He paused to stare as the machine circled, and saw Vic and Paul surging up behind. Somehow Vic was grinning, even as he gasped for breath.

Then Frank knew. The guardian was protecting them, as Vic had thought he would if they got close enough—got within those ridiculous welcome legalities of the Tikh Cheki Matrix which applied around gates.

He let Vic and Paul catch up, and they stood there in a joined cloud of their own heavy breathing, watching the helicopter circle, watching the snow churn around them again. Then the chopper drew off, and they looked at each other. Vic was grinning, and Frank was surprised that he too felt no anger.

"You lead," he said to Vic. "I still don't know just where the gate is."

Shark stayed on the floor of the grid room for several minutes, then got up and staggered into the adjacent bathroom, where he was repeatedly sick. His head hurt fiercely, his face felt like an inflated balloon, and he trembled violently. When he was able to return, he got weakly into the grid seat but did not at once reconnect with the search. Huddled like an old man, he dialed a Coke. A tray extruded from a service cabinet beside him, the drink on ice, and Shark drank avidly, then sat gathering his willingness.

At last he sat back, pushed *reset,* typed in the general coordinates, then *view.* His viewpoint returned to a location far above Lake Superior, zoomed down to overview the central section of Isle Royale from a mile up, then zoomed down again to 300 feet above the gate. Snowshoeing toward it were three figures, while the helicopter circled well away. Shark realized with dull shock that the quarry—the dream wreckers!—had escaped into the neutral zone. He watched until they stopped, almost directly beneath his viewpoint.

That was it. They were at the gate. There was nothing further he could do except wait and hope— hope that they could not carry out what they were there to do.

# < TWENTY-NINE >

This time Frank saw it too, not stairs going down into a hole, but a small blockhouse, semi-transparent to him. It had a door like an elevator door, with a square outlined beside it.

"Go ahead," Vic said, and Diacono touched the square. Paul stared; to him it seemed that Frank had simply raised his hand and jabbed the air with his finger.

To Frank's and Vic's perception, a door slid open. Frank turned to Paul and grinned. "After you," he said, gesturing. The Indian stared at Frank, then at nothingness, then stepped forward and found himself in a large elevator. Vic and Frank followed. The door closed, and they could sense their slow descent.

Vic pulled off his heavy mittens and shoved them into the pockets of his mackinaw, which he unbuttoned, then raised the earlaps of his cap, and finally took off his snowshoes. The others did the same.

And still they descended.

"Well," Vic said, "we got here." He looked around as if talking to more than Frank and Paul. Watching him, both were suddenly struck by an intense electric rush that passed over their skin in a series of quick waves. Skin pebbled, hair alive, they too looked around, but failed to see what they had sensed psychically.

"It's okay not to see them with your eyes," Vic said.

"Are all three of them here?" Paul asked.

"Yup." And then, looking upward: "You-all want to give them a demonstration? Gently?"

Frank felt something ruffle his hair, saw Paul's move too, for several seconds. "How'd they do that without bodies?" Frank asked curiously.

"Intention. If your crew members have really formed a unit with you, like Carol's and Ole's and Jerry's have, you can exercise a certain amount of telekinesis when you don't have a body."

The elevator eased to a stop and the door opened. It seemed to Frank, as they got out, that they had come a long way down. A guide waited for them, tall and slender, Germanic-looking, dressed in a jump suit. His "follow me" was crisp but not unfriendly.

Their guide directed them a dozen yards down a corridor to an open door. Inside, the man who waited smiled but did not get up. Like Gandy, he appeared to be an Indian, but unlike Gandy, he was small, dapper.

"Well," he said briskly, "you made it. My name is Alfred; I already know yours." He sounded faintly English.

"You had me worried for a while, you know." He didn't sound to Frank as if he ever worried; he sounded polite, his interest professional, perhaps professorial. "I suppose you have some questions."

"We're looking for the surprise generator," Vic said.

The black eyes were steady and seemed slightly amused. "I see," said Alfred.

"We'd like directions to find it."

"Of course. You're free to go anywhere here that's

open to you. I'm not allowed to direct you, but this is not one of the larger installations; the layout is simple. Feel free to look about and find it for yourselves. Walter here"—he indicated the man who'd met them—"will accompany you, to help you avoid disallowed activities. It's not as if I won't know, or can't take care of things like that from here, but Walter's presence will keep you aware as well as informed. You'll find that ignorance is not an allowable excuse, and penalties hardly subject to appeals. So heed him."

"The activity we've got in mind," Vic said, "is to disconnect the surprise generator."

"I am aware of that. Be my guests." He looked around more widely than necessary to view just the three of them. "Gandy told me about you. In fact, since we talked, he and I, I've had a degree of attention on you."

"I didn't realize you guardians were in communication like that," Vic said.

"Indeed we are. In fact, Gandy and I made a wager concerning you."

"Is that right! Who won?"

"As a matter of fact, the matter is not yet decided."

Frank Diacono wasn't sure he was happy about the bet. If it was over whether or not they'd succeed in the disconnection, he hoped that Alfred's bet was *on* them, but somehow he didn't think it was. Hopefully, the guardian was too ethical to sabotage them. "What do guardians put up as stakes?" Frank asked. "I wouldn't think you'd have any use for money in places like these."

"That's right, Mr. Diacono. We wager favors; they're more interesting, anyway. In time we'll recycle back into the other side of reality, into what is thought of as 'the everyday side.' And once there, we'll no doubt become reinvolved with games and wars and so forth, just as you are. As we have been repeatedly before. At appropriate moments there, we take the opportunity to pay off obligations and wagers—perhaps save the other from a death or imprisonment, or provide him with something desired.

"And no," he went on, answering Frank's new, unspoken question, "we very rarely 'remember,' on the other side, that we had served as guardians or that a wager was owed. But we pay them off, willy-nilly. The knowledge is there, of course; we simply cloak it from ourselves."

His eyes twinkled. "Actually, Gandy thought more highly of your chances than I did. But as I said, I wish you well; to the degree that I feel a preference, I wish you well."

"How long have you been the guardian here?" Paul asked.

"I left the other side in A.D. 1897; I'm rather near the end of my term."

Paul looked at him almost broodingly. "Do other people come in here sometimes? Maybe a hiker now and then who can see the door?"

"You are the second—actually the second, third, and fourth—who've come in while occupying bodies. Walter, of course, arrived in the routine manner, as a spirit, cycling here after dying in the Battle of the Somme in 1916. An old Chippewa trapper and fisherman arrived like yourself, in the flesh, several decades ago. Of course, he did not see the entrance as an elevator, nor did he experience quite as you do what he found here. Your psychic preparation and relative technological sophistication help you to perceive things here quite accurately, actually."

"If you guys came here as spirits," Paul said, "how come you have bodies? Or are those an illusion?"

"Bodies are furnished, but the resemblance to your own is superficial. We wear quasi-organic androids, so to speak, which require neither delivery men, beds, nor cooks, among other things."

"Then you're not really an Indian."

"Correct. But in the Americas, it has become tradition for guardians to wear an Amerind body." Alfred looked appraisingly at Paul. "I suppose though that, in a sense, I am as much an Indian as yourself; I won't tell you who or what you were in 1873, just prior to your last death but one."

Paul regarded all this thoughtfully, nodding. His sessions with Vic had prepared him for it.

"Ninety years and only one visitor till now," Frank said. "Don't you get bored?"

Alfred shook his head. "Boredom is a state of mind, an emotion, actually, and one to which we are not much susceptible. We have ready viewing access, visual and auditory, to anything we wish to watch on the other side. Cabinet meetings, cabals, battles—we can be privy to them all. The London Philharmonic is a favorite entertainment of mine, and so are space activities. And I confess to an enjoyment of watching cinema, both the viewing and the making.

"No, Mr. Diacono, it is not boring here, within the time frame involved. In fact, it is something of a rejuvenative vacation. But when I recycle, I will not be unready."

He shifted his attention to Vic. "Perhaps I'll contact you then, in the current or whatever matrix," said Alfred thoughtfully. "You've come up with enhancement procedures that are not only effective and legal, but in part new, to the best of my knowledge. And I'm sure you realize how extremely unusual that is in the Tikh Cheki Matrix."

"Thanks," said Vic. "But right now I feel like it's time to find the surprise generator and get that job taken care of." He looked at Paul and Frank. "Is it okay with you guys to go now?"

Frank stood bemused. *"I'll contact you then,"* Alfred had said, *"in the current or whatever matrix."*

And said it so matter-of-factly! That and the wager with Gandy reflected a point of view, a perspective, that . . . Alfred would be virtually beyond fear or threat. Frank had come a long way himself, but he stood well short of that.

Yet Alfred looked up to Vic. Was Vic the more powerful, then? Clearly not. But Alfred's power came, at least in large part, with the territory—the job of guardian. And that would be lost, forgotten, when he recycled, while Vic had attained his knowledge and ability on the everyday side, working under the restrictions there. That's what had impressed Alfred; that's why he looked up to Vic.

Vic's hand on his shoulder removed Frank from his momentary reverie, and with Paul, they walked together into the corridor, Walter bringing up the rear. Vic turned right with the certainty of someone who knew where he was going, and Frank decided he probably did. *As a matter of fact*, he thought, *I suppose I do, too. In this universe I just don't always know what it is I know. Yet.*

Getting to the generator room was simple enough. There was no turn and no change in level, just a straight walk of about fifty yards. Without hesitating, Vic led them past several side doors to the corridor's end, which was a single door of corridor width. It opened at their approach, and they stepped through and stopped. They stood in a dome-roofed chamber about a hundred feet in diameter and perhaps twice as high, shaped like a bell jar. And somehow—somehow it was not underground, but seemed to stand free on a wintry plain like some clear, glass-walled edifice. Beyond its wall Diacono could see snow, and the night, and stars.

In the chamber where they stood were large geometrical objects—cubes, spheres, vertical helices, and others whose names Diacono did not know—all pulsing with soft light at different frequencies. They were arranged in six concentric circles around a hexagonal needle that reached almost or entirely to the chamber's highest point. Inside that towering needle, a continuous light seemed to move upward, a dual movement consisting of a rhythmical upward flickering through a slow even flow.

For a long moment they gazed about, especially at the needle. *So this is a reality generator,* thought Frank. *An ordinary electric power station is a lot bigger and more complicated-looking than this.*

Vic Merlin's attention was captured by an object on the side away from the entry, an object standing outside the outer hexagon of objects as if a reject. He walked to it, followed by the other three.

*Can that be it?* Frank wondered. *Something no bigger than that?* But it was—different. Every other object in the chamber was symmetrical; the one they went to was wildly asymmetric, like some gigantic blood-red ruby cut by a weirdly whimsical gem cutter. Chest high to Vic, it was also the only strongly colored object in the chamber. And its light did not pulse; it flashed, fluttered, and flickered, randomly, in a way that made it distracting to watch. It was also the only component there which stood on a separate base—a pentagonal metal plate—and on its top was what appeared to be a separate module, black and opaque.

Vic walked around it, looking for something which he appeared not to find.

"What now?" asked Frank. "The thing on top looks like something I could lift off. Shall I, and see what happens?"

They both looked at Walter, who nodded his permission. Frank took hold of the module and raised it. The machine proper continued its irritating irregular flashing, but at a notably slower rate. Frank turned and put the module on the floor next to the wall.

Paul studied the flickering red crystal. "Maybe just sitting on the base connects it," he suggested, and looked at Frank. "Maybe you and I can move it."

Vic turned to Walter. "Okay to try?"

Again Walter nodded. "That will be quite all right," he said. But now, beneath Walter's exterior nonchalance, Frank discerned a repressed excitement, a pleasure not entirely concealed. *This is the surprise generator, all right*, Frank told himself, *almost certainly. And these guys will be glad to see it go; or Walter will, anyhow.*

Paul and Frank moved to opposite sides of the object and lifted. Instantly the flashing stopped, leaving the object dull and lifeless. It was heavy enough that, being without good grasping angles, holding it was difficult. Briefly Frank considered dropping it deliberately, but decided against it. "By the wall," he said, "and let's lay it on its side." Together he and Paul shuffled to the wall and put it down on one of its larger facets, beside the black module. It remained dull, unlit.

Straightening, they looked at Vic, whose grin was back. "You think that did it?" Frank asked.

"Sure feels like it." Vic was positively beaming now. "How about it, Walt?"

"I'm not authorized to tell you that. It's the sort of thing you must decide for yourself."

Vic turned back to the others. "It's *done*," he said. "I'm sure of it."

Paul nodded. "It looks dead. And the place *feels* better."

"Maybe we ought to break it," Frank suggested. "So no one can put it back."

Walter interrupted. "Destruction is not allowed here. Not without special authorization, which neither Alfred nor I can give."

Frank ignored him, continuing to look at Vic. Vic shook his head. "We'd better leave well enough alone."

"That was easier than I thought it would be," Frank said. "What do we do next?"

"We go out, radio Lampi, and tell him to call the Michigan State Police and the F.B.I. Tell them we're out here, and there's a crew of armed hoods with a helicopter and automatic weapons trying to kill us. That ought to . . ."

Vic stopped in mid-sentence.

"That's right," said Frank. "The radio's back with my pack, where I dropped it, half a mile or more from here."

"Well," Vic said, "we'll just have to go out and see how things look."

Frank realized then that he didn't want to get killed when they went out. They'd won, and presumably the world was saved. He wanted to continue now with the life he had going; it wouldn't be fair to lose it after what he'd helped accomplish.

That's when it occurred to him that you couldn't rely on fairness in the Tikh Cheki Matrix. "Fair" seemed to carry no weight at all there, or at best not much.

# < THIRTY >

They stopped at Alfred's office long enough to tell him what they'd done. Not that he didn't know; it was a courtesy. Then the three of them rode the elevator to the everyday side of reality and stepped out into snow and subzero cold.

They couldn't see anyone.

"If a hit squad had been waiting for us here, could they have killed us?" Frank asked. "If they were standing here at arm's length with guns or axes?"

"I don't know all the legalities," Vic said, "but it seems to me like we'd be safe."

"Hnh!" Frank scanned the surroundings. "Maybe they just gave up and went home when they saw us go through the gate. They must have seen us.

"You know," he went on, "it would make more sense for you guys to wait inside the gate while I go get the radio. It ought to be warmer and safer down below. Warmer, anyway."

"I'm going with you," said Paul.

"Me, too," said Vic. "We'll stay together at least as far as where they tried to shoot us and couldn't."

Frank stood looking at that for a moment, then started out, the others following. It still seemed to

261

him that only one should risk himself—that Vic and Paul should go back below. As he snowshoed, he reached around psychically for the ghosts of Carol, Jerry, and Ole, but they were gone now. Instead, he touched an unseen someone he didn't know: one of the allies Vic had mentioned, it seemed to him. There was no sense of threat there, and after the touch, the other had drawn away with neither fear nor distaste.

Frank turned his attention to his physical environment and looked about him at the world of snow and starshine, Lake Superior black in the distance. Then their backtrail led them into the forest.

He noticed again how easy it was to see at night when the ground was snow-covered, even with no moon at all. Even in the timber, where most of the trees—aspens and birches—were bare. He glanced up at the forest canopy, its network of branches and twigs vaguely visible against the night sky's deep black, then briefly forgot himself in the pleasure of snowshoeing in that wild place.

Paul's near-whisper broke the spell. "It was about here where they first shot at us and missed. We were probably already in the neutral zone."

They stopped. "The packs are about three or four hundred yards farther," Frank murmured. "Five at most. I still think I ought to go alone from here. Not that I feel like anything's going to happen, but it makes better sense for two of us to stay in the neutral zone."

"There're three packs back there," Vic said. "You can't carry all three."

"If nothing happens, then you could go get your packs," Frank insisted quietly. It struck him as odd, then, how careful and uncertain he was being.

Vic stood thoughtfully for several seconds, and this was even odder; ordinarily, Vic knew exactly what he wanted to do, and acted without hesitation. He'd been tentative ever since they'd come back out the gate.

"Vic," Frank asked, "is anything wrong?"

Vic nodded. "I've got a feeling like something's going to happen, but I don't have any idea what it is, or what's the correct action. It's as if I've really thoroughly cloaked myself from knowing anything about it." He paused again. "All right," he said after a moment, "Paul and I'll wait here. And if you're not back in ten minutes, we'll follow you."

Frank nodded and set off alone, feeling edgy. It was about a quarter mile farther that he found the Duluth pack, but he went on to Paul's pack and then Vic's, draping one over each shoulder before turning back. He had set them down in the snow and was hoisting the bulky Duluth pack when he heard Paul's bellow of anger, faint with distance, perhaps hearing it more psychically than aurally.

For a moment Diacono stood there with the pack in his hands, his scalp crawling. He had no weapon except his body and the light cruiser's ax in the pack. Quickly he removed the ax, intending to leave the pack there for better speed, but on an impulse slung it onto his back instead, shrugging into the straps. With the ax in one hand, he started for where he'd left Vic and Paul, removing the ax sheath as he went and putting it into a mackinaw pocket. That done, he increased his pace to a swinging gallop on the now well-packed trail.

He'd gone about two hundred yards when he glimpsed movement ahead and left the trail downslope, intending to hide behind a thicket of young balsam fir. Whoever they were, they'd see his diverging tracks and come after him, and if they weren't Vic and Paul, he'd take them with the ax.

But he'd been seen; he got only three strides from the trail when automatic rifle fire began, bullets thudding and singing into and off the frozen trees around him. One struck his right deltoid, numbing shoulder and arm, and he felt another strike his pack. If there'd been any uncertainty about being outside the neutral zone, that settled the question. He speeded his pace down the ridge.

Even as he fled, his mind looked at the question: Should he be running? Or should he stay and try to help his friends? But the answer was unavoidable— the only product of staying would be his own death.

What was it Lampi had said? Down the ridge into the valley, and follow the creek there to Siskiwit Lake. But in this case, he wouldn't radio from there. He would bypass Siskiwit Lake, where he'd be too good a target on its snow-covered ice. He'd go on instead to Lake Superior and lose himself on its snow-free new ice, where he'd be hard to see and leave no tracks. He'd wait to radio until he was sure he'd shaken his pursuers—out where Lampi's plane, with its running lights off, wouldn't be spotted.

Assuming Lake Superior was frozen out far enough on the south side of the island. He'd have to take the chance. God knew, it was cold enough.

As soon as he'd seen Merlin and the other two disappear into the gate—just disappear!—Gracco had told the chopper pilot to swing around to Hatchet Lake and pick up the ambush party stationed there. He wanted ground troops. He radioed ahead, and they were waiting for him on the ice, inconspicuous in their white combat uniforms. When they were aboard, the helicopter lifted again, and he had it land on a stretch of open crest about half a mile west of the gate.

There Gracco himself, with five men, got out and snowshoed eastward along the crest to take cover in a patch of scrub. Crouching, they waited, watching the gate a hundred and fifty yards farther on, glad they'd been able to get electrically heated gloves and socks.

The next question was whether his quarry would pick up his presence psychically. If they did, they did.

Gracco didn't even try to raise Shark; something had clearly gone wrong there. He told himself that Shark had screwed up too often on this operation anyway—that he was better off operating on his own observations and judgment now. And he'd had a hunch again; he always felt better when he was acting on a hunch.

All he needed was for Merlin and his men to come back out. He knew just what he wanted to do then; he didn't need any goddamn kibitzing. He'd briefed his men when they had loaded; now, waiting, he took the opportunity to go over his full game plan with them. Maybe they could even pull it off in the neutral zone if they had to.

When the three reappeared, as if from nowhere, Gracco held back patiently, watching. Briefly the quarry stood by the gate, apparently in conversation, then turned east and began to backtrack. At that, Gracco led his white-clad men after them in a half crouch, moving without packs, their rifles slung. They had closed the gap to a hundred yards by the time Merlin and his men entered the timber, then speeded up, depending on the trees to hide their approach.

Things were looking good; there was no sign that Merlin had detected them. Now all he had to do was follow them outside the neutral zone and either shoot them down or drive them into the guns of the Chickenbone Lake party that was on its way now to take them from behind.

And if Merlin spotted them still inside the neutral zone, well, maybe he had that figured out, too.

Suddenly, Gracco saw two of them standing in the snowshoe trail not thirty yards ahead, and they saw him at the same time. Gracco broke into an awkward lope, his men following without unslinging their rifles. When Vic did not run, Paul too stood his ground.

At little more than arm's length, Gracco suddenly stopped. Vic, eyes calm, simply waited for whatever might develop, but Paul, abruptly, attacked, and the punch he started to throw locked his body immobile. Calmly then, even gently, Gracco removed Paul's mittens and cap, then clamped a handcuff on one of the Indian's wrists and its mate on one of Vic's, chaining the two men awkwardly together.

This done, Gracco took a knife from his belt and casually cut their snowshoe bindings, then sent two men ahead to catch Diacono.

Vic might have avoided his own manacles simply by withholding his wrists. Then Gracco would have had to apply force, and been himself immobilized. But Vic had let it happen. Somehow it had seemed the thing to do.

Now Gracco was grinning at him. His hunch had paid off; Merlin was outsmarted.

After a minute the cramps faded from Paul's body and the glare from his eyes. "I couldn't move," he said to Vic. "It was a gate effect, wasn't it?"

"Yep," Vic said. "I figured the neutral zone would keep them from even touching us here, but it seems like it only responds to violent actions, not harmful intentions."

He turned to Gracco. "That was really pretty slick," he went on, "coming up with that idea. But you're too late. You needed to catch us on our way in."

Gracco's grin didn't fade; it just hardened. He reached out to Vic's manacled hand, pulled its mitten off, and handed it to a grinning henchman. "Not too late for what comes next," he said. "I'm taking you to see the boss." He gestured with his knife, eastward along their old trail. "That's the way we're going now. Move it, or we'll stand here and watch

you two freeze." Lightly he plucked Vic's hat away.
"You won't last very long out here like that.

"But if you behave, maybe I'll give your mittens
and caps back."

Paul sized up the situation. The only way back to
the gate was over these guys, and that would take
violence. Without snowshoes they couldn't outflank
them. He looked questioningly at Vic.

"Let's go, Paul," Vic said, and they started wading
slowly through the snow, side by side because of the
way they were shackled together.

"How come we didn't feel them coming?" Paul
muttered.

Vic never got his answer out; instead, just then,
they heard a burst of rifle fire ahead. Paul's lips
tightened: the enemy had caught up with Frank. For
just a moment they stopped, almost crotch deep in
snow, then went on. Neither had any illusions now
about where they were going.

When they had gone another hundred yards, it
occurred to Gracco that this felt far enough. He
raised his rifle and fired a burst at each of them.
Both prisoners went down, and quickly the snow
darkened where they fell.

Diacono moved fast, his powerful legs striding rhyth-
mically. He knew he was being chased: it had felt
that way since he'd been shot. Then he'd been shot
at again, perhaps blindly, some two or three minutes
after the first time.

He had snowshoed quite a bit in the past—it
avoided the waxing problems of ski touring in
Arizona—and he knew how to make good speed
without excessive effort. But presumably the men
chasing him were competent snowshoers, too; whoever was in charge would have brought in men who
could operate in these conditions.

Then he heard a double burst of shooting far back

on the upper slope, and a pang of grief struck him with unexpected intensity, hurting his throat. Frank knew at once what had happened, and for a moment thought of turning back—finding and killing. But the urge, like the grief, passed quickly, for he and Vic had stripped away the positive feedback circuits that beefed up harmful emotions and held them in place.

So he simply kept striding through the forest at a half lope.

He knew his bullet wound wasn't severe—certainly not as bullet wounds go. It didn't hurt too much, and the arm still functioned despite the initial numbness of the shoulder. He had felt what had to be blood running down his arm, but it hadn't been enough to reach his mittened hand. Probably, he thought, the bullet had first struck a tree, losing most of its momentum before hitting him.

He became aware of blood drying on his arm and forearm, tugging the hairs and drawing the skin. Hopefully, that meant the bleeding had stopped. After a bit the shoulder began to hurt more and then to stiffen, but he'd played football with worse pain than that, he told himself, and probably with more damage.

It wasn't long before the ridge toed out into alder swamp. There the thick brush slowed him markedly, but also screened him effectively from the men who now would be closing the gap behind him. When they reached the brush, they too would slow down.

Then the brush thinned, gave way to a narrow open bog with scattered small spruce and dead tamarack snags. Frank speeded up then because he'd be exposed while crossing. The open bog presented another problem, too—one he hadn't anticipated: its sedges and dwarf shrubs had kept the snow from settling, so that he sank to his knees at every step, despite the snowshoes.

Giving it all he had, Frank lowered his head and

charged forward, bull-like. He made it across without being shot at, puffing violently, even sweating a little despite the cold, plunged into the brush and trees, and angled off to his left before his pursuers reached the opening.

When they did reach it, they paused long enough to spray bullets down his trail into the brush on the other side, then hurried after him, hoping to find him dead or down. But if they didn't, it would just be a matter of time, they were confident. He was breaking trail for them; he would wear down sooner or later, and they'd kill him then.

In the valley, Frank found the going rough, with abundant underbrush and blown-down timber. Even hiking on the creek he came to was not as much help as he'd expected. It was narrow enough that the tag alder which overhung its banks sometimes met over the middle, and there was no shortage of windthrown cedars lying across it. Furthermore, except on the small beaver ponds, the creek level had fallen notably since freezeup, and the ice had sagged, slanting down from the banks, now and then threatening audibly to break beneath his weight. So after a little he left it and forced a cross-country route away from the creek.

Diacono tired more than he thought he should, and credited this to the bullet wound. He was slowing, and began to entertain the possibility that he might not make it—that he might well be run down and killed. So when he came at last to Siskiwit Lake, he could not resist the faster, easier travel of its open, windpacked snow. It seemed to him he might as well chance it.

Even so, he did not strike off across its exposed width, but struck off eastward, virtually within arm's reach of its forested shore.

Pete Haugen snowshoed with an economy of motion, his eyes alert on the forest ahead, missing little.

He'd grown up in the backwoods near Ely, Minnesota, as a kid had trapped mink and beaver, poached deer, moose, and wolf. Both snowshoes and alder brush were long familiar to him, yet he told himself he'd never gotten mixed up in a pile of shit like this before.

Several times he seemed to catch his webs on snow-buried obstacles and fell sprawling face down in the snow. Once he pitched headfirst among dead branches, one of which stabbed him in the cheek. Getting to his knees, he'd taken off an electrically heated glove to feel the injury with his fingers; the goddamn sonofabitching branch could have put out an eye, he told himself.

As he knelt there, he heard Graham call softly behind him. "Jesus Christ, Pete, this is a fucking nightmare in here!" The man panted between sentences. "Every fucking branch I come to hits me in the fucking face. I vote for turning around. We're never going to catch that sonofabitch anyway!"

Haugen got up, turned, and waited for the man. "Look, asshole," he hissed as Graham caught up with him, "I'm telling you just once—I ain't quitting and you ain't quitting. We're going to catch that bastard and kill his ass for leading us in here, and then we'll take his scalp back with us for proof. You go back empty-handed and Olson'll gut you. Now quit your goddamn bellyaching. The quicker we get this done with, the better."

Then he turned and something caught a snowshoe again; again he fell. He got up cursing with every epithet he knew, and started rapidly down the trail.

Graham had exaggerated his snowshoeing experience. He'd been doing collections for more than a month, and that was dull shit; a secret mission had sounded interesting. His actual experience had been rabbit hunting on snowshoes a couple of times with his brother-in-law up by Mille Lacs, and it hadn't been that hard. He'd gotten the feel of it pretty good. But that hadn't been a footrace through the brush at night.

Something whispered in his mind that he ought to shoot Haugen for talking to him that way. But Haugen was a real killer, and Graham was afraid of him; Haugen was one of the guys Olson sent to take care of hard cases. If he shot at Haugen and didn't kill him instantly . . .

No way was he trying that! He'd just tough it out, that was all. Haugen was almost out of sight already, and Graham speeded up, lowering his head to do so. Nonetheless, somehow a branch slashed across his face, as if it had been drawn back and released. He swore, grabbing the branch in midstride and jerking, intending to snap it off, then stepped on one snowshoe with the other and fell again. A voice laughed, a voice soft but real, right there beside him. He raised his face and couldn't see anyone, not even Haugen up ahead.

The chill that ran through Graham wasn't from cold.

Diacono had gone the first hundred yards on the lake ice with as much energy as he thought he had to give, not even glancing back over his shoulder. Distance was what he needed; if they shot him, they shot him. After the first hundred yards, though, he looked back. There was no one in sight, and suddenly he found a little more energy, picking up the pace again. Maybe he'd been widening his lead all along, despite breaking trail; he must have!

Now he started glancing back every few paces.

"You don't need to look back," a voice whispered. "It slows you down." Frank almost stopped, it surprised him so. "I'll tell you when they come out," it went on. The 'voice,' though non-sonic, seemed clearly female, and for a moment he thought it was Carol's ghost, then knew that it wasn't. It was someone he didn't know, the same one he'd touched when they'd come out the gate.

Nonetheless, he was spooked for a few seconds, but kept going and stopped looking back. When there was no repetition, he wondered if perhaps he'd imagined it. But if it actually was a spirit—a ghost, or someone away from their body—at least it had been friendly, an ally. And he could use an ally out here, even an imaginary ally.

At three hundred yards he heard the shot, just one, and angled for cover. "Stay on the ice!" the presence commanded. "Something's wrong with his gun. Go as fast as you can!"

Frank went, as fast as he could. A minute later there was a short burst of fire—three rounds. But in the night there was no aiming—one could only point and fire—and he raced along unhit. And there were no more shots. He didn't let up for another minute, but then he had to slow. His breath was a heavy gasping, and it was beginning to burn in his throat, as if the subzero air was freezing his windpipe.

It occurred to him that with the lead he had, it was time to begin angling across to the southeast corner of the lake, where his mental image of the map told him there was a short trail leading to Lake Superior.

Except for its crystal decor, it could have been a corporate boardroom on the everyday side of reality. The principal furnishings were a long table and surrounding chairs.

Certainly it didn't look at all like a courtroom, though it was about to be the scene of a trial. Around it sat the principals and others involved in the matter at issue, along with the Games Master for planet Earth, two of her aides, and a master-at-arms. The master-at-arms, looking small and mild, was capable of immobilizing anyone there, simply by intention.

The principals were Peter Shark, Vic Merlin, Vincent Gracco, Kurt Hardman, Gandy, and Alfred. The others were Paul David, Olaf Sigurdsson, Jerry Connor, and Carol Ludi. There was no court recorder; the proceedings and the events at issue could be actually re-viewed at any time, in whole or in part, by the Games Master or any future authority.

Everyone wore a body, even those who had been without one when the court was convened.

Most of those present had no idea where the court was; they had simply and without warning found themselves there, in place, without traveling. But because of the history of man, screened though it ordinarily was, they were neither shocked nor confused at suddenly being there.

In a gown-like robe of pale lavender blue, the Games Master arose, tall, handsome, commanding, and looked around the table. "Everyone required to be here is here," she observed amiably, "so let us begin: Court is in session." She looked at one of the aides flanking her. "Malo, please read the questions which the Court is to examine and pass upon."

Malo did not stand, merely straightened and glanced down at a small object he held in one hand, reading easily in a mellow baritone. "The following are accused of deliberate and knowing violations of the neutral zone of the Isle Royale Gate: Peter Shark and Vincent Gracco. There are accessories, but none of them are chargeable in this court.

"The following is accused of deliberately and knowingly tampering with a reality generator in such a way as to alter in an illegal manner the broad course of events on the entire space-time-energy-matter field known as the Tikh Cheki Matrix: Victor Merlin. Accessories who are chargeable in this court are: Paul David, Olaf Sigurdsson, and Frank Diacono. Mr.

Diacono is not present; he is currently completing a cycle of action within the matrix, which will be allowed to run its course unless the findings of this court cancel that cycle before its completion."

Again Malo paused, to glance around briefly.

"The following are accused of malfeasance as gate guardians: Gandy and Alfred.

The following is accused of illegal technical abuse of disembodied players: Kurt Hardman."

Malo scanned the assembly again. "That is the statement of charges against the named persons. The other individuals present before the court are knowledgeable accessories not presently charged."

Malo drew his hand into his robes and sat back.

"Very well. Thank you, Malo." The Games Master looked the group over again. Two hands stood raised, and she looked at their owners: "Questions and comments will not be entertained except as I specifically request them. The first issue before the court is the violation of gate neutrality. The first principal is Peter Shark." She looked at him. "Peter Shark, you have heard the charge against you. How do you plead?"

"Don't I get a counselor?" Shark asked. "What kind of court is this?"

The Games Master was unperturbed. "If a counselor were necessary, I would provide one. As for the kind of court this is, it is an ethical court of absolute and unappealable judgment. And with the complete availability for viewing of all pertinent actions, the adversary system has no pretension to applicability here." She held Shark with mild eyes. "Would you care to be tried mute? That can easily be arranged."

Shark shook his head.

"How do you plead?"

"Not guilty."

"On what grounds?"

"On the grounds that there was no violation of

gate neutrality. No one was harmed within the neutral zone around the gate."

"Um. Do you deny that an armed helicopter, indirectly under your command and inside the neutral zone, attacked and killed persons outside the neutral zone? And that those persons were on business within the gate? We can re-view any of this if necessary."

Shark looked jarred by the question. "But— Your Honor, I didn't realize that was a violation."

"Your claim of ignorance is noted. However, in this court, for anyone deemed sufficiently responsible to stand trial, there is no ignorance. There is only acting in disregard of the law."

Her calm eyes fixed him in his seat. "You are herewith found guilty as charged."

Shark stared agape. "And that's all there is to it?"

"Correct."

"But I haven't been confronted by my accusers! There's been no cross-examination! There's . . ."

"Your accusers are not persons. Your accusers are the facts. The events have been replayed and the facts are not arguable. You may argue only with proposed corrections and amends which the Court, in due course, will impose. You might also have argued with interpretations of the law, had there been any. But the law and your actions are and were unequivocal in this instance."

She looked at the others around the table. "Because of the interrelatedness of the various charges, corrections and amends will not be decided until after all charges have been examined and found upon."

Her eyes went then to Gracco. "Vincent Gracco, you have heard the charge against you. How do you plead?"

Gracco grunted. "Well, at the time, I thought . . . Oh, hell. Guilty. Besides the chopper, I also caught two of them inside the neutral zone and took them outside and killed them." He grinned. "Guilty as hell." Then, turning, he looked at his recent victims. "Although right now they don't seem any the worse for wear."

"Thank you, Mr. Gracco, but I'm afraid you deprived them illegally of game and roles." Her eyes went to Vic Merlin.

"Victor Merlin, you have heard the charges against you. How do you plead?"

"Not guilty, on the grounds that what we did was remove an unauthorized addition to the reality generator."

The calm eyes regarded him thoughtfully. "Unauthorized? Please elaborate for the court."

"My time track research shows that the original reality generator was designed and installed by High Interest Playgrounds." Vic glanced at his teammates. "That's a pretty close translation of what it was called," he added.

He turned again to the Games Master. "Afterwards, unauthorized circuits were patched in from time to time by Prank and Associates, known later as the Seven Lords of Disaster and similar names—one more reason why every now and then the equipment had to be redesigned and overhauled.

"The most recent redesign resulted in the present equipment, which generates the Tikh Cheki Matrix. It includes ingenious design characteristics that keep anyone, including Prank, from getting access to the generator and altering it *except from the everyday side*. And being on the everyday side, Prank and his folks had to operate within the constraints of that side. Apparently they got less and less powerful the longer they stayed there, until after a while they weren't able to design system-compatible alterations anymore."

"Remarkable!" said the Games Master. "How did

you manage to access this information from the everyday side?"

"I looked. I'm good at that, although I'm not sure why."

"Hmm. Continue."

"Now this next part I only got onto recently, and it's partly induction from things that other folks came up with. But somewhere down the line—it almost had to be in the first cycle of Tikh Cheki—Prank and his folks were able to design and install an adjunct to the Tikh Cheki reality generator that introduced destructive impulses into the matrix. It's been called the surprise generator, and it sure makes for surprises all right, but 'chaos generator' might fit it better. I suppose maybe some guardian or other got busted for letting it get installed.

"Anyway, although the matrix has been reprogrammed quite a few times since then, the surprise generator has never been removed. But apparently it was never formally approved and authorized; it was just sort of left on because it made the matrix more interesting."

He smiled at the Games Master. "You can see I'm doing some supposing in here. Anyway, somewhere along the line, Prank installed an addition to the surprise generator: call it an output accelerator. That probably had to be in the first cycle, too. And when some feedback indicator read at a critical level, the accelerator would begin to increase the output of 'surprises,' or destructive impulses.

"Anyway, that's how I put it together."

He met the Games Master's eyes.

"The way it looks to me," he went on, "this accelerator was set to kick in whenever the players were about to develop a major new level of games—like interstellar space flight, or an effective and legal psychic technology. Anyway, about three years ago it kicked in, and ever since then, things have been going to hell fast. But by the time we got enough information to realize what was going on, there was only a few months left before the chaos level in human activity would go critical and shut the matrix off for reprogramming—'the end of the world'—and we'd have to start over again.

"Well, it seemed like about time to break that climb-and-crash routine, so we got together to disconnect the chaos generator.

"But we never tampered with the reality generator itself. No way! What we did was 'untamper' it. That's why we're not guilty as charged."

The Games Master's eyes had withdrawn; she looked contemplative. "A very interesting position," she said. "But the surprise generator—the 'chaos generator,' as you so colorfully put it—has been accepted as a *de facto* part of the reality generator ever since, as you supposed, the first cycle of Tikh Cheki, even though it had not been part of the formally agreed-upon design. From that point of view, you *did* tamper with the reality generator. Certainly you changed reality, rather drastically.

"But insofar as it pertains to the question of your guilt, you have a viable argument."

She stood up. "This court is herewith recessed while the Games Master confers with the Board of Adjudications."

# < THIRTY-ONE >

After Haugen finished swearing at his rifle and prying out the jammed cartridge case, he turned and shouted to Graham to hurry. When the panting Graham caught up, Haugen snatched the man's rifle and snapped off a short burst. Then it jammed, too, when the action didn't slide far enough and a cartridge case failed to fully eject. Haugen cursed some more.

Again he drew his knife, and pried out the case. *That's what comes from having people running things who don't know what the hell they're doing,* he told himself. Gracco hadn't known enough to get the oil wiped off the actions before sending guys out where the mercury was going way below zero. Now it had gotten cold enough that the oil had turned sticky, and he found himself with a steel and plastic club instead of a gun.

"Here!" he said, shoving Graham's rifle back at him. "The oil's got gummy. Carry it inside your parka and warm it up so it'll work."

"How can I carry it inside my parka?"

"Just *do* it, for chrissake!" Haugen barked, then took off his own parka and slung his weapon butt

279

upward from his right shoulder. Graham copied his action. His parka back on, Haugen peered ahead across the ice. The sonofabitch they were chasing was way to hell and gone ahead now; he could hardly see him. The guy was angling off across the lake.

And then it hit him—out on the ice away from cover, the guy would be a sitting duck for the chopper. Quickly Haugen took his radio from a parka pocket and switched it on, noticing the tiny red light come on to indicate power. The batteries were surviving the cold, anyway.

"Vulture One, this is Haugen. Come in, Vulture One. . . . Vulture One, this is Haugen. Come in, Vulture One."

There was no response, and Haugen glared at Graham as if he were to blame. "Gimme your radio!" he demanded. Graham dug it out and handed it over; again there was no reply. Haugen handed it back, his anger suddenly broken to mere resentment. Either the radios were junk that wouldn't reach the chopper, or someone was asleep on the job.

"Let's go," he growled, and set off, departing Diacono's tracks, cutting the angle to gain ground on the man. They'd have to bag the guy themselves. Or probably *him*self; that finky Graham wasn't likely to last much longer.

Frank could feel the tiredness again, and wished briefly that he could ditch his pack. But once he lost his pursuers, out on Lake Superior, he'd need his radio and his sleeping bag and ground pad while he waited for Lampi to come get him, and his flashlight for a beacon when Lampi was looking for him.

There were some small rocky islets at this end of the lake, near the shore. Diacono paused, and from behind one of them looked back, trying to spot the gunman or gunmen. He couldn't see anyone, and it occurred to him that they might have given up.

"No," a voice whispered in his mind. He'd forgotten the voice in the minutes since it had spoken to him earlier. "They're still coming—two of them. They're hard to see because they're quite a long way behind you and they've got white uniforms on."

"Thanks. Who are you?"

"My name is Miki. Miki Ludi."

Ludi; that was Carol's last name. "Are you a ghost?" This time he didn't take the breath to ask out loud. He thought the question to her.

"No. I'm a sort of—a psychic would be closest, I suppose; I wouldn't qualify as a witch."

"Do you have straight black hair, bobbed?"

"Yes. How did you know?"

"I dreamed about you. Maybe you visited me in my sleep."

She didn't answer, just continued with him as he strode along. He was maintaining a good pace, but not trying to go really fast. If they gained a little on him, Diacono told himself, well, he'd soon be off the lake, on a regular forest trail this time. And his pursuers must be tiring, too.

"How about it?" he asked. "Can you tell if they're tiring badly?"

There was a moment without answer, then: "One of them is. He's falling way behind the other one. The leader seems to be doing all right, but he doesn't look any fresher than you do. What do you have in your pack?"

"More bulk than weight. A short-wave radio that weighs a few pounds, a flashlight I'm going to need, my sleeping bag and Vic's, a couple of rolled-up ground pads to put them on, and enough trail rations for a couple of meals."

"Is Vic the older one with the beard? Not very large?"

"That's him."

"Then—he's dead."

There it was. He'd known it, accepted it, but to have someone say it jolted him for a moment.

"You could throw his bag away," she suggested.

"It's not worth stopping to do it. It probably weighs ten pounds; maybe twelve with the ground pad. And I may want it as a quilt when I bed down on the lake. I will for sure if a breeze comes up."

He kept striding, the only sounds his breathing and the slight sound of snowshoes in dry snow. "Can you check Lake Superior," he asked silently, "and tell me if it's frozen for a few miles out? Check it from down by the surface; new ice won't have snow on it, so from up a ways it'll look black, like the water."

He felt her withdraw. In a minute or two she was back. "It's frozen out quite a way. Maybe two miles—I'm not good at estimating that kind of thing. And it seems fairly thick; I can see cracks in it that look like wide gauze ribbons from the top of the ice to the water, and it looks like it might be ten inches or a foot."

The information gave him new optimism, and close ahead now he could see a little bay. The trail would be at the end of the bay, if he remembered correctly. If not, he'd simply take off cross-country.

Hell, he had this as good as whipped. All he had to do was keep going.

The once-Lefty Nagel didn't have brush and branches to work with now, and found that either he could not affect Graham's body directly, or could not bring himself to. But Vic and Tory had given him some heavy counseling in enabling him to escape the holding bottle; he could probably create some visible effects, he decided.

Positioning himself in front of Graham, he groaned

into the man's mind. Graham looked up from the snow in front of his snowshoes and saw something resembling cheesecloth, roughly in the shape of a person, a decayed cheesecloth body with its head a semi-transparent caved-in skull. The gunman stopped in his tracks as a coldness gripped him that had nothing to do with the minus twenty-eight-degree temperature of the air.

"Pete!" he husked, staring. Haugen was a hundred yards ahead of him. The ghost hung between them, one arm pointing back the way he had come. "Pete!" This time it was a croak. A thought came to him— that if he went on, he would surely die.

"Yes, sir!" whispered Graham, his head bobbing rapidly. "Yes, *sir!*" Turning, he started on the back trail across the ice and didn't look back for a quarter mile. When he did look back, he couldn't see Pete anymore. He couldn't see the ghost, either. It occurred to him that he was in trouble now for sure. He couldn't tell Gracco he'd run—that a ghost had chased him off. He didn't know what the hell to do.

He started hiking again, still headed down the back trail for Greenstone Ridge. When he got back, he'd just have to lie, and hope for the best. That had worked for him before, more than once. Maybe Pete wouldn't come back. No ghost would scare Pete away, but maybe it would kill him. Maybe Haugen would die out here in the snow.

Lefty joined Leo in accompanying Pete Haugen, and let the other ghost know what he'd done. They should do the same to this man, he suggested. Leo thought back at him that Haugen was a tough and forceful man, a man who ordered himself, even when the impetus came from some boss. He wasn't someone easily shoved around.

These communications weren't in words. The two of them were advanced enough that, unconnected as they were to bodies, they communicated easily and efficiently with one another by concepts. And despite Haugen's toughness, they decided to work on him. Lefty created a wind gust, sending a thin cloud of snow swirling up from the surface in front of Haugen, while Leo groaned into the man's ear. Haugen scowled but did not slow. A breeze had risen, he told himself; and the ice was freezing thicker, groaning in contraction. As if in agreement, the ice gave forth a long snapping, cracking sound under the stress of increasing cold.

Lefty sent the snow swirling more thickly, so that Haugen walked through it squinting, half blinded, and this time Leo groaned Haugen's name. "Peter Haugen! Peter Haugen!"

Haugen stopped in consternation, cold chills rushing over him. "Who the hell is that? What's going on?"

They created ghostly shapes in front of him, pointing. "Go back," they moaned in chorus. "Go back or you'll die."

"Eat shit!" he swore at them, and unzipped his parka, his mittened hand going to his rifle. "Get your asses out of here! Now!"

He couldn't have said anything more effective to a ghost than a firm and fearless order to leave. They found themselves instantly a considerable distance overhead, seeing Siskiwit Lake as a seven-mile, fish-shaped white oblong surrounded by dark forest. Mentally they shrugged at each other: there still were definite limitations to this ghost business. Perhaps, though, they could harass the man covertly again, as before, when he reentered the forest—as long as he didn't realize his power and once more order them off.

Soberly, they relocated themselves where they could watch his wolflike half-lope along Diacono's snowshoe trail. He seemed to be going faster now.

* * *

At the lower end of the little bay, Frank found not a trail to Lake Superior, but a narrow channel that took him to a much smaller lake. He'd remembered the map wrong. Not surprising, he told himself. There'd been a lot of map, and he hadn't put much attention on this part of it. So he kept hiking, though not as fast as before. He could bypass the feeling of tiredness temporarily, by intention, but then it would hit him again.

"Miki," he thought, "how am I doing? Is he gaining on me, or am I getting farther ahead?"

She withdrew for a moment, then was there again. "One of them has turned back," she said. "You can forget about him. The other one is gaining on you. He seems to be very tough, and he has no pack."

"How close?"

"I would say—perhaps a half mile."

He nodded and picked up his pace again. Quickly he was approaching the far corner of the little lake, and a post on the shore. As he came up to it, he saw its small sign just above the snow: "Whittlesey Lake Portage/0.5 mile."

It puzzled him. "Doesn't this trail take me to Lake Superior?" he asked.

Again Miki flicked away, and he stood there, stopping for the first time since they'd shot him back on the ridge. Half a minute later she was back.

"It goes to another lake—a very narrow lake with steep ridges on both sides. The lake must be two or three miles long, and at the other end there is forest again. Beyond that is another long, thin lake. Lake Superior is off to your right."

She thought to him a picture of the scene as she'd seen it from high above narrow Whittlesey Lake. "But partway up this trail you cross a hill." She let him see that too, as she had, from a point near the ground. "The hill leads toward Lake Superior."

He nodded, and started off again.

The trail was free of brush and blowdowns, but it led uphill, and he realized he was tireder than he'd thought. At its top he left the trail, turning right along the crest.

The forest here was of fir and spruce, with dense sapling thickets that he had to find his way around. Here too he had to go uphill for a while; when he topped out, it was gratefully. On a hunch, he angled left a bit, and was soon in a heavily wooded draw. Before long it ended at a tiny cove, across which he saw Lake Superior with a narrow white shelf of ice. Beyond that was blackness which stretched to a horizon lost against the sky.

He barely paused, striding out on the snow-covered cove with a feeling of grim satisfaction. Though no longer free-swinging, his pace still was quick, and the safety of snow-free ice was in sight. It took a minute or two to clear the mouth of the cove and reach the open sweep of the great Lake, then he continued straight ahead, as if he thought he could walk all the way to Michigan.

He'd gone scarcely a quarter mile when he heard a burst of gunfire behind him. Instantly he broke into a clumsy gallop, not trying to dodge, seeking the relative safety of the black new ice just ahead. The shooting stopped while the gunman dug another clip from his pocket and seated it, and as soon as Frank was on new ice, he cut left. Surely his pursuer couldn't see him now.

Another burst of gunfire blasted from the direction of the shore. He fell heavily, not from bullets but because he had slipped; his snowshoes gave poor traction on bare ice. Pain stabbed the wound in his shoulder when he fell, but he got up immediately and continued with a crouched and shambling, half-skating gait.

For a couple of hundred yards he hurried parallel

to the edge of the older, snow-covered ice, then veered outward again away from it. In his dark pants and mackinaw he was hidden by blackness now, well away from the snow that had framed him for so many miles and had shown the clear marks of his passing.

When he'd come out of the forest onto the shore of the cove, Haugen had realized at once what his target had in mind. He could barely see the man, in line with the straight trail he left in his wake. Again Haugen unzipped his parka, throwing it at his feet, to take the rifle from his shoulder.

At that moment both Lefty and Leo sent snow swirling up in front of Haugen, screening his target. The gunman fired anyway, emptying his clip, then seated another as the snow continued to swirl around him. He stood there in angry chagrin for a moment, not realizing that he need but repeat his earlier order to leave. Then once again he fired blindly, emptying a full clip in one long burst, heating the chamber and barrel so that he could smell the now-hot oil.

When the swirl of snow had died, Haugen reslung his rifle, shook the snow from his parka and put it back on. Then he started down his quarry's trail once more. As he strode, his eyes scanned ahead, right to left and back again. At the edge of the black new ice he stopped and stood a long minute, searching, finding nothing, tasting bitterness.

Then he turned slowly and headed back the way he'd come.

Diacono kept hiking, still quickly at first, then more slowly. When the edge of the snow was a half mile behind him, he stopped. Miki told him that the ice went on only another mile or so, and he didn't want to hazard Lampi breaking through it when he landed.

Miki checked on Haugen and reported that the gunman had started back up the hill toward the portage trail.

Frank set the pack down on the ice, took off his mittens and dug out the radio, intending to call Lampi. There was a bullet hole in the side of the pack, as he knew there would be, but even so he was not prepared for what he found. The slug had ripped through the radio, ruining it; there would be no call to Lampi.

He had snowshoed at least a dozen miles that night, maybe fifteen, some of it through brush, and broken trail the whole way through virgin powder snow, carrying a pack. He hadn't eaten since a mid-afternoon meal in Duluth. On top of that, he'd been shot, although the wound was minor.

And now this!

In utter chagrin he stood there, then shook it off and tried to think what to do. "Miki," he said, "there should be a park headquarters eastward along the shore somewhere. I'm sure I saw it that way on the map. Can you check it out for me? Give me an idea of how far, and help me find it?"

Again she flicked away, skimming along the shore, seeking, and he stood waiting in the minus-thirty-degree cold. His eyes traveled up the sky to scan the silent panoply of stars, then panned the horizon all around. There might not be another human being for thirty or forty miles, he thought, except for a few who wanted to kill him. *This is the wilderness, all right,* he told himself. *A man could die here and never be found.* He slapped his left thigh with the mittened hand of his unwounded arm. *But some of us are damned hard to kill.*

Then Miki was back. "I found it," she told him. "It's east, all right, on a long island just off the shore. And there's a light in one of the buildings, and a plane parked on the ice by them."

"How far?"

She didn't answer at once, and he could sense that she hated to tell him. "I think it must be ten miles, at least," she said.

Unexpectedly, he laughed. "Hell, kiddo," he said aloud, "I can do that walking on my hands. Let's go."

But his right shoulder hurt so sharply when he swung the heavy pack onto his back that he almost passed out, and as he began to walk, he could feel blood running down his arm again.

# < THIRTY-TWO >

It seemed as if only about fifteen minutes had passed when the Games Master reappeared in her seat. Carol wondered if her conference had been so brief or if perhaps time here was flexible—an hour in some conference room fitting into a quarter hour here. But if so, why not an hour in the conference room to two minutes here, or zero minutes? Or why not a telepathic conference without leaving?

Apparently the place had its own rules and limits; it would be interesting to know what they were. Clearly, they were much different from those she was used to. For one thing, she was here, and Jerry and Ole. Yet she clearly remembered the helicopter, the automatic weapons fire, bullets slamming her, and falling into the snow. Then she had looked down at her body and watched the snow turn red—black, actually, by starlight. Her body had looked really, really dead, like something dumped there, and she'd thought it was interesting that she could look at it like that without feeling upset.

Next she'd checked the bodies of Jerry and Ole. Ole—himself, not his body—had joined her. Jerry had still been hanging in there, his heart pumping.

When it stopped, all three together had gained elevation, a few thousand feet of it.

It was beautiful—the night, the snow, the wilderness island spread beneath them. And after their psychic experiences under Vic's and Ole's "counseling," they had found no trauma in death. In fact, for a few minutes they did not think to look for Vic and the others; importances had altered somewhat, and they had enjoyed a purely spiritual experience.

Now here she sat in what appeared to be her old body. It wasn't, though; although it did feel the same, it wasn't bullet-torn. She wondered what sort of punishment they visited on dead people here, but somehow the question didn't trouble her.

"All right," said the Games Master, interrupting Carol's thoughts, "court is now in session." She looked at Vic. "Mr. Merlin, the Board of Adjudications has found that you did not act illegally—far more boldly than we are accustomed to, but not illegally. You are therefore, of course, not guilty. On the same grounds, Misters Sigurdsson, David, and Diacono are likewise not guilty."

Ole stood and applauded, grinning broadly, his tall rawboned frame looking hard and vigorous, not at all dead, the sound of his big hands loud in the room. Jerry stood, too, and Carol, joining him in applause. Paul smiled, and Vic grinned as if amused as well as pleased; still seated, they added to the clapping.

The Games Master did not gavel them down, nor tell the master-at-arms to bring order. Instead, she waited mildly for the ten-second outburst to end on its own. When it had, she spoke again.

"Now," she said, "the court will examine the remaining issues, commencing with the charges against Gandy and Alfred." Her eyes went to the two guardians where they sat side by side looking altogether unconcerned. "You have been accused of malfeasance. Alfred, I am dropping the charges against you because the Court has determined that the persons you allowed into the generator room did not act illegally there." She glanced at Vic and Paul, then back at the guardians. "And, of course, their entering was no crime in itself; anyone who has the power to enter is free to, at his or her own risk.

"However, Gandy, the charge against you still stands. It appears that you took an effective partisan role in this contest. How do you plead?"

Gandy sat with arms folded, seemingly unworried. "Not guilty. I took no partisan action."

"You gave useful information to one side in the contest."

"Granted. But I was not partisan. I would have given any permissible information to the other side, too, if they'd asked for it. In fact, I was rather surprised that they didn't at least come to learn what I had told their opponents. Considering their abilities, I presumed they knew that their opposition had been through the gate."

The Games Master shook her head. "Not a valid defense. The information given to the Merlin group was vital to their success and not otherwise available to them. It was the single action which decided the contest, or at least, without which they could not have won. On the other hand, the Shark group did not need your information. They drew the correct conclusion without it."

Vic's Texas voice came in when she had finished. "Be all right if I say something about that?"

"If it is relevant."

"I could have found out where the surprise generator was without Gandy's help."

Her eyebrows rose. "Then why did you go to the Sipapu Gate?"

"Two main reasons. First off, I'd made a lot of progress on counseling techniques, since I'd been through a gate before. My first two times through a gate, it hit me pretty hard, and it really kicked back on me afterwards, physically and mentally. And it felt as if, to handle the surprise generator, I'd need to take at least one of these new folks along through whatever gate was the one. Besides which, we'd need to be able to operate when we got there. That meant we needed a test run, and Sipapu was the handiest gate.

"But if Gandy hadn't told us, I could have found out anyway. What he did didn't make that much difference."

"And how," asked the Games Master, "would you have found out?"

"You asked a while ago how I'd accessed the information I gave here. I said I got it by looking. I'd have gotten this information the same way, if I'd needed to; it just would have taken me maybe two or three days. Or maybe less, depending on how things worked out. I already knew the location of eight gates, and before we went to Sipapu, I put my attention inside each of them, one after another, looking for anything that looked like it didn't belong there. I looked backwards at them so I was seeing them in the past; that way, I wouldn't disturb their guardians. But I didn't find anything that looked promising.

"If Gandy hadn't told us where it was, the next thing I'd have done was check out other places where the pattern indicated there ought to be gates. And if the surprise generator wasn't at any of them, I'd have extended the pattern . . ."

"Thank you, Mr. Merlin," the Games Master interrupted, "I see the procedure. An obvious and workable approach for someone who knows as much as you. You *have* made remarkable advances. I'm amazed you survived your early research, booby-trapped as the area is. I would have expected it to lead to insanity or death instead of to workable procedures."

She turned her attention to the Guardian of Sipapu. "Gandy, I find you not guilty of malfeasance."

"Wait a minute!" Shark protested. "What do you mean, 'not guilty?' He had no way of knowing that Merlin could do those things! He took sides!"

"There is a saying on your world," the Games Master answered mildly, " 'no harm, no foul.' On the same basis, it is results we evaluate here. There are no accidents, there is no luck. There are only results—the combined effects of scripts, intentions, knowing and actions. And in truth, *knowing* goes far beyond the concept of knowing usually recognized within the Tikh Cheki Matrix."

She turned then to Kurt Hardman, who sat glum and apparently inattentive. "Mr. Hardman, the Court has decided to remand your case to a referee's hearing."

With that, Kurt Hardman simply disappeared—presumably, Carol decided, to reappear in the office of some referee.

"And now," the Games Master continued, "the Court will decide what to do about the disconnection of the so-called surprise generator, chaos generator, confusion generator—call it what you will.

"The fact is that the players of Tikh Cheki, in their billions, have become used to the richness of troublesome surprises which the surprise generator has provided. In fact, it would long ago have been taken off-line, had there not been rather general approval of its effects. Therefore, it is the preliminary consideration of this court that it should be put back on line." She looked at Vic. "Are there any comments or objections?"

It was Jerry who spoke. "Yeah, I've got an objection. The damned thing was about ready to destroy the world. Now, I know there'd be a replacement world, and everybody who lost their body when the present reality blew would be eligible for a new one, if they wanted, as bodies became available."

He pointed a finger like a gun at the Games Master. "But I'd like to know just what the hell constitutes that 'general approval' you talked about. I don't recall hearing about any survey, let alone a vote.

"Vic told us that at the end of each cycle, the reality generator gets reprogrammed to, ah, correct what seemed to need correction in the previous matrix. Is that the way it works?"

The Games Master's eyes were on him intently. "Basically, yes."

"He also told us that with each reprogramming, the rules become more restrictive, and the level of play—I don't recall just how he put it, but the way it came across to me was, it got grungier. Less rich. Is that right?"

"I suppose it could be looked at that way. It is a viable point of view."

"So *why?* Why is it that way? What the hell is going on to make it like that?"

Her mildness had changed now, the apparent boredom beneath it replaced by growing interest. "You are the one who is pulling this string," she said. "Continue pulling, and tell us what you find."

"You bet," he said. "So in each cycle, humankind starts from scratch. Some of us. Others say to hell with it and quit playing—go outside the matrix and watch, like McBee. Or maybe hang out, waiting till the matrix has enough bodies so there's one for them; or try a different sector or universe somewhere. Right?

"And over time here we build things back up. What are we building toward? Some level we want that we think is desirable. And we have to do this against obstacles for it to be interesting. So we try this and that—religion, philosophy, science, what have you—and bit by bit, we gain."

His eyes fixed the Games Master in her seat. "And

then what the hell happens? The surprise generator speeds up and blows the whole damn thing! What the hell kind of a game is that, where you can't win? People have even stopped thinking we can make it! When we start to get close, our progress jabs all those painful other times when we were starting to win and then had the world end on us. Down underneath we expect it all to collapse again."

Suddenly Jerry grinned, a big now-I-got-it kind of grin. For a moment he said nothing, until the Games Master prodded him. "Mr. Connor, you seem to have had a major realization. I trust you aren't going to keep us waiting for it."

"I might." His grin didn't reduce a bit. "But I won't. The Lords of Chaos, Prank and Associates—whatever—fooled hell out of us, and I bet they're laughing right now, wherever they got hauled off to. They put in the chaos generator knowing damn well that the difficulties it added to games would make things a lot more interesting. And correct me if I'm wrong, but we'd been playing games for trilennia before Tikh Cheki, until we had ennui out the kazoo! We'd learned that things had to be really challenging to keep our interest over the long haul; otherwise, forever would be unbearable.

"So okay, you were right: People *didn't* want to scrap the surprise generator.

"But there's one thing wrong: the surprise generator is a trap! It lets mankind think he's coming along—three steps forward and two and nine-tenths back, but he's coming along. And then, whammo!

"What's wrong with the surprise generator is simply that it accelerates every time we reach the point where we're really threatening to win as a species! So all you need to do is fix it so it doesn't accelerate; *then* you put it back on line. That way we keep our barriers, our degree of difficulty, but give ourselves a chance to actually advance to a whole new level of activity."

He looked around the table. "And that's all I've got. Don't ask me how to do it. I imagine you've got engineers who can solve that for us."

He sat back down. This time there was no applause, but Vic and Ole, Carol and Paul, grinned and glowed at him. Then Vic stood up.

"I'm pretty sure it won't be any big deal to do that. Like I said before, I'll bet just about anything that the accelerator was added on after the surprise generator had been on line a while. It's a module that was sort of plugged in on the top. Check it out and see if that's not the way it was."

The Games Master stood. "Thank you, Jerry Connor and Victor Merlin." Her eyes fixed on Jerry. "I believe you have provided us with the proper resolution of the problem.

"Court is recessed while I have the generator and module examined. When that has been done, I believe we can make a final disposition of the entire matter and get on with other activities."

# < THIRTY-THREE >

For the first half hour after starting for Park Head-quarters, Diacono made decent time. Not as fast as when he was being chased, but he strode along at a pretty good pace. The first thing he did was to angle shoreward, to get on the firm, windpacked snow along the edge of the old ice. The traction it afforded made walking both easier and faster.

After a few minutes, the wound again seemed to have stopped bleeding, and he could feel the clotting pull on his skin. The pain had slackened.

At one point he saw something lying in the snow not far ahead, and went to it: the bones of a moose, with blood and a few scraps of hide around. There were a lot of wolf tracks, and the tracks of scavengers— ravens and fox. It all seemed several days old; the wolf tracks had ice crystals in them that had frozen out of the air when the arctic cold moved in.

A half mile farther on, he had stumbled—stepped one snowshoe onto the toe of the other—and fallen heavily with the pack on his back, again catching himself reflexively on his mittened hands. This time the stab of pain in his shoulder was so bad that he stayed on his hands and knees for a minute or so before getting up and going on his way again. After that the shoulder bled much worse than before, until the thick woolen inner mitten was sodden with blood that squished when he flexed his hand. He decided that the bullet, probably flattened by hitting a tree, must be lodged in the deltoid, and in the fall had damaged a vein or artery more severely.

For just a moment he considered trying to do something about it, but that was clearly impractical. He'd have to strip to the waist, and to bandage the deltoid effectively would require a body bandage, applied somehow with his left hand. It couldn't even be undertaken with a mitten on, and barehanded, his fingers would be useless within a minute or so. Then he'd still have to put on his undershirt, shirt . . .

No, he'd just have to tough the wound out like an old grizzly.

Before long he noticed he was leaving a blood trail; the leather outer shell of the mitten was full, and blood was dribbling from it. He pulled it off and dumped it out, then slid his hand back into it, all without stopping his steady stride. The bleeding would stop soon enough, he told himself, or if it didn't, it didn't.

To Miki it seemed he couldn't long continue like that. With a quick mental "I'll be back," she flicked away.

Farley Waner had gone to bed about twelve-thirty, having stayed up to finish a novel he'd been reading. His pilot, Chuck Carnes, had been asleep for almost three hours. In the morning they would begin their aerial survey of the island's moose population.

Both men were asleep when Miki arrived. She spent five minutes trying to waken Waner, sensing that he was sleeping less deeply than the other.

Finally he sat up, looked at the clock, muttered something about "crazy dreams," and got out of bed. As he started for the refrigerator, she undertook to put an image of herself in front of him.

He paused, blinked, shook his head. For a moment he'd thought he was looking at a beautiful nude woman, but women were not semitransparent. He walked right through the image, opened the refrigerator door, and took out the bottle of scotch. *What the Park Service doesn't know,* he thought as he tipped the illicit bottle, *won't hurt them.* Then he tipped it a couple more times, trying to ignore the thoughts stirring in his mind.

After that he went back to bed.

Miki decided then that she would try to produce poltergeist effects. If she succeeded, that would surely get their attention. But first she would return to Frank, just for half a minute, long enough to tell him she was trying to get help.

With the thought, she left the building. She did not make an instantaneous transfer; if she had, her experience might have confused her even more than it did. Instead she sped from the building, angling toward Saginaw Point and around it, zipping along above the old shelf ice to meet Frank. It took finite time, seconds, and had she looked back before rounding Saginaw Point, from her elevation she might have seen the lights flash on in the cabin, where suddenly Waner was putting away the dishes while Carnes talked of going to bed early.

Her eyes were on the ice ahead, though, watching for Frank. Seconds later she slowed, thinking she should have seen him by then. There was no sign of him. Alarm flashed through her; perhaps he'd passed out from loss of blood.

But she could not even find his tracks! She came to the remains of the moose, the days-old tracks of wolves and the rest, but nowhere, nowhere was there any sign that Frank Diacono had ever been there. It wasn't as if he'd fallen through a hole in the ice, or been attacked and taken away. It was as if he never was!

There was a moment's panic, the panic of a strong and competent person confronted with evidence of her own insanity. She fought it down, and psychically called his name.

At once she was caught up in a vortex, a whirling darkness without snow or stars or any light at all . . .

And opened her eyes in her bedroom, fully clothed. The clock read six oh-five—early evening. She had just been somewhere. The memory was fading quickly, like a dream, but she clutched one piece of it: She had been with a man called Frank Diacono. And . . . he was in trouble . . . and the clock should read much later than five minutes after six! She whispered the name aloud to herself and put her attention on the mental image that came to her, of a man pouring blood from his mitten. From that she gradually pulled the rest of it back, including his inexplicable erasure, the evidence of hallucination.

But this still left her in mystery. She did not know of the Games Master's court, or that its final disposition was underway, the source of her bewilderment. She might have poured herself a drink. She might have said "enough of that," and stayed away from out-of-body travel for days or weeks. What she did instead was close her eyes and psychically seek out a vaguely remembered Tory Merlin for advice.

Peter Shark paused in his orderly scanning of the night to look at the distant lights of Thunder Bay, Ontario, some thirty miles north. That wild Canadian shore seemed to him a strange place for a city of a hundred thousand. But minerals and natural harbors were wherever the matrix put them, he reminded himself, and man was hungry for both. The business of minerals was itself a major game for beings to play, with many roles, as well as being a necessary background element for most other games in the Tikh Cheki Matrix.

He didn't remember ever thinking this before.

Shark resumed his scanning then, rotating his viewpoint clockwise away from Thunder Bay, around to the east, the south, the west, with nothing to see in any of those directions except night and nature. No sign of man, no plane, no lights except the silent stars in a sky from which all moisture had been frozen.

Even Peter Shark could appreciate a sky like that, could feel its beauty. He gazed upward for a moment, then continued his scanning of the night around the island, watching and listening intently for the plane that would bring Merlin and his people to their death.

He gazed down briefly at the ridgetop below him, but saw no one, nor any tracks in the snow. The six snowshoers moving through the forest below escaped his vision, for they were skirting around the ridge crest openings, avoiding exposure, keeping carefully to cover.

They entered no opening until the last fifty yards to the gate, a mile west of Shark's position. The last of them carried a small, bushy fir sapling, which he used as best he could to obscure their tracks. Then all six snowshoers got into the elevator. The big man who'd broken trail for them chuckled as they started down.

"This is the damnedest thing I ever heard of," he said quietly, flexing his now-unwounded shoulder. "And here I am living it: the shooting of an altered scene in real life!"

* * *

Basically, the Merlin group had been given another chance. Merlin and Jerry had been allowed to rescript the scene, which they did in conference with Frank and Ole, Paul and Carol, under the Games Master's surveillance.

The result wasn't at all what Hollywood would consider a shooting script, or even a master scene script. Or even a treatment. It required only a brief discussion and decision, and nothing was written down. Simply, the Games Master would return them to the time and place at which they'd started up the trail above Chickenbone Lake. From there, all the principals would pick up life again as if the rejected scene had never been lived, would create anew on the stage—ad lib. The surprise generator would still be on line, or be on line again, depending on how you looked at it, complete with accelerator. And again Shark would watch for them, with full intention, and ability, to prevent their success.

This time Frank would follow a covered route. And when they reached the surprise generator—*if* they reached the surprise generator—they would leave it on line, only removing the accelerator. Alfred and Walter were authorized and instructed to then trash the accelerator.

With the accelerator gone, the output of the surprise generator would return to the preacceleration level: The human race would have another chance in this cycle to make good its potential.

It was far from the first time a scene had been reshot with a revised script, but it was one of the very few times that any of the principals remembered afterward that there had, in fact, been a reshoot. Shark did not remember, nor did Gracco; to them there was only the revised reality. But those with whom Vic had worked, remembered. Both versions were accessible to them.

* * *

When the Merlin party came back out the gate, fifteen minutes after entering, they exposed themselves only briefly again, with Paul once more wielding his crude fir brush to their trail. Then they trekked through the timber, down the slope toward Siskiwit Lake. It took them somewhat longer to reach Lake Superior than it had taken Frank in the original version, because Vic and Ole in particular were worn out.

And of course there was no great hurry now; they had only to move fast enough to keep from freezing, for this time there was no alarm. Gracco slept. Shark never spotted them, saw no tracks; and the chaos generator never went off-line, so there was not that to shock him. Sleepless and restless as he was, awake only through the frequent ingestion of caffeine tablets and coffee, Shark failed to notice the change in the matrix when the accelerator was removed.

When finally the Merlin team was well out on the new ice, they radioed Lampi, then crawled into their arctic sleeping bags fully clothed, to doze fitfully in the minus-thirty-degree cold. An hour later, they were in the air on their way to Duluth. In the noisy cabin of the De Haviland they again dozed fitfully, except for Diacono, who rode up front with Lampi, keeping him company and telling him as much as he thought the pilot was ready to hear.

Lampi didn't know he had hitchhikers; Lefty and Leo were inconspicuous and weighed nothing at all. But about the time the plane reached the Minnesota shore, below Beaver Bay, the ghosts "disappeared," whether to recycle, or tour, or leave the Tikh Cheki Matrix, they didn't say. The ghost who is free both of compulsions and current purposes is very free indeed, free even of old associations, and has many alternatives available.

Finally, Lampi set his six passengers down on the ice at the edge of Grand Lake. Frank's pickup was waiting for them undisturbed, and surprisingly (or perhaps not surprisingly) it even started.

Back in the warmth and relative quiet of the motel, the victorious team members debriefed one another. They were emotionally high, though their bodies were tired. Jerry told Frank more details of the trial, with occasional input by others. Frank told about his flight through the woods, and the role that Miki Ludi had played; they never learned how the ghosts had harassed his pursuers. Tory, through Vic, told of the assaults on Hardman and Shark by Miki Ludi, the ghosts, the Van Wyks, and herself, along with another whom they had not identified but whom Ole suspected was Madame Tanya.

Miki, who'd arrived with Tory sans body, wasn't ready yet to share her story with these tired but exuberant others. But after Frank was in bed, she told him silently what had happened at Park Headquarters, laughing about it now, and what she had found, or failed to find, when she'd gone back to look for him. That had been right after the transition, when the original scene had just been scrubbed.

Next they made plans, she and Frank. Miki would visit him in Flagstaff, and look into the possibilities of a fitness salon there. If that didn't look good, Frank would send coaching resumes to high schools and colleges in the Los Angeles area. Once established together, they could evolve a new project, whatever that might be.

While Ole was getting ready for bed, Jerry borrowed his car keys and left their room to knock on Carol's door. She was waiting. Together they went to an all-night restaurant and talked over coffee.

It didn't take them long to make their decisions:
When they got back to L.A., they'd get married.
They would also have Ole train them as operational
psychics. He had offered to, had said that with what
he, and they, had learned from Vic, it would be easy.
They already had come a long way.

Carol and Jerry agreed that they didn't want to be
in the psychic business, but psychic abilities would
be a boon in whatever they did decide to do.

Tired as they were, when they got back to the
motel they started to kiss goodnight at Carol's door,
then instead went inside together. Ole could have a
room to himself that night.

When Jerry left with the car keys, Ole Sigurdsson
didn't go to sleep at once. He lay there with his big
hands behind his head, fingers interlocked, gazing at
the ceiling. For a while he would work with Vic and
Tory on their research, he decided, from L.A. as
much as he was able, and in Arizona when necessary. He'd learn from them and help them as much
as he could. They had the master key, and the doors
were there waiting; with the surprise generator sta-
bilized, it looked as if there'd be time to finish
exploring.

There still were nuclear weapons, fanaticism, and
all the other threats, but those were only dangers,
not certain doom. And now that Merlin's research
had enabled them to handle the problem of the
accelerating chaos generator, what other effects
might they create—especially as the research advanced.

While Frank and Miki conferred, Vic had left
his body in bed and relocated himself in the ranch
house. Tory's body was asleep, but that was no
problem.

"Howdy."

"Well, hello there! I enjoyed the debriefings, and I expect I'll remember them when I wake up. I'm doing better and better on that these days, seems like."

"I'll phone you when I get up," Vic thought to her, "and remind you, just in case. We'll be starting home on toward noon."

"Sounds good to me. How'd that Shark dude come out that we jumped all over? Nobody said, and I never thought to ask."

"That's right! And you never peeked in on the trial; or anyway, I never noticed you there."

"Couldn't break in there nohow; I knew there was something going on, but it was strictly no trespassing."

"Well, the only reason Shark and Gracco are still around was to do the reshoot tonight. They had to rescript for fatal accidents tomorrow, although in this universe they don't remember doing it. The Dallas house is going to burn to the ground, and there's going to be a bad helicopter wreck on Lake Superior. And they won't get to recycle back in until each one prepares a script with an amends project in it, and gets it approved."

"Huh! Then The Four are down to zero! That ought to help." Tory paused thoughtfully. "You know, we got kind of spoiled lately, what with Ole and the Van Wyks showing up and bringing all that excitement with them. We're going to have to mock up something new to keep life interesting."

"I was looking at that, flying back to Duluth," Vic replied. "It seems like we've got a possible new shortcut in science. We could research physics and the other basic material fields like that by examining the programs in the reality generator. We'd look at the program instead of the output."

"I don't get it."

"Well, the reality generator is the computer for the video game of life, right? And the usual approach of science is to research the *output* of that computer—the Tikh Cheki Matrix, the physical world, the setting for games. Scientists don't let themselves know that's what they're doing, but it is. But with the progress we've made on being able to look at the other side of reality, it seems like we could work out a way to examine the programs for it directly. That ought to be a lot quicker, and we'd make a lot fewer mistakes."

Tory looked at the idea. "We'll have to talk about that," she said. "Maybe we ought to hold it down to a major new breakthrough or two. Otherwise, we might spoil a lot of other people's games. All those physicists and mathematicians and such like want to have fun, too."

She paused. "Might be we could try mapping out what lies behind the *arcade* universe. Leif Haller's peeks into that always looked pretty interesting to me." She changed the subject. "When do you-all expect to get home?"

"We'll sleep late this morning and then head west through North Dakota and Montana, and south through Utah. There could still be hostiles watching for us on the route we came up on, so we might as well play it safe. We'll be home about Thursday."

He paused, pointedly. "There's someone I'd like to bring home with me to stay four or five weeks—the Indian, Paul, that we picked up over east of Tucson. He was with us through the whole thing. I gave him a few sessions along the road, and he's pretty powerful. He wants more, and wants me to train him so he can go back to Oklahoma and pass it on among his folks there."

Tory didn't hesitate. "It's all right with me, for a

few weeks. If he's as strong as he looks, maybe I can get him to build me that concrete cistern I've been after ever since last winter, in exchange for the training."

Mentally Vic grinned at her. "I'm going to be glad to see you. My feet have gotten awful cold, sleeping alone."

"Mine, too. We'll have to have us a big old foot-warming when you get here. I'll have the boys bring home a jug of peach brandy. It's good for things like warming feet."

When everyone had gone to sleep, the group and a number of past and present associates had a party in the Maxfield Parrish universe. Theirs wasn't the only celebration there, of course, because the whole population had a strong interest in the Tikh Cheki Matrix. But theirs was the most special.

And the most confidential; they all agreed that would be best. Basically, theirs was a planning party: they made a broad-brush integrative script, and created some personal, highly varied outline scripts to start on it with. None of them hazarded a guess as to how long it would take to carry out—how many lifetimes—but now it seemed feasible, and given their recent success, they were rather optimistic about it.

"Word" got "around" the non-material non-universe very quickly: Not only had The Seven Lords of Chaos been extradited from the Tikh Cheki Matrix, but now the generator had been debugged—renovated without a shutdown. Thus in the Maxfield Parrish universe—a "waiting room" as well as the "mezzanine" or "arcade" for the Tikh Cheki Matrix—there were a lot of new applicants. McBee was one.

So the players in the Tikh Cheki Matrix were

quickly under pressure to provide more bodies for interested candidates, and a baby boom could be expected that would give sociologists grist for a thousand erroneous papers. The human race would just have to come up with a faster-than-light drive again to handle the population stress.

# WE'RE LOOKING FOR
# TROUBLE

Well, feedback, anyway. Baen Books endeavors to publish only the best in science fiction and fantasy—but we need you to tell us whether we're doing it right. Why not let us know? We'll award a Baen Books gift certificate worth $100 (plus a copy of our catalog) to the reader who best tells us what he or she likes about Baen Books—and where we could do better. We reserve the right to quote any or all of you. Contest closes December 31, 1987. All letters should be addressed to Baen Books, 260 Fifth Avenue, New York, N.Y. 10001.

At the same time, ask about the Baen Book Club—buy five books, get another five free! For information, send a self-addressed, stamped envelope. For a copy of our catalog, enclose one dollar as well.